PRAISE FOR CORINNE SULLIVAN

Yours Always

"*Yours Always* is a twisty, turbulent ride filled with psychological tension and an unpredictable cast of characters that kept me on my toes until the novel's bombshell ending. Don't miss Corinne Sullivan's first-ever thriller—I pray it's not her last!"

—Carola Lovering, author of *Tell Me Lies* and *Bye, Baby*

"Corinne Sullivan has written a terrific thriller. *Yours Always* is tightly plotted, told in deliciously cutting prose, twisty—and twisted in the best way. It pulled me right into its intricate web of secrets and deceit, and I enjoyed every minute of it."

—Clémence Michallon, internationally bestselling author of *The Quiet Tenant*

"Steeped in the claustrophobia of Austin's dating and tech scenes, *Yours Always* is a deliciously dark treat that I couldn't stop consuming, rushing home from an evening out to finish the last few chapters. Sullivan does an excellent job of wriggling her way into each character's head, making even the most despicable dating app user sympathetic to her readers. I could not recommend this twisty, gossipy psychological thriller more!"

—Flora Collins, author of *Nanny Dearest* and *A Small Affair*

Indecent

"[A] surprising debut . . . an affecting novel, examining self-doubt, self-sabotage, and the lasting impact of both."

—*Publishers Weekly*

"Sullivan's debut is a smart and delicious page-turner."

—*Booklist*

"[A] steamy debut, in which infatuation crosses the line into obsession . . . Imogene's backstory . . . will have readers sympathizing with her as she works through her past."

—*Library Journal*

"The disturbingly painful depiction of the struggle to be at home within one's skin will move teens with its well-written, haunting, and illuminating story of a young woman spinning out of control."

—*School Library Journal*

"*Indecent* is a fresh twist on the prep school novel, a thrilling ride that masterfully explores class, sex, and obsession. Sullivan's debut novel is a sharp and complex coming-of-age story that will keep you hooked until the last page."

—Jennifer Close, author of *The Hopefuls*

"A suspenseful and excruciatingly true portrait of what it's like to be young, female, and desperate to be loved—by the wrong person. Corinne Sullivan's style is effortless and completely absorbing."

—Swan Huntley, author of *We Could Be Beautiful* and *The Goddesses*

"A heartbreaking, entirely believable exploration of an illicit affair. *Indecent* captures the white-hot haze of first love, as obsessive and delicious as it is blinding and dangerous. You won't be able to put this down."

—Georgia Clark, author of *The Regulars*

"A page-turner with characters so fresh and real it's scary, *Indecent* will take your breath away. Sullivan explores subject matter that could be merely titillating—sex, power, desire—but is so ruthlessly honest about them that in the end she challenges everything we thought we knew."

—Rufi Thorpe, author of *The Girls from Corona del Mar* and *Dear Fang, With Love*

"*Indecent* is so astutely observed, so expertly crafted, I didn't realize I was riding a roller coaster until I was already buckled in and halfway to the top. A fractured coming-of-age story, a one-two punch about self-sabotage and obsessive love, *Indecent* is a page-turner of a debut by a ridiculously talented young writer."

—Lauren Fox, author of *Still Life with Husband*

"*Indecent* asks the hard questions about just how low low self-worth can make a person go, and the even harder questions about what it means to truly grow up."

—Elisa Albert, author of *After Birth*

YOURS ALWAYS

OTHER TITLES BY CORINNE SULLIVAN

Indecent

CORINNE
SULLIVAN

THOMAS & MERCER

Published by Thomas & Mercer, Seattle

www.apub.com

EU product safety contact:
Amazon Media EU S. à r.l.
38, avenue John F. Kennedy, L-1855 Luxembourg
amazonpublishing-gpsr@amazon.com

ISBN-13: 9781662535628 (paperback)
ISBN-13: 9781662535635 (digital)

Cover design by James Iacobelli
Cover image: © lambada / Getty

Printed in the United States of America

For Mickey

Prologue

Her first thought upon waking: *Is it over? Am I safe?* Her second: *I can't move my arms.*

As she steadily slips back into consciousness, the room around her begins to take shape, and she identifies what she can—a window darkened by plastic blinds, a whiteboard decorated with illegible notes, an IV leading from the inside of her elbow to the machine beeping insistently next to her head. *Hospital,* she thinks, dredging up the word with some effort. *I am in a hospital.* Then she feels it all at once: the white-hot, all-consuming throb of her left shin, wrapped in layers of gauze so she can't see the damage. She wonders if it looks as bad as it feels; that doesn't seem possible.

It comes back to her in flashes.

Shouting. Struggle. The deafening blast of a gunshot. Searing pain.

And blood. So much blood.

Through a plexiglass window in the door, she can see a uniformed officer standing outside the room. *See?* she thinks. *Safe. You are safe.*

"Water," she attempts to croak, but her voice fails her. She tries to wave her arms, to call out again, but it seems her whole body is paralyzed. Instead, she closes her eyes, settles back into her pillow, and concentrates on her breathing: in and out, in and out. She tells herself, *It's all over now.*

But a voice deep inside her head whispers that's not quite true.

Because it's only over if they believe her.

Chapter One

Townsend

Twelve Weeks Earlier

Townsend Fuller watches as his friends unload cases of Lone Star from his buddy's G-Wagon, feeling low-key pissed off.

Jackson, Brett, Warren—they're the same guys he's known since his St. Augustine Episcopal School days, whose families also have memberships at the Verano Country Club and boat slips at the Lake Austin Marina. Theirs is a friendship of proximity, not affinity, and while Townsend could once at least relate to these guys, that is no longer the case. They have no idea how it feels to be strapped to a ticking time bomb.

As if on cue, Townsend's phone buzzes in his pocket. He doesn't read the notification. He knows who the message is from—who all the messages are from. He's been ignoring them for weeks, but it hasn't proved much of a deterrent. They come when he's taking his phone out of his locker at the gym. As he walks into a meeting with potential investors. The second after he closes his eyes at night.

You can't ignore me forever Townsend.

Fxck you.

You'll regret this.

Before Brett can close the door of his Benz, Townsend tosses his phone into the back seat. He doesn't need to feel her watching him all afternoon.

Townsend is too old for Party Island, but it's Saturday, and it's mid-May, so that's where he's going. On the south side of Town Lake, he can see them: the bronzed bodies and pastel paddleboards, bobbing in a festive mass near Lou Neff Point. He wonders how many of those partygoers are worried about sunscreen, or algae blooms, or about the body pulled from the water just last week.

"Hey, Fuller, you going to help or just going to fuck around?" Jackson says this affectionately, almost like an apology, and Townsend realizes this is his way of asking *Are you okay?* He hates their pity.

"Says the king of fucking around." He smiles back, his way of saying *I'm good.* Then he strips down to his swim shorts and grabs a case of beer.

Together, the boys head down to the boat-rental shack to meet up with Nicole, Brett's on-again, off-again girlfriend. She's brought along one of her faithful blond retainers. Both women are in jean cutoffs and bikini tops, and when they greet the guys, both have the same pervasive vocal fry. This habit of traveling in packs was cute when Nicole and her friends were freshmen and Townsend and his crew were seniors, but now those girls are all at least thirty, while Townsend is less than a month away from thirty-four.

"I'll go get the shit," he tells his friends.

At the counter, he pays for six kayak rentals, feeling a pang in his gut as he hands over his credit card. It's like a small death, every time he remembers his funds are no longer unlimited.

After divvying up the beers and collecting their paddles, they get in their kayaks and head toward the action. For a moment, Townsend tunes out his friends and focuses on the familiar sight of the Austin skyline shimmering in the distance: the Texas State Capitol building, where he'd spent countless school field trips; the Austinite, where he's lived for over a decade; the Frost Bank Tower, where he'd worked alongside his dad up until a month ago, when everything went to shit.

"So. Townsend." The blond girl—Chrissy, apparently—floats alongside him, blocking his view. "I don't think I've seen you since Nicole's Christmas party. How have you been?"

"I've been . . ." Townsend hesitates, searching for the right word. *Exhausted. Strung out. Fucked up beyond all reason.* "Fine. I've been fine, I guess." He racks his brain for something he can ask her in return, but considering he couldn't even remember her name before Nicole reminded him of it, he's got no shot at recalling her job or interests.

Chrissy has wedged herself next to him, so close their kayaks touch. "I heard about your dad. I'm so sorry for your loss."

Over the past month, Townsend has heard these words more times than he can count: *I'm sorry for your loss.* Sometimes people mixed in other platitudes as well, such as *He's in a better place now* or *At least he didn't suffer*. But it's *I'm sorry for your loss* that bothers him the most. People like Chrissy can't begin to understand the extent of what he lost.

"It's fine. It's whatever."

By the time they hit the sandbar by Lou Neff Point, Party Island is in full swing. Brett realizes he forgot his floating grill in the car and paddles back to get it, while the rest of them float among the hundreds of half-naked young people, stretched out on paddleboards and kayaks, guzzling beers and roasting in the sun. To Townsend's left, an intense game of beer pong is taking place on what looks like an inflatable mattress. To his right, a man in a canoe holds a giant Bluetooth speaker over his head, blaring trap music. Townsend tucks his oar into his kayak and cracks open a Lone Star. Perhaps he can drink enough to forget how little he wants to be here.

"Yo, guys," Brett says when he returns. "The grill master has arrived. And I brought a surprise for you, Townsend."

From behind, Townsend can hear the slaps of Brett's paddle as he approaches, as well as a woman's timid giggle. His heart seizes—did she follow him here?

Watch your fxcking back Townsend.

You can't escape me.

Your mine forever.

He turns slowly, suspending the moment—but when he sees who sits in Brett's boat, he feels a rush of relief. It's not her, thank Christ. Instead, it's the last person he expected to see.

Her hair is shorter; she's cut it into a coquettish, chin-length style with choppy bangs that frame her heart-shaped face. Her skin is a bit tanner, her body is a bit leaner, her lips are painted a dark-red shade he doesn't remember her ever wearing before, but it's unmistakably her.

"Talia."

"Townsend, wow." Her lips twist into a shy smile. They match her dress, a short thing with frills on the shoulders and a low-cut neckline. "Hi."

"Hi." It's all Townsend can manage. She looks good. *Really* good. He squeezes his beer in his hand and tries to collect himself. Then he gives a little cough to clear his throat and turns to the rest of the group. "You all remember my—you remember Talia, right?" He trips over the unspoken modifier: my *ex-girlfriend*, Talia.

When he used to imagine what it would be like if he ever ran into Talia again, he assumed she would be cold toward him. God knows she has plenty of reason to be. But with that soft half smile on her face, Talia doesn't *look* like she wants to kill him, and Townsend is happy to take a win where he can get one. They dated for about six months last year—what feels like a lifetime ago to Townsend. Would it be so crazy to think she's moved on too?

"Hey, everyone," Talia says, lifting a hand in greeting. "Good to see you all again." Townsend knows she's just being polite. He'd invited Talia to hang with his St. Augustine friends a few times over the course of their relationship, but they never really seemed to gel. Looking back, Townsend can recognize that Talia was probably bored by the rehashing of high school drama that always seemed to occur when the crew got together.

"Babe, come on. I think I see some girls from Regents." Nicole starts to paddle in the direction of a floating trampoline.

"Coming!" Brett calls after her. "Right, so . . ." He hesitates, twisting back to where Talia is still perched on his boat.

"Oh, sorry!" Talia says. It's clear she's not being invited along to chum it up with Nicole's gaggle of prep school friends. "Of course. Should I . . . ?" She gestures to Townsend's kayak. "Do you mind?"

"No, of course not, please." With some effort, Townsend navigates his kayak next to Brett's. Talia holds out her hand expectantly, and he takes it, pulling her aboard. She smells just as he remembers, like rose oil and sandalwood.

"Hi," she says again.

"Hi."

The rest of the group follows Brett and Nicole, paddling off toward the party, but Townsend just lets his kayak bob in the water. A beat of silence. He and Talia smile timidly at each other, unsure, as people whoop and laugh around them. "Can I get you a drink?" Townsend finally says, cursing himself for the cliché. He's nervous.

"Sure."

He hands her one of the beers rolling around in the bottom of the kayak, then he picks up his oar and starts paddling aimlessly, just looking to get away from the noise. Talia leans back into her seat and sips her beer, her face mostly hidden as she faces the water ahead.

"So," Talia begins, right as Townsend starts to say, "How you've been?"

She huffs out something like a laugh, then peeks over her shoulder before turning away again. In that glimpse, Townsend can see her cheeks have turned pink, but it's been so long, he's not sure how to read her blush. Is she embarrassed? Pleased? Regretting whatever life choices led her back into Townsend's shitty orbit?

It's painful, this awkwardness. Townsend should just row her back to shore and say goodbye. But for some reason, he finds he doesn't want to. There's something compelling him to keep Talia on his boat. Guilt, maybe. Or attraction. She really does look good with this new haircut. Then he gets an idea. "Have you ever been to the Congress Avenue Bridge at sunset?"

She swivels to face him. "Is this a line?"

"No, it's a genuine question."

"I have not."

"You have to see it. There are these bats—it sounds weird, but it's actually incredible. We should go now before it gets too late." He pauses for a moment. "If that's okay with you."

Talia crosses one long, skinny leg over the other. "That's okay with me."

"Cool." Townsend paddles with confidence now, pleased with his plan and with the extra time he's bought himself with Talia. "So. Want to explain how you ended up in my buddy's boat?"

As they make their way toward the north shore of Town Lake, Talia explains how she ran into Brett in the parking lot, where she'd just been leaving after having a picnic with a friend in the park. "Remember my coworker at Cuff, Meera? With the daughter?"

"Yeah, that name sounds familiar." Townsend doesn't want to talk about Meera. "And Brett just invited you to come chill with us?"

"Yep. Kind of a weird coincidence, I guess."

"What is it they say? Maybe 'coincidence' is just another word for 'fate'?"

"Oof." Talia rolls her eyes. "Now *that's* a line."

"Is it working?"

"Maybe," she admits with a sly smile. She seems lighter, more carefree than he remembers her being. It's undeniably sexy—but in a more sophisticated, self-assured way than the likes of Chrissy with her tiny bikini. Was Talia like this when they were together? So cool and confident?

Still keeping a good pace (he wants to make it to the bridge before sunset), Townsend tells Talia about his dad's recent heart attack, about how his health issues had pushed Townsend to finally launch his holistic health care start-up.

"You told me about this. AutoInTune—like 'autoimmune'—right?"

"Yes, that's it. I can't believe you remember that."

"I remember everything," says Talia, and for the first time since they spotted each other in the middle of Party Island, Townsend sees something like mistrust in her eyes.

"Tal . . ." He says her name softly, hoping she can hear the apology in his voice without him actually having to say the bitter words.

He knows that, with Talia, he screwed up. He was careless. Arrogant. Easily bored. Everything came easy to him, so he wasn't afraid to lose what he had. Even after she started to refer to him as her boyfriend, he kept an eye on what else was out there, mindlessly swiping through Cuff, the very dating app Talia worked for, while she slept next to him. He liked Talia, sure, but it was obvious that she was looking for something more serious than he was willing to give at the time. She was always talking about future plans, like what they would do for Halloween when it was still July. She used to show up at his apartment unannounced with homemade cookies, like some cross between a Girl Scout and his mother. So when he came across the Cuff profile of a shapely blond whose bio simply said "Aspiring nepo baby," he took his chances. He got sloppy. Maybe, deep down, he even wanted to get caught. And eventually, he did.

While he's been lost in his thoughts, they've reached the Congress Avenue Bridge. Townsend is saved from figuring out how to apologize to Talia when, all of a sudden, thousands of bats emerge at once from the underbelly of the bridge, flapping wildly against the darkening sky.

"Oh, look! Look!" Talia pulls out her phone from the sporty little belt bag strapped across her chest and starts taking pictures of the sunset. As she snaps away, he admires her delicate wrists: paper-thin skin, prominent tendons, bluish-purple network of veins.

Talia sighs, her eyes following the bats as they soar in frenzied circles. "They're so beautiful."

Townsend watches, too, but mostly he watches her. With her face lit by the glow of the distant skyline, she looks to him like the promise of something new—or, rather, the promise of a second chance at something he once had.

Sitting in his car later that night, staring into the blue glow of his phone in the dark, Townsend finally reads through the dozens of messages he received from her that day.

Your a piece of shxt.

I love you Townsend.

I still know the key code to get into your place.

Ignoring her is the easiest thing to do, but he's tired of taking the easy way out. He quickly types out a message and sends it before he can regret it.

This is over. We are over, he writes. Leave me the fuck alone, or I will make you leave me alone.

Chapter Two

TALIA

Talia Danvers knows what she wants, and it isn't this.

It feels uncharitable to think that way, especially since Gracie is pretty funny and sweet. But looking around Meera's cramped two-bedroom Tarrytown condo—every surface crowded with unfolded laundry and Barbie dolls and Gracie's art projects from school—Talia doesn't feel envy. She may be thirty-one and childless, but she knows when it happens for her, it's going to happen the right way.

On the couch next to Talia, Gracie watches cartoons while upside down, her bare feet dangling over the back of the sofa and her head grazing the carpet. She's still in her pajamas, though Meera has asked her three times already to get dressed. Talia wasn't allowed to watch TV growing up, but she can at least identify this character on the screen as SpongeBob SquarePants.

"Why don't you want to go to your dad's?" Talia asks.

Gracie's eyes don't leave the screen. "Because his house is stupid, and every meal has to be GGB."

"We don't say 'stupid,'" calls Meera from the bathroom, where she's dragging a mascara wand through her eyelashes.

"What's 'GGB'?"

"Stupid," Gracie mutters.

Meera ignores this. "Grain, green, and bean," she tells Talia. "It's her dad's requirement for all meals. Hari's girlfriend is a vegan now, apparently."

"I see." Talia kicks off her flip-flops and swivels her body around so that, like Gracie, her legs hang over the back of the sofa and her hair grazes the carpet. Blood rushes to her skull, but Gracie giggles, delighted to find Talia's head hanging beside hers.

"I don't like beans," she whispers to Talia.

"I don't like beans either," Talia whispers back. "They make me fart."

Gracie laughs again, her big brown eyes crinkling in the corners.

"Do you like your dad's girlfriend?"

"She's okay." Gracie turns her attention back to the TV screen. "I'd rather hang out with you and Mom."

From upside down, Talia watches Meera frown into the bathroom mirror. She hates seeing her friend stress.

"You know what's cool about your dad's house, though?" she asks Gracie.

"What?"

"Marty lives there, and you get to spend the next two days playing with him."

She doesn't respond, but Talia can tell Gracie is trying not to smile; she loves her new dachshund puppy.

"And I bet Marty will eat all of your beans for you, even if they make him a little gassy."

"He will." Gracie nods, her dark ponytail bobbing with her.

"Your dad will probably be here soon to pick you up. Want me to help you pick out an outfit? I bet he'll have Marty with him."

"That's okay." Gracie plants her hands on the carpet and performs an effortless backbend kickover off the sofa. Talia can't really remember being seven, but she feels certain she could never move her body like that.

With some struggle, she gets herself upright again on the sofa, and Meera joins her. Together they watch as Gracie disappears behind her bedroom door.

"I don't know how you did that, but thank you," she says.

"Anytime," Talia replies, and she means it. She's good with kids, and it feels nice to have this skill, one she knows men appreciate. Of course, she knows not to seem too interested in children, lest a guy think she's desperate to procreate. Dating means having to navigate a thousand contradictions, but if Talia's instincts are right (which they usually are), she'll never have to go on another first date again.

After Meera's ex arrives to pick up Gracie, she and Talia head to brunch at Maudie's Café in Westlake, which Meera claims is the best Maudie's location. Personally, Talia doesn't love the idea of breakfast tacos, but there are few things Meera likes about Austin, and Tex-Mex is one of them. For her best friend, Talia is willing to stomach a plate of greasy chorizo migas.

The host sets them up on the patio facing the parking lot, where they perch on wobbly metal chairs and bake in the heat of exhaust fumes and the already-hot sun. Struggling to peel her laminated menu off the table, Meera wrinkles her nose.

"I thought you loved Maudie's," Talia says, teasing.

"I do. Just not between the months of April and October."

"Manhattan gets hot too."

"Yeah." Meera finally unsticks her menu from the table. "But even when it's hot, it's still cool."

It's been eight years since Meera's then-husband convinced her to leave New York City to move to his hometown in Texas, and she's still bitter about it (mostly because Hari ended up leaving her just a few years later). But Talia—who moved from Lee County, Alabama, about three years ago—loves life in Austin, where being over the age of thirty without a ring on your finger doesn't invite strange looks. At Auburn University, she was one of three girls in her sorority who didn't get engaged before graduation. Here in Austin, there's far less pressure to settle down—though that doesn't stop Talia from putting pressure on herself.

Meera fans herself with her menu. "Fuck. I don't know how anyone functions in this heat. How am I supposed to go on a date when I can't stop sweating?"

"Have you?"

"Been sweating? Yes, a fuck ton."

"No." Talia swats her friend. "Been dating."

"A little. As it turns out, no one wants to date a thirtysomething, chronically ill divorcée who's still carrying baby weight, even though her kid is seven."

"C'mon. You're a knockout, and an awesome mom, and a badass engineer. Any guy would be crazy not to want you." Talia doesn't quite believe the words she's saying any more than Meera probably does, but it feels like the right thing to say. After all, Meera didn't expect things to end up like this.

Meera was still married and had already been at Cuff for a year when Talia was hired as a machine learning engineer. Talia had never imagined herself working for an online dating service—she'd hoped to become an AI trainer—but Cuff had just been acquired by Match Group and wanted to expand, so getting an entry-level position was easy. Talia liked to say it was fate that she and Meera were paired together for Talia's first assignment (though being the only female engineers on the machine learning team probably had something to do with that decision).

Initially, Meera seemed like someone who wasn't looking for new friends, what with her handsome husband and handful of a toddler at home. But still the two bonded over Shonda Rhimes shows and sushi restaurants and the pitfalls of being women in STEM. And when Meera's marriage started to crumble, Talia was the one who kept Meera from falling apart too. Three years and a messy divorce later, Talia considers Meera the closest thing she has to a sister—despite having an actual sister, to whom she hasn't spoken in years.

"Yeah, okay." Meera flips her off with both fingers. "What about you, hot stuff? Whatever happened with that lawyer who took you to the fancy omakase restaurant? Has he gotten a chance to see your new little French-girl haircut?"

The server arrives then, saving Talia from having to answer right away. As he fills their water glasses and takes their orders, she steels herself. Then she takes a deep breath and tells Meera the news she's been both eager and reluctant to share all morning.

"He was nice, but I don't think I'm going to see him again. I think I'm seeing Townsend again, actually."

After that night a few weeks ago when they watched the bats take flight, she wasn't sure Townsend would call. She hoped he would, obviously, but she's been working on letting things unfold at their own pace. For years, she was always hurry up and go, impatient to get to the happily ever after she'd always longed for. Now, however, she knows that some things just take time. For the right guy, she's willing to wait.

Like a perfect gentleman, Townsend rowed her back to shore, kissed her chastely on the cheek, and said they should see each other again soon—on purpose, next time. It was a piecrust promise, she figured. Easily made, easily broken.

But he did call. He called her the next morning (a phone call, not even a text) and asked her to dinner that night. For nearly four hours, they laughed over pre-Prohibition cocktails and pommes frites at Péché in the Warehouse District, where the lighting was so dim and the drinks were so strong that Talia was tempted to kiss Townsend right there at the table. But she didn't kiss him then, and she didn't kiss him three nights later, either, when he took her to Red Ash and ordered a $950 bottle of Barolo and finally, fully, apologized for how their relationship had ended last year. No, it wasn't until their Saturday-night date at the Blue Starlite Drive-in—one week after they'd reunited—that she leaned over the center console of Townsend's silver sports car and kissed him, just as she'd been dying to do for the past six months since their breakup. Neither of them cared about the movie (some slasher flick about an aspiring actress stalked by a vicious killer in 1980s Los Angeles), so they left and returned to Townsend's condo, where they had sex twice before falling asleep in each other's arms. It was the happiest Talia had felt in a very long time. Perhaps ever.

In the morning, they stayed in bed and talked, the conversation spanning from a childhood trip Townsend took to Monterey, to Talia's childhood fear of stingrays, to Townsend's dream of spending one more afternoon with his father, to Talia's wish that she could have been there for him when his dad passed.

"It just means the world to me that you're here now," he told her. "With all the fucking pressure I'm under right now, I feel like you're the one person keeping me sane."

"I'm here for you," she promised him. "I'm not going anywhere."

She didn't ask him to make the same promise, but somehow, he sensed she needed to hear these words back: "I'm not going anywhere either."

Across from her now at the table, Meera goes still, and for a moment, she looks pissed. But her face softens again just as quickly. "Tal, really? Townsend? Do you think that's a good idea?"

"I ran into him a few weeks ago at Town Lake. Or, really, I ran into his friend, and he invited me to go out on his boat to . . ." Talia hesitates, debating how best to describe Party Island. "It's just, like, a huge group of people who hang out near Lou Neff—"

"I know what Brotilla is," Meera says. "I'm a mom, not an alien."

"Right. Well, Townsend and I started talking, and he took me to watch the bats at Congress Avenue Bridge—"

Meera scrunched her nose. "Ew."

"It was cool, believe it or not. And we've been hanging out ever since." She pauses and then adds, "I was with him last night. He asked me if I want to be exclusive."

If she closes her eyes, Talia can take herself right back to that moment, to lying naked beneath Townsend's buttery-smooth Egyptian cotton sheets with her back pressed against his chest and his fingers in her hair. The mahogany sleigh bed, the handwoven shag rug, the heavy velvet curtains blocking Townsend's view of downtown from the forty-eighth floor—just a few weeks back together, and it already feels so familiar again. And while it's easy to be wooed by the opulence, Talia knows that isn't the reason Townsend's bed feels like home. It's the way he makes her feel when they're together, like he'll keep her safe and warm in that pretty room forever.

"He wants to be exclusive? That doesn't sound like Townsend. What did you tell him?"

"I said I'll think about it," Talia lies.

Meera sighs. "Okay, look, I'm glad you're happy. But I'm telling you now, this isn't going to end well. Did you already forget what happened last time?"

"He's changed. He's going out a lot less often and putting a lot more work into his start-up. And his dad died."

"People don't change, Tal, and his dad dying doesn't change what he did to you."

Talia opens her mouth to reply, but no words come out. She could say Meera isn't one to judge, seeing as she's a single parent with no prospects of her own. She could say it is possible for people to change, because Meera's ex-husband certainly did. She could say Meera is just jealous, because she doesn't have anything like what Talia has with Townsend, and it's likely she never will. But she doesn't say any of that. Meera is her closest friend in Austin—her only friend, really—and she doesn't deserve to be burdened with the truth. Whoever said truth is a deep kindness clearly didn't understand female friendships.

"I don't understand why you don't like him," Talia says instead.

"I don't understand why you *do*. I hate to say it, Tal, but he's an entitled prick who's just going to hurt you all over again."

"No." Talia shakes her head. "He's not." She wishes she could describe for her friend the intensity behind Townsend's eyes when he kissed her goodbye that morning or the way his mouth curled up on one side as he said, *Talia and Townsend. T 'n' T. We're dynamite together, baby.* But these fragile, fleeting moments will fracture if they're laid out on the table for everyone to appraise. Talia needs to keep them as safe as she feels in Townsend's arms.

"Okay. I hope you're right. Just know that, in my experience, history repeats."

Their food arrives—huevos rancheros for Meera, sweet potato hash for Talia—and they eat in tense silence, Talia glad for the excuse not to speak for a bit. At the table next to theirs, two women who look to be in their mid-twenties are laughing at something on one of their phone screens.

"Where did you guys meet?" the one with red hair asks.

"On Cuff," says the brunette.

Talia and Meera meet eyes and grin knowingly. It's always amusing to hear about other people's experiences with the app. Cuff employees are, of course, encouraged to use it themselves, though most don't. Seeing how the sausage gets made takes some of the magic out of the experience—not that there's a whole lot of magic to begin with when it comes to online dating.

Still, Talia is one of the few who take advantage of the free membership. She's always believed the adage that you have to kiss a lot of frogs before you find the one that turns into a prince. And sometimes, she's begun to suspect, you have to kiss the same frog twice.

She's not an idiot, despite what Meera clearly thinks. She knows that the last time she and Townsend dated, he was an ass to her. She can still remember the searing jolt she felt when she let herself into Townsend's place that Saturday night and found him in bed with another girl. And maybe she's just setting herself up for disappointment once again, but it's a risk Talia's willing to take. Her favorite podcast, *Spot of Positivitea*, always talks about the power of positive thinking. How we have the ability to shape our own realities. Someone like Meera, who assumes the world is out to get her, usually has her biases confirmed. Talia doesn't want to live like that. She wants to be hopeful.

The girls at the next table over are now discussing how the brunette's Cuff date was in bed, and the redhead seems angry suddenly. "Jen, you shouldn't have gone to that guy's apartment after the first date."

"Seriously? You're slut-shaming me?"

"I don't care if you have sex on a first date. But you met this guy on a dating app. Do you know how many girls have been murdered by dating app matches? You don't know him at all."

Murdered. The word hangs in the air, heavy as the sweet potato hash already churning in Talia's stomach, but it's the last line that really sticks in Talia's head: *You don't know him at all.* She knows this woman isn't speaking to her, probably isn't aware of her at all—but still, her words feel like a direct attack. It seems Meera's cynicism is contagious.

She does know Townsend. She *does.*

"Damn," Meera hisses, nodding her head in the direction of the two girls. "Are you listening to this? Shit got dark fast."

Talia manages a smile, though she still feels uneasy. It seems things are okay between her and Meera, at least.

She finishes her meal and lets the conversation drift to Gracie and whether she's going to sign up for ballet or soccer in the fall. But in the back of her mind, Talia keeps repeating to herself that she knows Townsend. Getting back together with him has its risks, but it's the right choice. He's everything she's always wanted.

Besides, people *can* change. She certainly has. She's no longer that desperate, cloying girlfriend who drove him away. Her past experiences were a result of her past thinking, but the present is hers to mold like clay in her hands.

And she's going to make it perfect.

Chapter Three

Meera

It's not unusual for Meera Ratnam to be the first one on the floor. At least, not since nearly losing her job.

Her chronic illness isn't her fault; she knows that. Still, she can't help but feel guilty for the hours of work she missed while fighting her fucked-up thyroid. After being diagnosed with Hashimoto's disease a year ago at the ripe age of thirty-three, Meera spent an inordinate amount of time in and out of doctors' offices, desperate to feel less achy and irritable and utterly drained. She even went on temporary disability to get her symptoms under control, and though her manager claimed to be understanding, she could just imagine what he was thinking: Weak. Lazy. Underachieving, just like her thyroid. She can't trust that her job is safe, and so—as of last month—she always shows up early and stays late, hoping her commitment makes up for her routine blood tests and persistent brain fog.

Unfortunately, Meera is finding it more difficult than usual to concentrate this morning. Last week, she'd been tasked with creating a presentation on new machine learning operations tools, and it's still not finished (even though it's due to be presented to the summer interns at noon). She needs to stay on task, but her nagging suspicion wins out over her need to achieve. Work can wait. It will only take a few minutes to find what she needs.

Just to be sure she's alone, Meera stands up from her desk, which is bare, save for a framed copy of Gracie's latest school-picture-day photo and a half-dead succulent. ("Half *alive*," Talia, ever the optimist, corrects Meera when she says this.) In the wake of the pandemic, Cuff hired an architect to design what the company coined "mod pods": a series of modular mini offices that contained each team within its own mega cubicle. The hope was to offer more peace and privacy than the traditional open-office concept, but really, Meera just feels like she's trapped in a jury-rigged fort with the whole ML team. At least she can see most of the floor from her spot near the doorway, including the corner dedicated to the offices of the C-level executives.

She confirms it: No one is in. Not even the office custodian, Aarav, who's made a habit of frequenting Meera's desk (and showing her pictures of his grandchildren) ever since learning that she also speaks Tamil.

She knows that what she's about to do is a fireable offense. It could even be considered a federal offense. But there are only two people in the world who would compel Meera to take this kind of risk: her daughter and her best friend. And right now, Talia needs her. Even if she's not willing to admit it.

At Cuff, Meera's job isn't about the customer; it's about developing algorithms and cleaning data. And while all Cuff employees have limited access to user accounts, it's really only the membership experience and security teams who have reason to access individual customer information. But because she knows her login will give her the info she needs, Meera enters the company's database and searches for Townsend Fuller.

Along with 401(k) matching and monthly date stipends (which Meera always spends on solo take-out dinners), Cuff offers all its employees free Cuff Plus memberships, giving them infinite swipes and Winks (the Cuff equivalent of likes). Meera doesn't use Cuff anymore; to her, it feels like pissing in her own swimming pool. "Everyone is on the apps these days," Talia always tells Meera. "You're not just going to bump into the right guy. You've got to actively pursue him."

But Meera did bump into the right guy, once upon a time. During her first year in NYU's Interactive Telecommunications Program, she and Hari Balaji took the same Synthetic Architectures course, where they became seatmates, and then study buddies, and then so much more. They bonded over their similar backgrounds (both had Sri Lankan Tamil parents who came to the States as refugees during the Sri Lankan Civil War) and their shared dreams of using communications technologies to make a difference in the world.

After graduating from NYU, they moved into a one-bedroom apartment in the East Village, where they spent their weekends trying new restaurants and attending immersive art exhibits. They made friends. They got married. They were deliriously happy. Then Hari's dad had a ministroke, and Hari insisted they move down to Texas to be closer to him. Meera didn't see an alternative.

Within a month, they traded their apartment with its lofty tin ceilings and view of Tompkins Square Park for a three-bedroom bungalow in charming, tree-lined Tarrytown (just west of Downtown Austin), where they spent their weekends grocery shopping and mowing the lawn. They got office jobs. They had a baby. They were making things work.

Then Hari's girlfriend sent Meera an email, explaining that her husband no longer loved her and would be leaving her.

He hadn't intended for her to find out this way, Hari said. Jessica was a good person but a little impulsive, he said. But Meera knew exactly what Jessica was: a Machiavellian Mary, a toxic feminist, a woman so afraid of not getting what she wants that she'll go to any lengths to succeed.

Once upon a time, Meera could relate to women like Jessica. When she was younger, Meera was driven. Motivated to succeed in a male-dominated industry. Determined to support her parents in their old age and prove them wrong when they worried that their daughter's attempts to "have it all" would end disastrously. But it turned out they were right. She lost the husband and the house and was clinging to her career by her fingernails. Not even two years later, Meera was struck down by a disease that disproportionately affects women, which felt like cosmic punishment for a lifetime of claiming she wasn't like other girls.

Being different hadn't served her well, but still, Meera doesn't want to be on the apps like everyone else. She doesn't want to spend her free time sifting through a slush pile of hopeful singles, assessing their capacity to love based on a half dozen photos and a few cherry-picked interests. *So-and-so likes wine, basketball, and dogs.*

Meera doesn't care about that; she wants to know how these prospective matches feel about machine sentience, or quantum computing, or interstellar travel. Or infidelity.

She knows how dating app algorithms work because she helped create those algorithms, and still, they don't work in her favor. No matter what Talia says, Meera won't use Cuff herself, even after three years of being single—save for the brief dalliance she indulged in about a year after her divorce. Talia doesn't know about that; Meera plans to take that mess of a relationship (if she could even call it that) to the grave.

Sitting now in the Cuff office, Meera slurps her iced coffee and stares at her screen, where the search results have proved her right. Despite asking to be exclusive (according to Talia, anyway), Townsend still has an active Cuff profile, with his account showing activity as recent as the night before. Meera is disappointed, but she isn't surprised.

Men like Townsend always disappoint, especially when given a chance with women like Talia.

It was just about a year ago when Talia and Townsend first met on Cuff; Meera can still remember her friend's excitement. "He's an Ivy League grad and an investment banker and he's unbelievably handsome," Talia had gushed while twirling around Meera's kitchen. "We've been talking nonstop for a week. He wants to take me on a date. He seems too good to be true."

"Well, when something seems too good to be true . . ." Meera looked at her meaningfully.

"I know, I know. It probably is." Talia sighed. "But I don't want him to be."

Outside the Cuff office window now, horns beep and voices call out as Downtown Austin stirs to life. Her coworkers will be arriving soon. Meera taps a meticulously sharpened fingernail on her mouse, debating what to do. Knowing that Townsend has an active Cuff account is enough for her to prove to Talia that the man hasn't changed, but still she's tempted to look at more—to see who he's swiped right on, who he's sent Winks to, who he's made promises to.

And if he's uploaded photos through a social media platform, she can access even more data: his interests, his music tastes, his most frequently used words, the images he likes, the people he likes, the average time he spends looking at a photo . . . She could know everything there is to know about Townsend Fuller with a few strokes of her keyboard. It never ceases to amaze Meera just how willing people are to bare the whole truth of themselves on the internet for all to see. Or, at least, for those who know where to look.

But regardless of what she finds, Meera knows she needs to tell Talia that Townsend isn't who he seems. It will be difficult, because the truth is the hardest thing to see, but Meera just needs to sit her friend down, look her in the eye, and say—

"What are you doing?"

Meera jumps, her elbow knocking her iced coffee off her desk and onto the carpeted floor, where it creates a Rorschach-style splatter. Behind her, Talia stands expectantly, dark hair freshly blown out and lips painted berry red. Sometimes, Meera wonders if she's not a little bit in love with her best friend. But that can't be. This is just what it feels like to care deeply about someone, the way she cares deeply about Gracie. The way she once cared deeply about Hari, before he fucked that up.

"Aren't we jumpy. Did I catch you looking at porn on the job?"

"You very well know all the good sites are blocked here." Meera catches her breath and forces a smile. Out of the corner of her eye, she checks her screen—the only thing visible is her Outlook inbox, the company database minimized out of view. "You owe me six bucks, by the way."

Talia looks bewildered. "For what?"

"For the coffee you just made me drop. That shit's expensive."

"Take mine. I need to cut back on caffeine anyway." Talia holds out her own coffee, a gesture so generous it nearly makes Meera cry. Must be her out-of-whack hormones.

"I'm not taking your coffee, you martyr." Meera waves her off. "I will take the shirt off your back, though. That top is cute."

"I would give it to you if I were wearing a better bra today," Talia jokes. She's too kind to mention that Meera could never fit into her clothing. Too kind to be deceived by someone like Townsend Fuller.

"Spill?" Aarav appears in the doorway by Meera's desk, sneaking up on her just like Talia did moments ago. She really needs to be more vigilant. In his hands, he holds a roll of paper towels and a bottle of carpet cleaner.

"Yes, sorry, Aarav. That was me. You don't have to clean it up—I can take care of it."

"No, no. I will clean." She watches as Aarav kneels on the floor and begins to soak up the milky-brown puddle. After a moment, he looks up at Talia, who smiles politely. Then he turns to face Meera, and in Tamil—so quietly she can barely hear him—he says, "Don't worry. I won't tell."

Meera freezes. It's unclear whether he's referring to the coffee spill or the illicit snooping, but before she can ask for clarification, Talia speaks.

"Lunch later?"

"For sure, if I get this stupid MLOps-intern presentation done before then."

"You'll get it done," Talia says. "You always do." Ever the optimist.

Meera watches as Talia heads off to her desk, and then turns to find Aarav. But he's no longer crouched on the floor beside her; only a wet splotch stinking of ammonia remains.

She'll warn Talia about Townsend soon, Meera tells herself. The next opportunity she gets. She doesn't relish the idea of breaking her friend's heart, but telling her about Townsend's Cuff profile is the right thing to do. Though whip smart and ambitious, Talia is also—in Meera's opinion—a little naive.

And Meera knows just how easy it is for someone like that to get hurt by someone like him.

Chapter Four

Kaitlyn

Kaitlyn Reade has never broken into an apartment before—but then again, she's never had good reason to do so before now.

She also never expected it to be so easy. All she had to do: Tell the landlord that she needed to water her sister's plants and she forgot her spare key.

The landlord—a squat man with a wispy gray ponytail—squinted at her in response. "You're Amanda's sister?"

"I am." Kaitlyn knew exactly what he was thinking, what everyone seemed to be thinking when they compared the two sisters: *So how come she's hot and you're not?*

Luck, she wanted to tell them. *Good luck for her, bad luck for me.*

"She's months behind on rent. She's going to get her ass kicked out of here soon."

"Have you seen her recently?"

The landlord shook his head no. "She's avoiding me."

Join the club, Kaitlyn was tempted to say, but instead, she just followed the landlord up the stairs.

She hoped—perhaps naively—that she would find her sister still in bed, sleeping off a hangover. She hoped to hash out their issues and finally understand why she'd been cut out of Amanda's life. But standing now in Amanda's empty studio apartment, it's clear that her sister hasn't been here in quite some time.

She's only been to Amanda's place in East Austin once or twice, but she remembers it being messy to the point of feeling squalid: crusty dishes stacked in the sink; clothes—both washed and unwashed—thrown over the furniture; rolling papers and parking tickets and crumpled wads of bills scattered on every surface, like proud evidence of a life lived fast. But surveying the four-hundred-square-foot space now, Kaitlyn can see little evidence of life at all—the place is immaculate. No dirty dishes, no unfolded clothes, no clutter.

She wonders, for a moment, whether the landlord let her into the right apartment, but then she notices the black-and-white modeling shot hanging in the kitchen: her sister, smirking at the camera lens, one hand cupping a bare breast and the other offering a middle finger to the photographer. Yes, this is her sister's apartment, all right.

Of course, Amanda isn't a real model, just as she isn't a DJ or makeup artist or aspiring fashion designer or any of the things she claims to be. And even with the tens of thousands of followers Amanda boasts on social media, Kaitlyn isn't positive her sister can be considered a professional influencer, as there is nothing professional about Amanda Reade—though she is certainly influential when she wants to be.

All Kaitlyn knows for sure about her little sister is that she's very good at landing on her feet . . . though where she's landed now, Kaitlyn can only imagine.

Despite being born just fourteen months apart, the sisters aren't close and have never pretended to be. Kaitlyn used to joke that Amanda (conceived by accident) just couldn't resist stealing her spotlight, and she's been stealing it ever since . . . along with Kaitlyn's clothes, and money, and friends. But that joke stopped feeling funny after their parents died in a car wreck two years ago, leaving Kaitlyn the executor of their will and the recipient of a mere ten thousand dollars. The rest of the estate—modest, though not insubstantial—was left to Amanda. As her parents explained in the will, Kaitlyn is a paralegal. Kaitlyn is salaried. Kaitlyn is stable. And since Amanda is none of these things, she's more in need of financial assistance. Kaitlyn would understand their decision, they were sure.

Kaitlyn can't fault her sister for this. Amanda didn't ask for the unexpected windfall, just as she didn't ask for a perfectly symmetrical face, or the thick blond waves that fell to her elbows, or a natural hourglass figure that stayed trim no matter how many french fries she ate and beers she chugged. And for all her flighty tendencies, there wasn't a malicious bone in her sister's body—which is why Kaitlyn believes Amanda isn't ignoring her on purpose. It's not uncommon for three weeks to go by without her sister returning a call or text. But this time, it's been nearly three *months* since she last heard from Amanda. That isn't normal.

The last time Kaitlyn saw Amanda was late February. They got brunch at their favorite diner in Georgetown, Spooners, which was just a few minutes away from Southwestern University, where their parents had both been professors. Amanda had grumbled about making the trip up there so early on a Saturday (their hometown being over thirty miles north of Austin), but Kaitlyn knew her sister was feeling just as nostalgic for Georgetown as she was, what with the two-year anniversary of their parents' death approaching. It was on that car ride that Kaitlyn asked Amanda about her plan.

"My plan?" Amanda parroted from the passenger seat. Even though they were in Amanda's car—a pearly-white 2024 Honda Accord purchased with inheritance money—Kaitlyn was the one driving, as Amanda claimed she needed to finish her makeup.

"Yeah, your plan." From the corner of her eye, Kaitlyn watched as her sister admired her face in the visor mirror. "The money from Mom and Dad won't last forever, you know. I think it's time to find something steady."

"I'm supposed to become a boring paralegal?"

Kaitlyn let the insult roll off her back. If she let every snide remark from Amanda get to her, she'd never stop snapping. She didn't want to be responsible for ruining the day. "Being a paralegal isn't the only job option."

"I know that," Amanda said. "Do you?"

Kaitlyn sighed. They'd had this same conversation too many times over the past two years, and they were both tired of it. "If you could do anything, what would you do?"

"What I'm doing right now." Amanda leaned closer to the mirror, puckering her lips. "I'm twenty-four. I don't have to have things figured out. I'm enjoying myself, and I'm enjoying life. You should try it sometime."

"Twenty-four is when you should start to figure things out." By twenty-four, Kaitlyn had already spent two years working as a paralegal at Stevenson Ellis, one of the most prestigious law firms in Austin. She would have liked to pursue her law school dreams, but the loss of her parents (and her inheritance) made student debt seem like an unnecessary risk.

"I have almost thirty thousand followers on Instagram," Amanda said. "I could get a brand deal."

"You could. But have you?"

Amanda didn't answer.

"I can help you," Kaitlyn added, more gently this time. "I can help with content or with putting together a pitch to brands."

For a moment, Amanda was quiet, and then she said, "I'm thinking of subletting my apartment and going to Europe this summer."

"To Europe? Where in Europe?"

"Anywhere. Everywhere. I mean, I've barely left Texas my whole life. I want to see the world." Amanda waved the lip gloss wand in her hand for emphasis. "And I can get great content while I'm there. I'll get tons of new followers."

"Going to Europe isn't a plan, Amanda. You need a job. You need structure. Do you know how much money it would cost to traipse around Europe for a summer?"

"I saw a TikTok from a girl who backpacked through Europe for two months and spent less than four hundred dollars."

"And where exactly was she sleeping? A new guy's bed every night?"

"Maybe she was. There's nothing wrong with that." Amanda paused and then added, "I wouldn't be doing that, though, 'cause I have a boyfriend."

That caught Kaitlyn off guard even more than the Europe plans. "A boyfriend? Since when?" She'd heard about several of Amanda's boys over the years, but she'd never heard her sister refer to anyone as a boyfriend.

"Since about a month ago, when he asked me to be his girlfriend." Even without looking at her, Kaitlyn could tell her sister was beaming. She'd clearly been dying to bring this up. "He's gorgeous and has this incredible condo downtown, and he's so, so good to me. He took me to dinner at Jeffrey's in Clarksville for Valentine's Day. The bill was insane, and he just put down his credit card without even looking at it."

"So he's rich." Kaitlyn tried to keep the edge out of her voice and failed. "Is he older?"

"Only by, like, a decade."

"Seriously?"

"Relax. Age is just a number." Amanda laughed at the look on Kaitlyn's face, which was no doubt aghast. "He's a banker or something, but I think he also has a ton of family money. The waiter at Jeffrey's knew his name. And instead of just ordering, like, the cheapest bottle of red, he asked the wine guy for something from the Piedmont region. I don't even know what that means."

"Sommelier."

"What?"

"That's what a wine guy is called. A sommelier. And Piedmont is a region of Italy near the Alps."

"Well." Amanda crossed her arms. "I'll get to visit it myself when I go to Europe this summer."

"Is your boyfriend going with you on this trip?" A thought occurred to Kaitlyn. "Is he paying for this trip?"

"Maybe," Amanda said, though it wasn't clear which question she was answering.

They pulled into the diner parking lot. After getting out of the car, Kaitlyn frowned at the exterior, already scratched and coated with dirt. "I don't know why you went with a white car, Amanda. It's already so grimy."

"I can clean it."

"But you won't." Kaitlyn went around the back of the car, continuing her inspection. "And you put a bumper sticker on it! You've ruined it."

"It's not ruined. And it's a decal, not a bumper sticker, thank you very much." Looking proud, Amanda touched the decal—which resembled the Roman numeral for *two*—on her back window. "It's the Gemini symbol. It represents the twins, Castor and Pollux."

"It looks cheap." Kaitlyn doesn't believe in Greek mythology, or astrology, or any of the woo-woo shit Amanda is into. She believes in logic and reason and accountability.

"Says you," Amanda retorted, looking hurt.

The brunch had ended on a sour note—more bickering, more headbutting—and the two drove home in silence. Soon after, Kaitlyn blocked Amanda on Instagram; she was done with her sister's salacious snapshots showing up on her feed. And at some point, Amanda decided she was done with her, too, because the only way Kaitlyn could get into her apartment today was by breaking and entering.

It creeps her out, just how deadly quiet Amanda's studio feels. Kaitlyn sits on her sister's bed, attempting to feel less like an intruder and more like a guest. It's possible Amanda went through with her plan to spend the summer in Europe; it's possible she left the apartment spotless for a subletter, who could be arriving any minute. But the longer she sits here, the more bothered she becomes by a lingering stench, something pungent yet sterile. Bleach, she realizes. But it doesn't smell clean; it smells like something covered up. Unsure what else to do, Kaitlyn pulls out her phone and rereads her last three texts to Amanda, the most recent one sent less than a week ago.

> **Sun, Mar 17 at 11:57 AM:** I'm sorry for the shitty things I said at brunch last month. I only said them because I care.
>
> **Sat, Apr 20 at 3:39 PM:** You can't still be pissed about brunch. You said mean things, too.
>
> **Thu, May 30 at 8:11 AM:** Happy birthday, A. I love you, even if you are still mad at me.

Though Amanda had sent Kaitlyn a message for her own birthday back on March 3 (an obligatory "happy b-day" text, no exclamation points, no emojis), she hasn't said a word to Kaitlyn since. Almost three months of silence—it just doesn't feel right. And it's not like she can reach out to friends or family to ask after Amanda's whereabouts; Kaitlyn has no idea what sort of crowd her sister is hanging out with these days, and save for a weird aunt in Buffalo, they have no family aside from each other.

A thought occurs to her: Amanda may be ignoring her older sister, but surely she can't be ignoring her followers.

Feeling shaky, Kaitlyn logs onto Instagram and unblocks Amanda's account. Then she clicks on her latest post, which immediately makes her feel sick to her stomach. There isn't anything wrong with the photo: It's a shot of her sister taken from behind, her body illuminated by the giant picture window in the background and naked, save for a pair of men's boxer shorts. It's the date when it was posted that bothers her: March 6. For years, Kaitlyn has known her sister to reliably add photos to her Instagram grid at least twice a week. Now she hasn't posted a photo in months—not even on her twenty-fifth birthday. Amanda loves her own birthday, more than anyone Kaitlyn knows.

For months, Kaitlyn has ignored her nagging suspicions, reassuring herself that Amanda is just . . . being Amanda. But now she can't shake the feeling that something is wrong.

That her sister isn't just absent, but *missing*.

Panic setting in, Kaitlyn begins to tear through the apartment, looking first through the drawers in the kitchen and then moving on to the dresser. She doesn't know what she hopes to find—a note explaining Amanda's absence, maybe, or any sort of clue as to where she may be. But all she finds is silverware and cooking utensils and neatly folded clothes: nothing that would suggest her sister is across the ocean or, worse, in danger.

The only thing she finds that feels out of place: a thick gold ring engraved with a shield—a school crest, perhaps. Kaitlyn picks it up off the bedside table and slips it onto her thumb. It's way too big, likely made to fit a man's finger. A Latin phrase is written around the outside of the crest: *Dominus regit me.* According to Google, this roughly translates to "The Lord is my shepherd." Unless Amanda developed bloated fingers and an interest in the Old Testament since Kaitlyn last saw her, this ring belongs to someone else.

In the car on the way to that ill-fated brunch, Amanda mentioned a new boyfriend: an old money, blue blood type who likely attended some fancy prep school. The news hadn't sat well with Kaitlyn at the time, and shamefully, she figured she was jealous of her sister's good fortune. But now she feels something new: suspicion. Her sister is beautiful, yes, but she's not prim or polished. She's not the kind of girl you would take to the country club to meet your parents. And yet, somehow, she landed a guy who could afford dinner at Jeffrey's and possibly a heavy gold class ring. Someone who might have whisked her off to Europe, or at least have an explanation for why Amanda is MIA.

Kaitlyn pockets the ring—hoping she can later track down its owner and get some answers—and turns her attention back to Amanda's most recent Instagram post. Though her photos often generate hundreds of comments, this one has generated thousands, most of which have been written in the last few weeks: Where is she? Why hasn't she posted? Does anyone know what's up?

The realization sets in—a whole virtual community noticed Kaitlyn's sister was missing before she herself did. Shame settles over her skin, making her itchy to do something. To make up for lost time. Kaitlyn grabs her purse and exits the apartment, thanking the landlord on her way out and asking if it's okay for her to hold onto the spare set of keys so she doesn't have to bother him next time. As she steps out of the building, she thinks how disappointed their parents would be. It's her job to look after her younger sister, to guide her, to protect her. But she failed.

Three weeks earlier, after a disastrous date at Latchkey on East Sixth, Kaitlyn almost went to see Amanda. It was rare that she found herself in East Austin, and Amanda's apartment was only a block away. She could stop by, Kaitlyn thought. Her date (a chatty data science professor who kept blowing her nose and then inspecting the contents of her tissue) knew Amanda; they'd waitressed together at a sushi restaurant, and Amanda had been trying to set her and Kaitlyn up for months. Kaitlyn could tell Amanda that she'd finally reached out, despite having no desire to date at the moment. Maybe she'd even admit that she only went on the date to make Amanda happy. To get Amanda to talk to her again.

Kaitlyn even went so far as to walk right by Amanda's building—but then she remembered: It was a Saturday night. There was no way Amanda was home, and even if she was, there was little chance of her wanting to hang out with her dorky older sister, whose texts she'd been ignoring for months.

Kaitlyn was just about to cross the street to the bus stop (unlike Amanda, she didn't have the cash handy to buy herself a brand-new car) when it happened: A speeding silver convertible plowed past the stop sign, nearly swiping her in the process. In her surprise, Kaitlyn stumbled backward, tripping over the curb and landing hard on her ass. In all likelihood, the driver (some privileged asshole, she was sure, though she didn't get a good look) had simply been careless, but something about the near miss felt intentional. Like they had been trying to hit her.

In her head, she imagined what Amanda would say: *Or they just didn't see you, because you insist on wearing all black like a fucking emo kid.*

Leaving Amanda's apartment now, Kaitlyn looks both ways before crossing the street, half expecting the same silver sports car to come speeding toward her again. It doesn't, of course, and she feels stupid, both for expecting to see that car again and for not stopping by her sister's weeks earlier when she had the chance. What if Amanda had been home? What if that had been Kaitlyn's chance to fix things and she missed it?

Kaitlyn hasn't been able to keep Amanda from finding trouble, like her parents wanted. But she has a ring, and a description of a boyfriend, and a hunch.

It isn't much, but it may be enough to help find Amanda.

Chapter Five

Townsend

Townsend can't recall the last time he invited a girl to have a meal with his family—college maybe? Or perhaps they met that Ballet Austin company dancer he dated for a bit in his mid-twenties. He really can't remember—but he knows that he'll remember this, the first time his mom met Talia, forever. Of course, he'll only remember it because it's already going so exceptionally poorly.

Mother invited them to brunch at Foothill Grille—the members-only dining room at Verano Country Club—to belatedly celebrate Townsend's thirty-fourth birthday. Despite the casual dress code (it's clubhouse fare, after all), his mom insisted on wearing one of her fussy retro skirt suits, complete with painful-looking pointed-toe pumps and an impractically small alligator leather purse. When they first sat down at the table, Talia joked that she must not be able to fit much more than her phone and ChapStick in that bag. In response, Mother said it was a Mini Kelly, and from the look on Talia's face, Townsend could tell this didn't make any more sense to her than it did to him. That, at least, made him smile. He loves that Talia isn't fashion obsessed like other girls he's dated and that she doesn't pretend to know about things she doesn't. Talia is confident. She is real.

A month has passed since they got back together, and already, Townsend feels like another person. Inspired by Talia's regular Pilates classes, he's taken up running again for the first time since he trained for the Austin Marathon back in 2019. He's cut back even more on alcohol, and he's started drinking chamomile tea with Talia before bed rather than ending his nights with a glass of scotch. He's waking up earlier, singing in the shower, smiling at strangers on the street, leaving money in tip jars everywhere he goes—and it's all because of Talia.

Best of all, he's no longer afraid of his phone. There haven't been any threatening messages in weeks, not after he made it clear that things were over. He feels proud of the simple, efficient way he handled things—just like his father used to dispense with employees who weren't performing. Without trying too hard, Townsend can convince himself that the whole interlude never even happened. It was just a nightmare he can only remember now in patchy fragments.

As the new and improved Townsend, he hadn't intended to be late to brunch. Talia just looked so good in her little floral minidress when he picked her up this morning that he insisted on having her right then and there. But when they arrived at the country club at quarter past (they'd been expected at ten), his mom's annoyance was palpable. Also evident: her distaste for the short little dress Townsend found so sexy. As Mother looked his girlfriend up and down with casual dismissiveness, Townsend wondered if he should have suggested Talia change into something with a longer hemline. Or perhaps he should have suggested Talia not join them at all.

The hostess sat them at their usual table in the back, a secluded spot overlooking the pool. After getting settled and ordering (lox bagel sandwiches for him and Talia, Greek yogurt for his mom, greyhounds with Tito's and grapefruit juice for all), Mother turns to Talia with a tight-lipped smile.

"Talia," she says, "remind me what it is you do?" Townsend knows he never told his mom about Talia's job—or about their previous relationship and why it ended—so this overfamiliarity is strange. A tactic for getting Talia to drop her guard, he figures.

"I'm a machine learning engineer at Cuff." Talia pauses, and then adds, "Cuff is a dating app." Her cloth napkin still sits on her plate, wrapped around her silverware, and Townsend wills her to spread it on her lap. He knows she didn't spend her weekends in etiquette class from the age of ten like he did, but still, she should know the basics by now. His snobbery annoys him; Mother is getting in his head.

"And what does machine learning entail?"

"Basically, I work with the artificial intelligence team to develop the AI-enabled features on the app. That can range from building millisecond real-time predictions at scale, to automating the ML-model life cycle, to building support for generative AI models."

"My goodness." Mother sips her water, being careful not to leave lipstick stains on her glass. "Isn't that interesting." He knows Mother doesn't understand what any of that means, and even if she did, she'd hardly find it interesting. The woman still uses an ancient iPhone 6 and has told Townsend many times during the creation of AutoInTune that, while she's proud of him, she can only handle so much of his "computer talk."

"A lot of my job revolves around ensuring our AI system complies with data privacy laws and ethical AI development. AI is scary to a lot of people, just because it's a largely unregulated business technology, which naturally leads to privacy concerns." Talia must be nervous; she's talking too much. Townsend needs to bail her out.

"She's kind of a genius, if you can't tell." He places his hand softly on the back of Talia's neck, and she leans into it, looking grateful and a little exhausted.

"Where did you go to school?"

"Auburn University."

"Never heard of it."

"Yes, you have, Mom," Townsend says. "It's one of the largest universities in the South."

"It's in Alabama," Talia adds.

"Is that where you're from?"

"Yes, ma'am. Right outside Opelika." Townsend cringes at the use of *ma'am*; Mother finds certain Southern traditions affectatious, despite growing up in Austin herself.

"I believe there's a Greater Lee County Chapter of the NLJC. Is that right?"

"I'm not . . ." Talia trails off, seemingly at a loss.

"It's the National League of Junior Cotillions," Townsend tells her. "Mom, Talia didn't do cotillion."

"I see." Mother pointedly eyes the napkin still sitting on Talia's plate. Taking the hint, Talia unrolls it and spreads it on her lap, the tips of her ears burning pink. Fortunately, the server appears with their drinks, giving Townsend the opportunity to change the subject.

"Speaking of cotillion," he says, "Mom, do you remember my friend Brett Livingston? He's a St. Augustine guy, and we did cotillion together."

"The doctor, yes?"

"He didn't actually finish med school. He decided to join his dad's company instead. But yes, him."

"A shame," Mother says.

Townsend ignores this. "Well, his brother is a venture capitalist at Silicon Hills Venture Partners, and I have a meeting with him to talk about expanding my platform."

"Your what?"

"For my start-up," he says, resisting the urge to cap off his reply with *Duh.*

"Right. Your start-up. Remind me what it's called?" Townsend knows he's told Mother the name of his start-up before—several times, in fact. It's been months since he publicly launched to consumers (after operating in private beta for nearly a year), but he doubts she could recall the name even with a gun to her head.

"AutoInTune," Talia answers for him. "It's a platform for holistic autoimmune care. You should see the pitch deck for his expansion plans. It's very comprehensive."

Townsend smiles, touched by Talia's support. "It was Dad's rheumatoid arthritis that inspired me to create it. You know, maybe if he'd been diagnosed earlier and had access to a virtual team of experts, he wouldn't have developed heart disease. Maybe he'd still be alive."

"So you're diagnosing autoimmune diseases? With your bachelor's in finance?"

Townsend takes a generous swig of his drink, attempting to keep his cool. "I'm not diagnosing people. I'm offering personalized, evidence-based care. AutoInTune assigns members to a team of health experts, like dietitians and sleep coaches, to help them manage autoimmune symptoms. It's only been four months since I launched our virtual platform, and nearly ninety percent of users have already reported a reduction in hospital visits. The next step is expanding our reach and lowering out-of-pocket costs for users." He's been practicing his pitch for Brett's brother; he knows this spiel by heart.

"And how do you plan on doing that?"

He takes a deep breath. This is his chance. "Well, as you may remember, Dad was a generous contributor during my seed-funding round. I'm working on developing enterprise partnerships now, but if I really want to reduce costs at scale, I need more money."

"Oh?"

Under the table, Talia grabs his hand and gives it a squeeze. He briefed her on the car ride to the club, so she knows what he's about to ask. "Which is why I'm hoping to gain access to my trust."

They hadn't been particularly close, Townsend and his dad, but still, his unexpected passing devastated Townsend. The man was his father, and he'd looked out for Townsend in ways Mother never would or could. And though his dad had seemingly encouraged Townsend's entrepreneurial ambition in life (why else would he have provided early-stage capital to AutoInTune?), he'd revealed his true feelings in the most cowardly way: after death.

Townsend can still remember the gut punch he'd felt, learning that his inheritance—his birthright!—had been put into an inaccessible trust. To add insult to injury: As the trustee, Mother was the one who'd determine when he acquired the funds. It made sense that his little sister Blake, eight years his junior, didn't have access to her trust—she's basically still a child. But he's an adult, a thirty-four-year-old man with a smart, serious girlfriend and a legit health care start-up. He'd even recently deactivated his Instagram, erasing the last vestiges of the scotch-swilling libertine he'd been in his twenties. There was no reason he should've been punished.

The food arrives then, and they hold conversation as the server sets down their meals. Townsend watches as his mom artfully drizzles honey over her Greek yogurt bowl and takes a slow, lingering bite—and he's about to make his request again, wondering whether she heard him at all, when she finally speaks.

"Isn't that what investors are for? Getting more money?"

"I'm meeting with some firms. But I already gave up a large amount of equity in my seed round. I want to retain some control." He doesn't want to get into the real reason he's reluctant to approach investors—not now, and not with her. "Anyway, I'm sure Dad would have faith in my company, seeing as he already invested in it."

"Townsend," she sighs. "We've talked about this."

"I'd like to discuss it again."

"The discussion is over. You'll gain access when you've proved you're ready for it."

"What more do I have to do to prove myself?" Townsend hates the petulance creeping into his voice, but he can't help it. He could be a drug addict, or a drunk, or a hard-partying playboy, but instead, he's a clean-cut Penn grad whose worst crime is occasionally showing up a few minutes late to brunch.

As though reading his mind, Mother says, "You could start by addressing your chronic tardiness."

"It's my fault we were late today, ma'am," says Talia, saving him. "I'm sorry for keeping you waiting. I was having trouble deciding what to wear."

Mother makes a face, as though to say *And that's what you chose?* But instead, she asks, "And would you ever ambush your family like this at what was supposed to be a nice birthday brunch?"

"I . . ." Talia hesitates. "I wouldn't, but that's only because I don't have a relationship with my family."

"I'm sorry to hear that, dear," says Mother—and though she's likely too tactful to pry further, Townsend wants to be sure she moves on from this topic. Plus, he selfishly wants to keep this conversation on track.

"Will you at least consider giving me access to my trust?"

In a singsong voice, she says, "We'll see." An empty promise that makes Townsend feel violent.

It isn't until the drive back to his condo—when his head isn't so clouded with outrage—that he notices Talia's silence. "You okay?" he asks.

She responds without turning away from the window. "All good."

By now, Townsend knows Talia well enough to assume she's still thinking about her family, who she's told him about in bits and pieces: her father (a butcher with calloused hands, a personal Bible on his nightstand, and a mean streak), her mother (a commission-based cold caller who either cried or drank herself to sleep every night), and her older sister (who—after getting pregnant at sixteen—was sent away to live in a faith-based maternity home called Neveah's Oasis). Leaving for college was what convinced Talia to cut ties with her family for good, but Townsend can tell that the decision weighs heavily on her, even to this day. "I'm sorry if my mom overstepped at all," he tells her. "She can be nosy."

"It's okay." Talia shrugs. "I like talking about my job."

"I was referring more to all the questions about where you're from. And, you know, your family." After a beat, he adds, "But if you ever do want to talk more about them, you know I'm always down to listen."

A long pause follows. "I appreciate that," she says carefully, "but I'd rather not get into it right now, if that's okay with you. We just had such a nice birthday brunch. I'd hate to kill the mood."

From the corner of his eye, Townsend sees Talia crack a smile, and he laughs.

"It's hard to say what your mom was more impressed by: my outfit or my pedigree," she continues.

"Or your job. She seemed positively enthralled by the world of ML engineering."

"She couldn't stop asking questions! I was like, enough, lady. I know my work is fascinating, but surely you're dying to hear more about Townsend's start-up."

Talia places a hand on the center console, and Townsend lays his hand on top of hers, interlacing their fingers. How lucky he is, to have this woman who can make him laugh—and who can laugh at herself—after such a disastrous morning. Any other girl would have run sobbing from the club following such an unpleasant brunch with his mom. But not Talia.

At the Austinite, he pulls in front of the building to wait for the valet. "Do you want to hit the spa this afternoon?" he asks. "Or we could go lay out by the pool."

"I'm happy to do either. Or both," Talia says. She glances in the rearview mirror. "Hey, are you expecting someone?"

"No. Why?"

"It just seems like that car behind us was waiting for you. They pulled up right when you got here."

Townsend turns around to look out the back window. Sure enough, there's a grubby white Honda right behind him that hadn't been there a moment ago, so close it's in danger of tapping his bumper. The windshield is too dirty for him to see the driver's face, but he can make out a baseball cap and what appears to be a long blond ponytail snaking over one shoulder.

"Do you know them?"

"I don't know," Townsend answers honestly. But he feels dizzy and off kilter, like he had five cocktails at the club instead of just one. He grabs the door handle, ready to get out and confront them, when suddenly, the car backs up and then peels away from the curb, passing by the left side of his roadster too quickly for him to get a good look. But he does see something that gives him pause: a decal on the rear windshield that looks like the Roman numeral for *two*. The Gemini symbol, he knows, because his ex had the same design tattooed on her right hip bone. For a moment, he's back in bed with her, kissing that spot on her hip as she whispers, "Two Geminis are so powerful together. We're twin flames, you and I." But just as quickly, he's brought back by the sound of the valet tapping on his window.

"You good?" Talia smiles uncertainly. "You look like you've seen a ghost."

"All good," he says.

He hands his keys to the valet and hustles Talia inside. It's a coincidence, he assures himself. A fluke. That couldn't possibly have been her car because she's not here.

She's not a problem for him anymore.

Chapter Six

Talia

Talia sometimes wonders if she's in a dream. Her fear: She's going to wake up alone to find that Townsend hadn't spent the night, and hadn't taken her to Congress Avenue Bridge to see the bats fly, and hadn't so much as spoken to her since their breakup last year. The past five weeks have felt like a romance novel come to life—but what if she's imagined the whole thing? No, her imagination couldn't possibly be so vivid. Next to her on the couch, Townsend tugs on her forearm like an invitation. She accepts and falls into him, burrowing her face into his chest. This is real, he is real. And he is hers.

Already, Talia feels like she and Townsend are an old married couple in the best kind of way. To her, the perfect Friday night now means splitting a Neapolitan pizza at The Backspace before returning to Townsend's condo to watch *Shadow of a Doubt* and cuddle on his Belgian linen Restoration Hardware sectional, just as they did tonight. The movie isn't very interesting; Townsend is way more into Alfred Hitchcock movies than she is. But she would watch a rotisserie oven infomercial if it meant being here, on Townsend's chest, forty-eight stories above the city below.

It's not about the things—though she does marvel at the fact that Townsend spent $8,500 on a bone-white sofa just begging to be stained . . . and the fact that his mother likely spent three times that amount on her tiny alligator purse. (After brunch last week, Talia looked up the resale price of a Hermès Mini Kelly. Her undergraduate education had cost her less money.) Unlike her sorority sisters at Auburn, Talia doesn't care about the logo on her bag or the color of the soles on her shoes. It's this feeling of belonging that she loves, especially since she belongs to someone as prized and powerful as Townsend Fuller.

With everything going so well, it's tempting to forget what Meera revealed a few days ago on their lunch break. "I've been keeping something from you," she told Talia as soon as they sat with their salads at Sweetgreen, and somehow, Talia already knew it must involve Townsend. As inexplicable as it was, Meera's disapproval of Townsend was obvious, and no matter how many times Talia insisted that he'd changed, Meera refused to hear it.

"He hasn't changed, Tal," she said. "His Cuff account is active. I'm pretty sure he's still talking to other girls."

"You're pretty sure or you're sure?" Talia asked. "And how do you even know this?"

"I went into the customer service data." Seeing the shocked look on Talia's face, Meera quickly added, "I don't trust him. I did it for you."

"I didn't ask you to do it for me," Talia said. "And *I* trust him, which is what matters."

They left it at that and proceeded to eat their salads, the subject changed to Gracie's summer soccer league. But even days later, Talia can't stop thinking about Townsend secretly swiping on his phone, sending messages to girls who aren't her. It's possible he forgot to deactivate his account. Or maybe he just likes to look, nothing more. Or perhaps what happened last time is going to happen with someone new, and Talia will end up betrayed, broken, all by herself. Again.

No, she scolds herself. *He's given you no reason to doubt him this time, and so you won't.* This relationship wouldn't end the way things did with Malcolm. She'd never repeat the mistakes she made with Malcolm.

On the TV screen where *Shadow of a Doubt* is playing, Uncle Charlie offers his niece, Charlie, an emerald ring. (Why are both characters named Charlie? To Talia, this seems needlessly confusing.) She squeezes Townsend's right hand in hers, realizing something as she does so.

"Hey, what happened to your ring?"

"What ring?"

Talia pulls his hand closer to her face to inspect it. "You used to wear a gold ring." She traces a loop around his bare ring finger. "Right here. You don't wear it anymore."

"No, I guess not," Townsend says. She can hear annoyance in his voice. He doesn't like talking during movies—unless, of course, it's to discuss the movie.

Just then, something strikes the door so loudly and unexpectedly that Talia and Townsend both jump.

"Was that your door?"

There's another bang, even more insistent this time. Townsend untangles himself from Talia and crosses the room in three steps. He looks through the peephole, and Talia thinks she sees his spine stiffen, just a little. Then he opens the door to reveal two police officers, standing side by side as though to block any means of escape.

"Good evening," says the one on the left, a tall Black woman. "I'm Detective Harris, and this"—she gestures to her partner, a hulking white man—"is Detective Burrows. We're with the Austin Police Department."

"Good evening." Townsend nods, looking much calmer than Talia feels. Being this close to a police officer always makes her palms sweat, even when she's done nothing wrong. "How can I help you?"

"We're looking for Townsend Fuller."

"He is me. I mean, I am him." A cough escapes from Townsend's throat; his composure is slipping.

"Right. May we come in?"

"Please." He steps aside, and the two officers file into the room. Talia quickly moves to the far end of the sectional, making room for

Harris and Burrows to sit on the other end. Should she introduce herself? Excuse herself? Offer them drinks? The etiquette rules for this situation aren't obvious to her.

And clearly she misreads the situation, as the detectives continue to stand. Once it becomes evident that this is intentional—they're choosing to hover above Talia as she cowers on the pristine white sectional below them—Townsend asks again, "So how can I help you?"

"Is it okay if I stay?" Talia doesn't mean to blurt this out, but she does. When everyone turns to look at her, she adds, "Sorry."

Harris pulls out a pad of paper and leans forward. It seems she and Burrows have decided she'll take the lead. "Your name?"

"Talia Danvers."

"And your relationship to Mr. Fuller?"

"I'm his . . ." Talia pauses to glance at Townsend. She's never actually said this word out loud in front of him before.

"She's my girlfriend," Townsend says, rejoining her on the couch. The word sends an unexpected flutter through her chest. *Girlfriend.*

"Right." Harris scribbles this down.

Talia is tempted to ask again whether it is, in fact, okay for her to sit in on this conversation, but she resists the urge.

"Mr. Fuller, we don't want to take up too much of your time," Harris continues. "We just want to ask you a few questions."

"Okay. What about?"

"Do you know an Amanda Reade?"

Amanda Reade. That name feels like a blow to the head. Talia keeps from letting out an involuntary gasp.

"I . . . yes. I do." Townsend is avoiding her eyes. It's clear he doesn't want to discuss Amanda Reade any more than she does.

"And how do you know Ms. Reade?"

Talia thinks of the various ways Townsend could answer this question: *I met her on Cuff while I was still in a relationship. I fucked her behind my girlfriend's back. I allowed her to ruin everything.*

"We dated briefly back in the beginning of the year," he says instead.

"Was the relationship serious?"

"No, no, definitely not. It was very casual. We were just . . ." Townsend hesitates. "We were intimate, but it wasn't romantic."

"Okay." Harris writes this down. "Did the relationship end on bad terms?"

Townsend shakes his head no. "I don't think so. It just sort of fizzled out. I wouldn't even call it a relationship, really." In his hands, he fiddles with the TV remote, repeatedly removing the batteries and sliding them back into place again. Seeing this, Talia gently takes the remote from him and sets it next to her on the couch. She doesn't like it, seeing him so rattled.

"Are you still in communication?"

"I haven't spoken to her in three months." Townsend pulls out his phone and crosses the room to show the officers the screen. Talia waits for him to show her, too, before remembering she isn't the one leading this investigation. "See? The last text I received from her was on March third, and I never replied."

"Got it." Harris makes a note and then closes her pad.

"Do you mind me asking what this is all about?"

Burrows speaks for the first time, his voice gravelly and unsettling. "We're following up on a missing person report filed by Amanda's sister, Kaitlyn Reade. She said she hasn't seen or spoken to Amanda for months, which she said isn't all that unusual for her, but she's starting to get worried."

"Amanda told me she wanted to backpack through Europe this summer. Could she be traveling?"

"Kaitlyn mentioned that as well," says Burrows, "but we don't have any evidence to suggest that she has traveled abroad."

"I didn't know her well." Townsend places his hand on Talia's knee, seeming to remember her for the first time since the police arrived. "But I did get the impression she was a little . . . wild. Like, maybe disappearing like this isn't totally out of character for her. She said she flew to Vegas once on a whim and ended up staying for almost two months."

"Is that right?"

"Apparently Amanda had some past brushes with the law," Townsend continues, his voice on the verge of eager. "She told me she had a few DUIs on her record, as well as a breaking and entering charge from a couple years back."

"Interesting." It's unclear whether this is new information to Burrows, but Townsend still looks pleased to have volunteered it.

"Hey, can I ask something?" Townsend takes his hand back from Talia's knee, and her skin immediately feels cold. "How did you get my name? Like I said, things were casual between us, so our relationship wasn't exactly public."

"Kaitlyn said you were the last person her sister dated. Did Amanda ever introduce you two?"

"No. Amanda barely mentioned her sister." Townsend clears his throat. "But she did tell me once that she and Kaitlyn didn't get along. Apparently, when their folks died a few years ago, they left the bulk of their estate to Amanda, and the sister was pretty bitter about it." He shrugs his shoulders. "I don't know if that's relevant at all. Just seems like something worth mentioning."

Harris exchanges a look with Burrows. Then she opens her pad and jots this down. "One last question," she says. "Where were you on the night of May eighteenth?"

"He was with me." The words fly out of Talia's mouth before she can stop them. Burrows raises an eyebrow, and Talia forces herself to take a deep breath before continuing. "We were with some friends, kayaking on Town Lake."

"And you left together?" Harris asks.

Talia glances at Townsend, who puts his hand reassuringly back on her knee. "No," he tells the detective. "We left separately, just after sunset. Talia went back to her place, I assume"—Talia nods—"and I came back here. Oh, I also stopped to pick up some takeout. Got home around nine thirty. My doorman can confirm the exact time."

"What'd you get?" Burrows asks in his gravelly voice.

"Hmm?" Townsend is now rubbing his hand back and forth on Talia's knee. She places her hand on top of his to still the movement.

"To eat," Burrows clarifies.

"Oh." Townsend gives a little laugh. "Tacos. From this little food truck called Granny's."

Burrows smiles. "I know that place. They run it out of that Airstream, right? Over off East Seventh?"

"That's the one."

Harris gives Burrows a subtle nod. "Thank you for your help, Mr. Fuller," she says. "I'll leave you my card, and you'll follow up if you think of anything else that may be helpful, yes?"

"Sure thing," Townsend says, though Harris isn't really asking.

They leave, and Townsend turns to look at Talia for the first time in what feels like hours.

"So," he says, "should we finish the movie?"

Talia's head is spinning with all the information that was just relayed—missing person reports, estates, DUIs—and she can think of a dozen questions she'd like to ask Townsend. But then she sees the pleading look in his eyes, a look that says *Please, can we talk about it tomorrow and just go back to our movie like none of this ever happened?* "Okay," she says.

Later that night, as Townsend snores, Talia scrolls through Amanda Reade's Instagram. Since learning about Amanda last year, she's visited this profile dozens—if not hundreds—of times, and by now, the pictures feel as familiar as her own. But no matter how many times she revisits these images, a blind rage consumes her, never dulled or diluted in the months that have passed.

The worst image: the most recent one, posted on March 6, which shows Amanda standing practically naked in front of the picture window in Townsend's bedroom. Talia recognizes the room, the view, and even the men's boxers slung around Amanda's curvy hips—a pair of silk pinstripe shorts from Derek Rose, Townsend's preferred underwear brand. There's a special place in hell for boyfriend stealers, Talia has decided—especially for those who do so without any discretion or apology.

For months, Amanda's grid has remained unchanged—no new photos, no new updates. But now, Talia notices a colorful ring around the profile picture in the top left-hand corner: Amanda has added to her Instagram Story. Her curiosity piqued, Talia clicks to watch, not caring that Instagram will tattle on her for snooping. A paragraph appears, written in white text on a black background, and as Talia reads it, her hands start to shake.

Hi all, the note reads. Amanda's sister Kaitlyn here. As some of you have noticed, Amanda hasn't posted for the last few months. Today I filed a police report—she is officially considered a missing person. If anyone knows anything about where she may be, please send me a message.

None of this is new to Talia; the police just told her and Townsend as much. What really unnerves her are these last few lines:

> And if anyone has info about Amanda's most recent boyfriend, Townsend Fuller, I'd like to hear from you. I can't say much here, but I will say this: I know he's involved in Amanda's disappearance, and I have proof.

Chapter Seven

Kaitlyn

It didn't take Kaitlyn long to find the name of the man Amanda had been dating. She started with her sister's Instagram grid, where she found a picture of Amanda from February 14 in what looked like a nice restaurant, holding up a glass of red wine to the camera. Lay the table with the fancy shxt, the caption read. She'd added Jeffrey's as the location, and she'd tagged a username as well: @t_fuller90. Unfortunately, the handle was a dead end; the account was deactivated. But now she knew this: The mystery man who'd taken her sister to Jeffrey's on Valentine's Day was likely named T. Fuller, and (as Amanda had mentioned he was a decade her senior) he was likely born in 1990.

She also had the class ring from Amanda's apartment, which—based on the shield crest and slogan—led her to St. Augustine Episcopal School in Austin. Then she just had to search "T Fuller St. Augustine" to find a photo of three men, taken at an alumni holiday party four years earlier. According to the caption, the tall one in the middle was Townsend Fuller, class of '08. Thick brown hair, aquiline nose, self-assured smile, and dimple in one cheek—yes, this man was most definitely her sister's type.

From there, she went down a Google rabbit hole, finding the landing page for a tech start-up that touted Townsend as its "Thinker in

Chief" and an obituary from April for a Randolph Fuller, who appeared to be his father. Then Kaitlyn coughed up the thirteen dollars and ninety-nine cents for a one-month trial of a reverse-search website that promised to provide home address and telephone information for Townsend Fuller (34, Austin, Texas). Once she had his number, she fired off a text.

> Hi, this is Kaitlyn's Reade, Amanda's sister. I haven't been able to reach her and I'm worried. Hoping you might know where she is?

After three days with no response, she tried again.

> Hi. Checking in again. Please contact me when you get this.

Again, nothing. She called; it went straight to voicemail.

That uneasy feeling she'd experienced sitting in Amanda's empty apartment came creeping back. Something wasn't right. Even if this Townsend guy had broken up with Amanda—which, given her sister's track record, was not unlikely—wouldn't a decent person at least respond to Kaitlyn saying he had no information? His silence felt significant. Kaitlyn's gut told her this man held answers to explain her sister's disappearance. And if he wasn't going to respond to her messages, she was just going to have to take a different tack.

On LinkedIn, Kaitlyn searched for St. Augustine alumni from Townsend's year still living in Austin, and after poring over dozens of profiles, she finally found William Dupont, a Southwestern University grad who worked as an associate at Rutland & Wiles, a rival firm to the one she worked for. Someone she could conceivably reach out to for networking purposes. It was too perfect. After confirming that William's connections on LinkedIn included Townsend Fuller, Kaitlyn sent him a message:

> Hi William! I'm a paralegal at Stevenson Ellis who's considering making the move to Rutland. I would love

> to hear from a fellow SU grad about the office culture there. Would you be open to meeting for coffee?

He'd responded within a few hours. Please, call me Will, he wrote. I'd be happy to grab coffee and chat. Go Pirates!

Kaitlyn wasn't thrilled about the prospect of rendezvousing with a stranger, but she felt calmer once they arranged to meet at Galaxy Cafe in Clarksville. It was a safe, neutral location. What was this guy going to do—murder her in broad daylight?

After the obligatory small talk about their respective firms, Kaitlyn brought the conversation around to Townsend as casually as she could.

"By the way, I think we know someone in common. Townsend Fuller?"

Will's eyebrows raised at the mention of his old classmate. "Oh, sure. How do you know him?"

"My sister is dating him, I think," she said carefully. "Or, at least, was dating him. I'm protective. I want to know if he's a good guy."

"A good guy?" Will laughed like he's just remembered an inside joke. "I don't know about a good guy, but he's definitely a legend."

Leaning back in the booth, Will proceeded to share stories about his old St. Augustine classmate, told with a blend of amusement and awe. He recounted the time Townsend won class treasurer and then didn't show up for a single officer meeting, and the time he threw balloons filled with piss at the beekeeping club, and the time he hooked up with three different girls during the two-day retreat before junior year.

After twenty minutes of this, Kaitlyn resigned herself to the fact that the only intel on Townsend she was going to get from this guy was a greatest hits of dickish antics. But then, as she debated how best to extricate herself from the conversation, Will unexpectedly shared a story that caught her interest.

"I remember there was this big house party in Barton Creek where he and all his friends lived. Some neighbor approached the house and threatened to call the cops, so Townsend shot at him with a paintball gun from an upstairs window until the guy finally left. Apparently, the guy suffered a corneal abrasion or something from one of the paintballs and showed up on the evening news, wearing an eye patch, complaining about the out-of-control parties in the neighborhood. Townsend wore a *Pirates of the Caribbean* T-shirt under his uniform the next day."

Will laughed, but the story didn't sit right with Kaitlyn. "He *blinded* a guy?"

"He, like, scratched his cornea. I'm sure the guy was fine." Will shrugged. "But I wasn't actually there. I just heard about it later. Everyone did."

"And everyone thought it was funny that he shot a guy?"

"It was a paintball gun. It wasn't a big deal." Will smiled in a way that said *Can't you take a joke?*

The image stayed with Kaitlyn for the rest of the day. She pictured the nosy neighbor writhing in pain, hand clutched to his face. A raw, bloody eye socket. Townsend standing in the window, finger still on the trigger, a look of cold amusement on his face. Nothing Will had said about Townsend was outright incriminating in regard to his relationship with Amanda, but there was just something about his description of the guy that made Kaitlyn's skin crawl.

I'll give it one more week, she told herself on the drive home.

Seven days came and went with no word from Amanda and no word from Townsend Fuller. Kaitlyn was forced to admit she was in over her head. She looked up the number for the Austin Police Department, hands shaking as she dialed.

"Hello? My name is Kaitlyn Reade. I need to report a missing person."

Riding the elevator up to the Stevenson Ellis office on Monday morning, Kaitlyn thinks about how infuriating it is, the fact that the world does not stop moving just because your own life has come to a standstill. Two women to her right chatter about the latest episode of some HBO true crime series. *Fuck your TV drama,* she wants to tell them. *My sister is missing—like, real-life missing—and no one even gives a shit.*

When she called to report Amanda missing, the officers had assured Kaitlyn they'd investigate, including looking into her sister's last known boyfriend, Townsend Fuller. But when she called back a few days later, they claimed he'd already been cleared. "We spoke to him, ma'am," a woman who introduced herself as Detective Harris said. "He's not a suspect at this time." She thought she was putting Kaitlyn at ease by saying this, but she thought wrong.

"How can that be?" Kaitlyn argued. "I saw his car outside of Amanda's apartment."

From the information database she paid for, Kaitlyn knew that Townsend Fuller was the registered owner of a silver BMW Z4 Roadster. When she googled the make and model, an image of a sporty coupe convertible popped on her screen and sparked a memory. The night of her disaster date with the data science professor at Latchkey, when she passed by Amanda's apartment building without stopping in, she spotted a car that looked just like it. She remembered it barreling through a stop sign right as she stepped into the crosswalk, nearly hitting her in the process. It had to be the same one, right? It had to mean something.

Kaitlyn had spent more time than she cared to admit hovering in the vicinity of Townsend's condo building, waiting to catch a glimpse of the roadster to confirm her theory. One Saturday in mid-June, she'd seen it pull into the circular drive. For a moment, she thought about getting out and confronting him right then and there, but she could see there was a woman in the passenger seat with him, and Kaitlyn hadn't liked the idea of having an audience.

"We asked him about that night," Harris had told Kaitlyn. "You thought you saw his car outside of Amanda's place around eleven p.m. on May eighteenth? It turns out he was just getting takeout from a nearby restaurant."

How convenient for him, Kaitlyn had wanted to say. But she simply said thank you and asked them to please keep her informed. It wouldn't do her any good to make enemies of the detectives working on the case. Not when she could tell they already thought she was just being hysterical. Already, they'd confirmed that Amanda wasn't abroad (they'd checked flight records) and wasn't traveling by car (her white Honda Accord was sitting in her building's parking lot). She could be traveling with friends or hitchhiking, they said. She could be totally fine. After all, wasn't this behavior pretty on-brand for her? Wasn't that why Kaitlyn waited three months to report her own sister missing?

They won't come out and say it, but she knows what the police believe, because it was what she herself once believed: that the only danger Amanda is in is the danger she poses to herself.

Over the years, Amanda has let Kaitlyn down in a hundred different ways. There was that time she skipped Kaitlyn's college graduation (without apology) to attend the Hangout Music Festival in Alabama instead. And there was that time she missed their family Christmas (without explanation) only to later post pictures from a nightclub in Miami. But flakiness can't explain the aroma of bleach permeating Amanda's empty apartment or her Instagram grid, not updated since March. It can't explain why she didn't show up to their father's grave for his birthday, like she'd promised she would.

The last brunch they shared in February ended with regretful words and hurt feelings, but still, the sisters had made a vow: They would visit Dad's gravesite on his sixtieth birthday in June, and together, they would celebrate the milestone he'd never reach. That day was a week ago, and though Kaitlyn showed up at the cemetery—wishing, hoping, praying that her sister would prove her wrong—Amanda did not. But when she shared this story with the police (which felt, in her mind, like irrefutable evidence of something gone very wrong), they weren't as convinced.

"You're worried because she didn't attend your dad's birthday?" they asked. "But he's deceased?"

They didn't understand why she found this so troubling. They didn't understand that—as capricious as she could be—Amanda wasn't callous. She wouldn't just vanish for months without a word. Even if she was busy drinking herself into a stupor in New Orleans last week, she would have found her way back to Dad's grave, to keep her promise.

Unless she ditched you, a voice hisses in the back of Kaitlyn's mind. *Unless she fucked off and didn't even bother to let you know.*

ShrinkGPT, the AI-assisted therapy app she'd started using a few months earlier, warned her about indulging these sorts of intrusive thoughts. After confessing once that she feared everyone would leave her, the AI-therapy chatbot had Kaitlyn repeat the phrase *Everyone will leave me* for a full minute, over and over, while the app timed her. And Kaitlyn did: "Everyone will leave me. Everyone will leave me. Everyone will leave me. Everyone will leave me. Everyone will leave me. Everyone will leave me. Everyone will leave me." When the minute was up, the chatbot said, "See? Doesn't that sound ridiculous?" But for the rest of the day, Kaitlyn just kept hearing the phrase (*Everyone will leave me. Everyone will leave me. Everyone will leave me*) until it felt like an incantation or a prophecy.

But surely Amanda wouldn't vanish from her life without warning like their parents had; surely she knew that Kaitlyn couldn't endure that kind of pain again. *Amanda would not leave me,* she tells herself, quieting that voice. *Amanda would not leave me.*

The elevator doors open on the twenty-fourth floor, and Kaitlyn makes her way to her desk, nodding at the few people she passes. No one asks about her weekend, and she doesn't stop to ask about theirs; it's known by now that small talk isn't her thing. An initial case assessment is awaiting her attention, but first, she has her own task to complete. Looking around first to make sure no one is peeking over her shoulder, Kaitlyn logs onto Reddit and navigates to the Missing Persons community. Then she checks on the post she submitted last night.

A short press release about her sister's disappearance had appeared on the Travis County Sheriff's Office website, which Kaitlyn submitted to the subreddit, hoping to pique the interest of a few bored internet sleuths. So far, the thread has generated one comment from a user named Stoner_Sandwich420: She looks hot.

She sighs. Not even Amanda's thousands of social media followers seem to care about her disappearance as much as Kaitlyn expected. After posting that call to arms on her sister's Instagram Story (it was a good thing Amanda used the same password—geminibaby530—for just about everything), Kaitlyn had expected to be flooded with tips, theories, and search party volunteers. Instead, all she received in response were a handful of likes and crying-face emoji reactions. It makes her furious, really, if she thinks about it too long. If a stereotypically "hot" white girl can't get the attention of the police, what hope do the millions of other women who go missing every year have?

Maybe Kaitlyn just needs to help move things along.

After looking over her shoulder once again to make sure her coworkers are preoccupied, she creates a burner account. No one will take her seriously if she comments on her own Reddit thread. And she's tired of not being taken seriously. With the new username, she posts a screenshot of the Instagram Story she created last week, ending with that damning last line: I know he's involved in Amanda's disappearance, and I have proof. If her warning about Townsend didn't get the attention it deserved from Amanda's Instagram followers, then perhaps it will here.

Does she have actual proof that Townsend did something? No, not really. Just a ring, and a speeding car, and an unnerving story about a violent teen with a paintball gun. Putting him on blast on the internet may be a massive mistake, but he's her only lead. And if she's going to get people's attention, she needs to give them something substantial. She knows this, because she's dying for something substantial to hold onto herself.

Alongside the screenshot, she adds a brief comment: Saw this on Amanda's IG last week. Anyone got info on this Townsend Fuller guy?

Kaitlyn waits for a moment, then she refreshes the page. Nothing—but what did she expect? The internet is vast, and her missing sister is just another contribution to the unrelenting stream of sob story click-bait. This tragedy isn't singular enough to cut through the noise.

The workday is endless, but eventually, Kaitlyn returns home. There she checks the page again and finds a miracle: A new comment has appeared on the thread under the screenshot.

She blinks in disbelief; is it just another troll? But this post from LivingstonTheDream seems to be genuine: I've actually met him. I work in VC and he pitched his healthcare startup, AutoInTune, to us last week. It was kind of a shitshow TBH. The user metrics seem like bullshit.

Once again, she refreshes the page. Another comment pops up from a different account. That does sound sus IMO. Plus his picture gives me the ick. Total psychopath vibes.

Then another. And then another.

Finally, she thinks. People are listening. People *care.*

Chapter Eight

Meera

Meera doesn't want to say *I told you so*—but the longer she listens to Talia speak, the more tempted she is to say it.

Meera expected to hear what she usually hears from Talia during their postweekend catch-ups: gushing proclamations about how thoughtful Townsend was, and how kind he was, and how well he treated her. She certainly didn't expect a story about an encounter with the police and a missing ex-girlfriend.

It's Monday, and the two are grabbing coffee at Mañana around the corner from the Cuff office before heading into work. From their table facing the door, Meera can see all the techy folks bustling in to grab their morning cold brew or cold-pressed juice before heading off to their jobs at Meta and Google. She loves working in the Seaholm District, with its stark industrial aesthetic and energized feel. What she doesn't love: the idea of her best friend falling even deeper for a guy she knows to be bad news.

But instead of saying this—or *I told you so*—Meera says, "Tal, do you hear yourself? This is insane."

"I know, I know." Talia shakes her head. "But he was just as surprised by the police showing up at his door as I was. He didn't seem to have any idea Amanda was missing—he just thought she was in Europe. He said they haven't texted at all since their breakup."

"And you believe him?"

"Yes, I do. He even showed the police their text history to prove it."

"He could have just deleted all their recent texts."

Meera sees a flash of annoyance in Talia's eyes. "Yeah, and he could be having sex with five other girls behind my back. But I choose not to assume the worst in people."

It's becoming increasingly common for their conversations to take a turn like this, to go from light and playful to tense and strained with little warning. Meera hates it. She wants things to return to the way they were before Townsend reentered the picture.

Like most women Meera knows, Talia jumps into relationships with both feet. (Meera doesn't judge her for this; it seems so long ago now, but surely her own relationship with Hari started off just as intensely.) When Talia first met Townsend, he was all she could talk about, all she could think about—and in Talia's eyes, he could seemingly do no wrong. For six months this continued until things blew up in her face, and while their breakup didn't bring Meera any pleasure (what kind of friend would she be if she delighted in Talia's heartbreak?), it was a relief to have conversations revolve around something other than the life-and-death dramatics of Talia's relationship again. They could finally just shoot the shit about trivial matters—like who killed The Notorious B.I.G. and whether or not Beyoncé pooped. They could just be Talia and Meera, two smart, accomplished women whose moods weren't dictated by the amount of time it took a man to reply to their text messages.

But now Townsend is back, and if anything, his hold on Talia is even more powerful than it was the first time around. Because Meera has never seen Talia in a relationship with someone else, it's hard to say whether Townsend possesses some formidable influence or this is just the way Talia is with men. Either way, the dynamic makes Meera uneasy. It's like sitting in the passenger seat of a car that's destined to crash; there's nothing she can do but brace for impact.

Eager to restore a genial mood, Meera says, "It's called hostile attribution bias, apparently. Hari accused me of having it right around the time we got divorced. I'm just a mean ol' misanthropist. That's why I need you, my little optimist, to balance me out."

Talia smiles at her from across the table. "Happy to be of service."

Her annoyance seems to have been forgotten; Meera knows she should leave well enough alone. But still, she can't ignore a certain nagging thought. "I hate to bring this up, but as a misanthropist, I have to ask something."

"Uh-oh." Talia takes a sip of her coffee and then leans back, crossing her arms. "Let's hear it."

"Have you considered the possibility that Townsend has talked to Amanda through something other than text?"

"Like what? Carrier pigeon?"

"He still has an active Cuff account, Tal. What if they've been messaging through the app?"

A strange look crosses Talia's face—Meera can't tell if she's shocked by this idea or about to sneeze. After a beat, she asks, "How would I find that out?"

Before she can think better of it, Meera says, "I can pull up their message history on the database."

"Meera." Talia gives her a look that's meant to say *You know better than that.* "That's a major privacy breach. You could get fired for that."

"Well, if it weren't for you, I'd probably already be fired." When Meera was first diagnosed with Hashimoto's a year ago, Talia covered for her on countless instances, explaining Meera's absences to their boss when she had appointments to attend or was simply feeling too shitty to leave her bed. Picking up the slack on projects Meera couldn't finish in time. Watering her sad, half-dead succulent in vain. "I'm happy to take the risk for you."

"You shouldn't," Talia says. "Unless . . . you're really sure you can do this without getting caught?"

Meera glances at her watch. "No one will be in for another half hour. Let's do it now while we have the chance."

Ten minutes later, they sit in the ML-team office, both gathered in front of Meera's monitor. As Meera suspected, none of their coworkers are in yet, including the office custodian, Aarav, who's usually here by now.

"You're sure you don't mind doing this?" Talia asks for what feels like the tenth time since they left the coffee shop.

"For you, not at all," Meera says, "but you need to stop distracting me so I *can* do this."

Once again, Meera logs on to the company database and types in Townsend's name. There is all the info she saw last time, including his account status (still active).

"Look." Talia points at the screen. "It says he hasn't been on Cuff in nearly three weeks. He probably has no idea his profile is even active."

"Maybe," says Meera, "but we should still check out his conversation history."

"Do you know how to pull up the chat log?"

"It should all be stored in a log file." Meera quickly scans the page, and there it is: the entire chat history between Townsend Fuller and Amanda Reade, complete with dates and time stamps. "Should we go all the way back to the beginning?"

Talia shakes her head no. "I don't need to see how things started. That would be too painful."

"Okay. When did things end?"

Talia is quiet for a moment, her brow furrowed. "Based on what Townsend has told me, he broke up with her in early March."

Meera nods and scans the log, working her way backward until she finds the first message where things seem to take a sour turn. "Here it is," she says.

Amanda [Sun, Mar 3 at 8:20 PM]: Hey baby. Just want to remind you that your the love of my life.

Townsend [Sun, Mar 3 at 8:22 PM]: I am not the love of your life. I am not anything to you. This is done.

Amanda [Sun, Mar 3 at 8:34 PM]: We're over?

Amanda [Sun, Mar 3 at 8:36 PM]: Seriously?

Amanda [Sun, Mar 3 at 10:12 PM]: Your going to be so fxcking sorry.

"Shocker that she doesn't know the difference between 'your' the possessive adjective and 'you're' the contraction," Meera jokes.

Talia fails to laugh. Eyes glued to the screen, she says, "Keep scrolling."

Together, they continue to read silently. From what Meera can see, Amanda harassed Townsend for months after their breakup, often sending twenty to thirty messages in a row before receiving even a single reply from him.

"Jesus," Meera says under her breath. "This is fucking nuts."

Amanda's messages are a mix of beseeching and cold-blooded; a pathetic entreaty for Townsend to take her back would be followed minutes later with threats to go public about his start-up's failings. It doesn't make any sense. It seems like the ravings of a madman—or, rather, a madwoman. Meera glances at her friend, expecting to see her bafflement mirrored in Talia's face, but Talia's expression is entirely unreadable.

"Is his company not doing well?" Meera touches her finger to the screen. "Did you get to this part? What is she talking about here?"

"Shh. I'm reading." Talia bats Meera's hand away, still transfixed by the screen.

The last exchange between the two seemingly took place in mid-May, where nearly a dozen messages from Amanda were followed by just a single response.

Townsend [Sat, May 18 at 11:04 PM]: This is over. We are over. Leave me the fuck alone, or I will make you leave me alone.

A few minutes later, Townsend sent a photo, seemingly taken through the windshield of his car. All Meera can see is a nondescript apartment building. She looks closer, noticing something in the corner of the frame: a vague black shape sitting on the dashboard. Something that looks very much like a gun.

Townsend [Sat, May 18 at 11:07 PM]: Don't forget I know where you live. Don't forget I know things about you, too. Things you'd never want to get out. This is your last warning.

These are the last words Townsend ever said to Amanda. A cold chill spreads through Meera's chest.

"May eighteenth," Talia says quietly. "That was the day I ran into Townsend at Town Lake. When he took me to Congress Avenue Bridge to see the bats fly. He must have sent this later that night."

Beyond the surprise and uncertainty, Meera detects the slightest hint of pride in Talia's voice. Like she's pleased that her serendipitous romantic evening with Townsend was apparently so meaningful to him, he wasted no time shutting things down permanently with Amanda.

But Meera's still focused on the intensity of the threat and what came after—or, rather, what *didn't* come after. "There are no more messages from Amanda after that. Doesn't that seem kind of odd, Tal?"

"She probably heard that Townsend and I got back together and decided to finally stop harassing him."

"Heard from who? It's not like they shared mutual friends."

"I don't know." Talia shrugs. "She was clearly obsessed with him. She was no doubt stalking him too. Maybe she saw us together herself."

"And you think she just decided to give up? After months of alternately threatening him and trying to get him back?"

Talia's eyes flash angrily. "What are you implying?"

Meera has to tread carefully here; she doesn't want to get Talia any more upset than she already is. "I just think it's strange," she says carefully, "that Townsend says he's going to make Amanda leave him alone, and then suddenly, he never hears from her again. And now she's missing."

"So what the fuck are you saying?"

Talia so rarely curses that this catches Meera off guard. Before she can stop herself, she blurts out, "I'm saying, what if Townsend followed through on his threat?"

The sound of laughter carries from down the hall, and they both jump. Their coworkers are starting to arrive. Meera quickly exits out of the database and turns to face Talia again.

"You need to at least consider the possibility that Townsend is culpable here," she hisses to her friend. "Okay? This shit is serious."

"Okay," Talia says, so softly Meera can barely hear her.

"Will you promise me to stay away from Townsend until we can figure out what's going on here?"

"I—" Talia stands, still avoiding Meera's eyes.

"Do you promise me?"

"I need a minute." Without looking back, Talia scurries off toward the restroom, leaving Meera alone with Townsend's threat still echoing in her mind.

A quick Google search later that night gives Meera the lowdown on Townsend's company, AutoInTune—a start-up that proclaims to be "changing the tune for the autoimmune." She reads through the company website, the launch announcement in *Forbes*, and the early glowing reviews ("Since becoming an AutoInTune member and taking a foundational approach to healing, I feel more energy and less pain than I've felt in years!").

Under different circumstances, Meera might've been impressed or even tempted to enroll herself—finally, a virtual solution for the millions of people like her living with an invisible illness! But she has reason to be skeptical about Townsend's ethics. And apparently she's not the only one.

In her search, Meera finds a Reddit comment about AutoInTune—a response to someone looking for information on Townsend linked to Amanda Reade's disappearance. The user metrics seem like bullshit, it reads. Like a direct confirmation of Meera's suspicions.

For a moment, she hesitates. Then she composes a message: Hi, LivingstonTheDream. Just curious what seemed off about AutoInTune's data? Then she clicks send, unleashing her query into the digital universe.

There isn't any need to tell Talia about this, Meera thinks to herself. In fact, it's better if she *doesn't* tell Talia about this. But if Townsend's company is anything less than legitimate, Meera wants to know, even if the information is dangerous for her to have.

Looking in on her sleeping daughter before putting herself to bed, she hears his ominous words again: *Leave me the fuck alone, or I will make you leave me alone . . . This is your last warning.*

Meera may be a misanthropist, but she likes to think she knows a dangerous man when she sees one—and Townsend Fuller is, without a doubt, a dangerous man.

Chapter Nine

Townsend

It's still dark when Townsend steps outside on Tuesday morning, and he can just imagine what Talia would say: *Men don't know how lucky they are, to be able to run alone whenever they want without fearing for their lives.* He doesn't think about his male privilege—or, really, the many types of privilege he holds—as often as he should, but he doesn't want to mull over that right now. Instead, he sticks his AirPods into his ears and heads down Congress Avenue toward Butler Trail, which meanders along the north shore of Town Lake. Right now, he just wants to listen to Jack Harlow and figure out what the fuck is going on.

The police don't think he's guilty; that much is a relief. Or, at least, they don't *seem* to think he's guilty—Townsend has watched enough episodes of *Law & Order* to know the police sometimes play nice with their prime suspect, hoping to catch them off their game. But Townsend knows better than to let his guard down with them. With anyone, really.

With Amanda, Townsend fucked up—not only because he got caught by Talia, but because he fell for her wiles in the first place. He can still remember the picture that made him swipe right: a blond in a leather mini perched in a nightclub booth, one hand clutching a pink drink and the other touching her lips, like an invitation. She looked like trouble, and after months of playing house with Talia, a little trouble felt like a welcome change. His dad was sick. His start-up was struggling. The holiday season depressed him. Townsend could think of a dozen excuses for why he did it, but really, he had no excuse. Boredom was the reason, and it wasn't an excuse.

He's jogging now by the park at Waller Beach, where he and Amanda attended a protest on one of their very first hangouts. Amanda, like many of her fellow hippie Austinites, was opposed to the Texas Department of Transportation's multibillion-dollar plan to expand I-35. He smiles despite himself, thinking about how pink her cheeks used to get whenever they debated the project.

"It'll improve congestion, and it'll provide better connectivity between the east and the west," he told her. "Not to mention it's projected to drive more than ten billion dollars in economic development over the next three decades."

Amanda had huffed at this argument. "Yes, it will benefit drivers and businesses," she shot back. "And in the process, it will displace people and homes and result in more tailpipe emissions than ever."

It was early December when she invited him to the protest. They'd been talking for a few weeks, and they'd had sex once—just an impulsive, late-night rendezvous at her grubby little studio apartment in East Austin. The protest was the first time they saw each other in daylight, out in public, and though he attended the event just to humor her (protests were futile, in his opinion, and the I-35 expansion was inevitable), she surprised him. He thought Amanda was just some silly party girl, but marching around Waller Beach, brandishing that **Wider Won't Work** sign above her head, Townsend saw someone new: A rebel. A fighter. Someone so unlike Talia, who wanted nothing more than to behave and be accepted and follow the rules. He fell a little bit in love with Amanda that day, and though she didn't change his mind about the I-35 expansion, she *did* make him believe that she'd be worth the risk. What a fucking mistake that had been.

Still keeping a respectable jogging pace, Townsend crosses over the not-yet-expanded I-35. He shivers with delight each time a car whizzes past, reminding him just how easily he could be pulverized, his flesh and bones turned to pulp on the asphalt. It's not like he plans to jump in front of a car and off himself, obviously. It's just reassuring, knowing how quick it would be.

After everything that's happened, Townsend is reluctant to admit it—but when things were good with Amanda, they were *so* good. The two started seeing each other more and more frequently following the protest, meeting up at Amanda's place as often as two or three times a week. There, he could unwind and unload his struggles with AutoInTune, and he didn't have to worry about Amanda pushing him to *stick to it* and *keep at it*, like Talia the cheerleader always would. Amanda, like him, was too jaded for toxic positivity. She'd just listen to him bitch, and then they'd smoke weed, eat burritos, and have insanely good sex.

Afterward, Townsend would return to his condo, where he would text Talia to complain about another late night in the office. With that throaty laugh and that sexy little hip tattoo, Amanda had him under her spell—and for a short time, Townsend genuinely believed he could have his cake and eat it too.

His critical error: inviting Amanda to spend the night at his place, all the while knowing Talia had the key code and could appear at any moment. It was a Saturday, just about a week before Christmas, when she caught them naked in his bed, and the look of betrayal on Talia's face is a memory he'll never be able to erase.

Still, as mortifying as it was, Townsend felt an initial sense of relief. At least now he could be with Amanda without sneaking around.

He should have known the universe wouldn't be so kind as to let him get away scot-free.

Amanda didn't change overnight; he would have noticed that. Instead, she sunk her claws in bit by bit, so slowly that he felt little more than a pinch. Their nights of weed and burritos and sex at her place turned into expensive dinners out and sleepovers at his, where she would hang around watching TV and eating his snacks until well past noon the next day. She'd steal his Canali dress shirts to wear, then return them stained with orangey makeup. When he bought her a mini woven leather tote from Bottega Veneta for their one-month anniversary, she asked if he could exchange it for the larger version.

Things really took a turn around Valentine's Day, when Townsend treated Amanda to an expensive prix fixe at Jeffrey's. After leaving his condo the next morning, she posted a photo from the restaurant on Instagram (and he recognized the image well, as she'd spent half the dinner coaching him on how to take it). Though he wished she hadn't tagged him, the caption was innocuous enough . . . but then the messages through Cuff started.

This feels like the beginning of forever.

I'm so fxcking in love with you.

Do you feel it too? What I feel for you?

When they first started seeing each other, Townsend had been reluctant to give Amanda his number. It seemed too risky. What if Amanda called or texted him and Talia saw? So they kept their messages to Cuff—the irony of which was not lost on Townsend. But he'd heard Talia wax on about the app's security and encryption protections enough times to trust that his communications with Amanda would remain private.

Even after Talia was gone and there was no need for cloak-and-dagger measures anymore, they continued to chat mainly through Cuff, mostly out of habit. But also because Amanda was always losing her phone and never remembered to back up her contacts.

Sometimes, she'd trick him into believing she was still the chill, free-spirited woman he once believed her to be. They'd hang out, Amanda letting herself in with the key code that he only ever shared before with Talia. They'd lay on the couch, fool around a little. Maybe smoke a joint. It seemed totally normal. But then she'd go home and send him messages on Cuff, asking crazy shit like what they should name their future children. I want to have five kids, she wrote once, and I want them all to have your eyes. It started out slowly, just one or two messages a day, but then she started to send them more frequently, and they became increasingly more intense. She wanted them to grow old together. She wanted to know if he believed in soulmates.

The final straw came the first weekend in March. That Sunday afternoon, she showed up without invitation, as usual, and surprised him with a fantastic blow job. Then she invited him to spend the summer with her in Europe.

"You know that backpacking trip I've been talking about?" she asked him, still crouched above him in bed. "I want you to come with me. I think we'd have fun together."

It was all too much: the over-the-top messages, the constant barging into his condo, the intensity of her stare as she looked at him. He broke up with her right then and there, and though she left in a huff ("Your dick is too small anyway," she called over her shoulder on her way out the door), a message appeared on his phone that night, calling him the love of her life.

I am not the love of your life, he wrote back. I am not anything to you. This is done.

He thought that would be the last he heard from her. If only he'd known.

The sun is getting higher now. Townsend feels sweat trickling down his neck, but still, he pushes himself harder, picking up his pace. He passes by Festival Beach and—before he can think better of it—turns left away from Town Lake, heading into East Austin, his least favorite neighborhood. East Austin, with its street art and dive bars and hipsters bitching about gentrification, not realizing that they are, in fact, the problem. Hipsters like Amanda.

A few days after the breakup, Amanda posted a picture on her grid, which he recognized as having been taken in his bedroom. At first, she appeared totally naked—but when he zoomed in, he saw she was wearing a pair of his boxer shorts, like a prize. True psycho shit. He unfollowed her, hoping to be rid of her for good. But the Cuff correspondence continued, her once-saccharine love notes turned far more sinister. Threats, taunts, lies—nothing seemed to be off limits. And though he tried to block her profile, her messages continued to come through, undeterred. Like she was impervious to being blocked.

He knew he should just delete the app—that would be the easiest way to put an end to things. But the idea of doing so felt like admitting defeat. Why should he let one crazy woman drive him off the only halfway-decent dating app left? As unsettling as her messages had become, they were just words on a screen, and for all her talk of exposing Townsend's secrets, she hadn't actually done anything. He told himself she was just desperate for attention, and if he withheld it from her long enough, she'd go away.

Townsend is outside her apartment building now. Somehow, his body knew he was coming here when he left his place, even if his mind wasn't consciously aware of it. As he feared, that familiar white Honda Accord is parked in the lot beside the building, the same one he saw waiting for him after the birthday brunch with Mother. He wasn't crazy; it *was* Amanda's car.

After he ran into Talia back in May, Townsend drove over to Amanda's place with a head full of steam. He didn't know what he wanted to do, exactly. Just scare her a little bit. Make it clear that he wasn't someone who could be pushed around. He had his paintball gun in the trunk from going to the range the weekend before with his friends. As much as he wanted to, he knew he shouldn't fire a round into Amanda's window. There were too many eyes around—everyone had a Ring camera these days—and he didn't want to risk getting tagged with a vandalism charge right before his next round of investor meetings.

So he just took a picture of the gun on the dashboard. In the shadowy light of the streetlamps, it almost looked like the real thing. He sent it to Amanda, along with the reminder that—even though he was stupid enough to have told her about some of his concerns about AutoInTune—she had shared things too. She'd admitted to not-so-funny stories of things she'd done while drunk or high, involving break-ins and fender benders and almost setting her shower curtain on fire with a curling iron. And one night, when they were lying in bed, legs tangled under the sheets, she confessed to something even worse, about her parents and how they died. She broke down crying, and Townsend felt a surge of protectiveness as he pulled Amanda's naked body tighter to his chest.

In that moment, he really thought he knew her.

Now, he's got the police at his door, questioning his whereabouts, looking for any sign that Townsend might have done something to Amanda. Thank God he was hungry enough to grab tacos on his way home from East Austin that night. At least now he has a verifiable alibi for being in that part of town.

He thinks back to the text messages and phone calls he got a week ago, allegedly from Kaitlyn Reade, looking for her sister. Townsend didn't trust them. He feared it might actually be Amanda, using her sister as a screen to get Townsend to answer her. But now he doesn't know what to believe. He hasn't told Talia about the harassment, about the constant unhinged messages. He almost did last night, but in the end, he didn't want to burden her. It wasn't worth pulling her into his mess when it seemed like Amanda might finally be gone for good.

But *is* she really missing? Or just lying in wait?

All at once he feels dizzy, and thirsty, and like he might be sick. He sits on the sidewalk, already sizzling hot from the late-June heat, and holds his head in his hands. He wants to cry from the injustice of it all—would he be punished forever for pursuing the wrong girl? But he can't stay here, where anyone could see him. He checks his watch; it's getting late. He stands, wipes his face on his shirt, and starts toward home.

Talia will be awake soon, wondering where he went, and he can't give her any more reason to question him.

Chapter Ten

TALIA

On Tuesday morning, Talia arrives at work and does not stop, as she normally does, at Meera's desk to say hello.

She's still angry at her friend. It's classic Meera, really, to jump to the worst possible conclusion about a man. She's always had what seems like a personal vendetta against Townsend—even before he made that mistake with Amanda. Can't Meera see that Townsend's words were empty threats said out of desperation? Can't she see that Amanda was the problem, that Amanda was the psychotic one?

Yesterday, after she and Meera read through Townsend's and Amanda's Cuff messages, Talia hid out in the bathroom for twenty minutes. Crouched on the closed lid of a toilet in the handicap stall, she held her face in her hands and tried one of the breathing exercises that her Pilates instructor taught her. *Press your tongue to the roof of your mouth and exhale fully. Then, inhale for a count of four, hold your breath for a count of seven, and exhale slowly for a count of eight.*

Townsend wasn't a killer; this much she knew to be true. He was a thoughtful gift giver, a meticulous bed maker, the proud creator of an exceptional chicken salad recipe. A murderer? Absolutely not. What bothered Talia most was the fact that Meera (and Amanda's sister . . . and perhaps even the police . . .) could even *think* Townsend capable of such a thing. Was it possible they saw something dark and disquieting in her boyfriend that she—the person who arguably knows Townsend better than anyone—had failed to see herself?

When she returned home last night, Talia poured herself and Townsend a glass of wine and sat him down on the couch. Then, as calmly as she could, she said, "I think we need to talk about Amanda."

Since that night at the Blue Starlite Drive-in, when they officially got back together, neither has addressed the elephant in the room: the reason they broke up in the first place. For Talia, avoiding the subject of Amanda had been an act of self-preservation—why poke a wound that's still healing? And for Townsend, she imagined it felt like a gift, not having to answer for his mistakes. But Talia knew they needed to discuss what happened if they were going to have a life together—a life in which Amanda Reade was nothing more than a teeny, tiny, insignificant blip.

"You're right," Townsend said. A moment of awkward silence. Talia stifled a sigh. Apparently, he needed to be fed his lines.

"Did you love me? When we were together last year?"

"Of course I did." Townsend touched her hand. "I still love you now."

Her heart fluttered—he loved her! But no, she wouldn't be distracted so easily. "Then why did you let her ruin everything?"

Townsend let his eyes float up to the ceiling, as though the correct response might be written there.

"Just talk to me. Look at me."

He did, and Talia was surprised to see that he was teary-eyed. "I was the one who ruined everything," he said. "I had the greatest thing going with you, and I was so afraid of losing it—of losing you—that I pushed you away. It was the stupidest decision I've ever made, and I feel like the luckiest guy in the world that you're here now, giving me a second chance I probably don't deserve."

He was saying all the right things, and Talia appreciated that. But he could never know how broken she'd felt in those months following his betrayal. Sitting on the couch in front of him that Monday evening, she wondered how a man could love two wildly dissimilar women at once without being fractured inside. It reminded her of what happened with Malcolm, which was something she tried to think about as infrequently as possible.

"Just . . . why her?"

"It wasn't even about her. She could have been anyone. I was just so hell bent on destroying my own happiness that I—"

"Did you like that she was younger? Blonder? Was she more fun than me? More adventurous in bed than me?" Talia knew how silly this line of questioning sounded, how shallow and juvenile, but she couldn't seem to stop herself. "Did you love her more than me?"

"Love her?" Townsend scoffed. "I'm not even sure I liked her. I thought she'd be someone who'd let me indulge my worst habits without judgment. As it turns out, her habits were way worse than mine." He gave Talia a tentative smile. "I guess it just goes to show that you never know what you're getting into when you meet someone on an app."

Reluctantly, she smiled back. "They really should hire better people to monitor those things."

"I'd say to hell with them all if Cuff weren't the reason I met you."

It was so tempting to end the conversation right then, when things finally felt good again. Still, she pushed on. "When you say Amanda had bad habits . . . are you saying you believe what you told the police? That she could just be off on some bender?"

"It's entirely possible." Townsend shrugged. "When I ended things and told her I didn't want anything serious, she told me to fuck off and said she was going to Europe for the summer. Maybe she made it there, or maybe she's off partying somewhere in the States. All I know is I have no idea what happened to her."

"And you don't think anything . . . *bad* happened to her, do you?"

"I don't think she's actually missing or, you know, dead or whatever, if that's what you're asking."

End this conversation now, Talia told herself. *Change the subject.* She didn't; instead, she asked, "How do you know for sure? How do you know something bad didn't happen to her in Europe or wherever she is?"

Townsend hesitated for a moment, as though there was something more he wanted to say. But instead he just shrugged. "I guess I don't know for sure, but it doesn't really matter, does it? She's not my problem. I can only assume she's off being her usual chaotic self, because that's what she does best."

Talia touched his cheek, and he put his hand over hers, giving it a squeeze. "You're right," she said. "She's not our problem."

Settling in at her desk, Talia dives into a deep work session, attempting to extract a training dataset from big, noisy, nonsensical data. When she first started working for Cuff, she saw nothing more than a dating app with silly prompts and a simple swipe mechanism. She'd never imagined the engineering potential the job encompassed—or her own potential for helping people swipe their way to The One. Her current project: developing a natural language–processing model that can weed out bad actors from honest-to-goodness Cuff members looking for love.

Despite the smirks she gets when she reveals her job, or the jokes she's seen circulating on social media ("Like it rough? Into butt stuff? Download Cuff."), Talia hasn't turned cynical. No matter how many people may be on Cuff for easy, meaningless sex, she still believes most users want more than that. Just imagine the time these millions of people have poured into their profiles. Writing a 150-word bio that's pithy and sharp. Choosing a half dozen photos that exhibit approachability and warmth in addition to a great ass. It isn't easy deciding how to present your best self (or, at least, whatever version of yourself you think will serve you best).

Talia wants to reward their efforts by giving them the best user experience possible. May they all be so lucky as to find their own Townsend on Cuff, just as she has.

There isn't anything wrong with finding love on an app—though to be honest, Talia never imagined her own love life would play out this way. If she had a choice, she would have met Townsend in some romantic, clandestine way. Like how the protagonist in her favorite novel, Kennedy J. Abbott's *Right on Track*, met the love of her life: on a midnight Paris-bound train from Vienna.

Or how Kennedy met her own husband. According to an Instagram post the author shared on their five-year wedding anniversary, she and Thad met at the grocery store when they both went to reach for the last pint of Ben & Jerry's Cherry Garcia. He let me take the ice cream, she wrote in her caption, and in that moment, dear reader, he scooped up my heart. A true-blue meet-cute; Talia would expect nothing less for a romance writer.

What's less expected is that someone as analytical as Talia would have an affinity for romance novels (or, as Meera refers to the genre, "rom-vom"). Working in a male-dominated STEM field, Talia feels pressure to be one of the guys—to join the office bracket pool during March Madness and wear Chuck Taylors to work rather than heels. But in the safety of her home, she'll always choose a bodice ripper over that night's game. These books have been her guilty pleasure ever since middle school, when she discovered the dirty Regency romance series hidden under her older sister's bed. And in Talia's opinion, no one writes a romance novel quite like Kennedy J. Abbott.

Kennedy's Gramercy Park Hotel wedding was featured in *The New York Times*, and Talia spent so much time poring over the pictures on Kennedy's Instagram grid that she could recall every detail, down to Kennedy's silky cyan-colored Manolo Blahnik slingback pumps—her "something blue," according to a photo caption. Now she and Thad lived on a palatial estate in Asheville, North Carolina, where Kennedy doted on their honey-blond twin daughters and penned novels that made Talia feel more loved and seen than any person ever had—that is, until she met Townsend. Until she experienced her own love story.

Their spark didn't ignite on a train bound for Paris or in the freezer aisle of a grocery store; it began on a phone screen. And while she probably won't find their story in the pages of Kennedy's novels, Talia has come to accept the origin of her modern romance. It's unconventional, but it's hers. It's *theirs*.

It seems like only five minutes have passed before Talia feels a light tap on her shoulder. She startles; she didn't even hear Meera approach her. "What time is it?" she asks, taking out her AirPods. Rap isn't her thing, but she's been giving Jack Harlow a chance for Townsend's sake.

"Almost six. Are you heading out soon?"

"I am. I have dinner plans with . . ." Talia suddenly remembers her audience and stops herself.

"With Townsend? It's okay. You can tell me."

"Yes. With Townsend."

Meera tucks her hair behind both ears, looking suddenly sheepish. "Listen, I'm sorry for what I said yesterday. I shouldn't have made an accusation like that without knowing all the facts."

Talia nods stiffly. Is she even angry at Meera anymore? She can't decide. Truthfully, she's been feeling more pity than anything when it comes to her friend these days. Meera has made a choice to remain single and bitter, but Talia can choose to reject negativity. You attract the energy that you give off (as the *Spot of Positivitea* podcast often reminds her), and Talia believes this to be true. She even bought herself a "Spread Good Vibes" decal for her Stanley tumbler as a reminder. "Apology accepted," she tells Meera.

"Good." Meera smiles, looking genuinely relieved. "I say this a lot, but I really am just looking out for you. I'm overprotective because I care."

"I know. And I appreciate it." *But I really wish you would get your own life and let me enjoy mine.* Talia wants to add this last part but thinks better of it. "Walk out with me?"

"Let's do it."

As soon as Talia stands, her computer dings with an Outlook notification. A new email has arrived at six on the dot, even though the office has a strict policy against sending emails at the end of the workday. Cuff is all about the "work–life balance"—but still, Talia knows many of the upper-level execs are complete workaholics and use the delayed-send feature so they can fire off emails at two a.m. (and have them arrive at a much more reasonable eight thirty).

Meera squints curiously at her screen. "Who's emailing you now?"

"I don't know." According to Outlook, the message was sent by someone named Amy Stake. The address itself is a nonsensical group of letters and numbers attached to a disposable email domain—a burner email address.

"Amy Stake," Meera reads. "Who is Amy Stake?"

"Amy Stake." Talia says the name slowly. "A mistake. I think it's supposed to be a pun."

"Clever."

It would be smarter to report this email as a phishing attempt, but with Meera standing over her shoulder—part protector, part audience—Talia feels emboldened to click. She opens the email and steps to the side so she and Meera can read it together.

> Don't think I forgot about you bxtch. I know your with Townsend now and I know it's not going to last. Watch your fxcking back. As soon as it falls apart I'm coming for you both.

"Holy shit," Meera breathes. "Amanda?"

"I don't—" Talia takes a deep breath to center herself. *Inhale for four, hold for seven, exhale for eight.* "Do you think it's really her?"

"Who else? Just look at it. They mix up 'your' and 'you're.' And they weirdly censor any profanity with x's. Even the syntax is similar."

Talia sits down at her desk again. "Would that mean . . . ?"

Meera nods. "Unless Amanda sent this from beyond the grave, I'd say she's very much alive. And from the sound of it, she's very much pissed."

Chapter Eleven

Amanda

It was his first message on Cuff that roped her in: You look like a good time. Flirty without being overtly sexual—it was a refreshing change from the sort of messages Amanda usually received on the app. Look at those dick-sucking lips. What's that kitty taste like? I can just imagine the sounds you'll make when I choke you. It was incredible what men were emboldened to say when they could talk to a woman without having to look her in the eye.

But Townsend wasn't like that. He was too educated, too well bred. And while the secrecy was fun for a while, nothing felt quite as delicious as getting that prissy bitch of his out of the picture. As her sister would confirm, Amanda had never been good at sharing.

The first time she saw Talia, she didn't even realize they were in competition. It was early December, and she was running late to a Pilates class taught by her friend Raquel (whose friends-and-family discount was the only reason Amanda could afford to step foot into that bougie studio). Having forgotten to take her Converse off at the door, Amanda was creeping across the crowded room, trying to find an open spot, when the toe of her sneaker landed on Talia's mat. The two locked eyes for only a moment, and though she didn't say a word, the look on Talia's face could only be described as pure disgust—toward not just the toe of Amanda's shoe, it seemed, but the entire core of Amanda's being.

Later, in the locker room, Amanda listened in while Talia chatted happily with another woman, apparently having recovered from the great upset Amanda caused earlier. As discreetly as she could, Amanda looked Talia up and down—fresh blowout, matching Alo Yoga set, toned physique. The rich-bitch type who'd looked down on Amanda her whole life. She and her big-boobed Indian friend were discussing something stupid—a new downtown facial bar, it sounded like—when Amanda overheard a name that made her ears prick up: *Townsend.*

"You've been dating Townsend for six months, Talia," her friend was saying. "You shouldn't be this stressed about what to get him for Christmas."

"But that's exactly why I'm stressed," the woman—Talia, apparently—argued. "Six months is half a year. And I really feel like this could be forever." She grinned, and then added, "He changed the key code on his door to my birthday. Isn't that sweet?"

At this point, Amanda and Townsend had been talking for a little over two weeks and had hooked up once, an impulsive move that he'd seemed to regret, based on how quickly he'd gathered up his clothes and left her apartment afterward. She thought he was ashamed of slumming it with a cocktail waitress—which is perhaps why he insisted on the secrecy—but now it made sense: He was cheating. Sure, she could have been talking about another Townsend (not that there were many of them). But somehow, Amanda knew without a doubt that she and this Pilates princess were fucking the same guy.

Amanda waited until the two had left the locker room, and then she sent Townsend a message on Cuff. (So *this* is why he insisted on them keeping their correspondence on Cuff, she realized. Texting was too obvious.)

I'm going to a protest tomorrow at Waller Beach Park, she wrote. You should come.

His answer was almost immediate. What's it for?

Does it matter? It's a chance to hang out with me.

She couldn't help but grin when she saw his response: When you put it like that, how could I say no?

The fact that Townsend had a girlfriend should have annoyed or upset her. It wasn't the first time she was the other woman, and it probably wouldn't be the last. Her sister Kaitlyn once asked her (after it was revealed that she'd been sleeping with their dad's married coworker), "Doesn't it bother you, being everyone's sloppy seconds?" But it didn't, because she wasn't anyone's sloppy seconds. Time and time again, men were willing to upheave their lives for the chance to be with her. That made her the victor, not the backup. And now it seemed she was going to win again.

In these relationships, she never even thought of herself as *the other woman*. While taking an Arthurian literature class for community college (which was as awful as it sounded—no wonder she never finished her degree), she was forced to read *Le Morte d'Arthur* by Sir Thomas Malory, which is where she first learned the term *paramour*. It sounded so sexy to Amanda—and Queen Guinevere, fucking around with both King Arthur and Sir Lancelot, seemed pretty sexy too. So what if she was sentenced to death for her actions? She had a good time while things lasted.

Amanda and Townsend continued to see each other casually for the next few weeks, their meetings always furtive and quick—because it was hotter that way, as Townsend claimed. And because she was always game to fulfill someone's fantasy, Amanda never mentioned Talia; she allowed Townsend to believe she was blissfully ignorant. Like most men, he didn't tell her she was the other woman until after they were caught . . . by Talia, in his bed, just about a week before Christmas. It was all just too predictable and, frankly, a little funny. Naked beneath Townsend's sheets, Amanda watched as Talia's mouth gaped like a fish's—the same look of disgust she wore when Amanda accidentally stepped on her precious Pilates mat—and she had to stifle her giggle.

Even though he was handsome, and sophisticated, and on the cusp of making even more money than he already did (as he kept telling her, alluding to some start-up idea), she thought things with Townsend would get boring once the chase was over. Surprisingly, they didn't. After things with Talia ended, Townsend began calling Amanda his girlfriend, and belonging to him—being *just* his—was more thrilling than she could have ever imagined. Maybe Kaitlyn had been onto something. Maybe being someone's person was even better than being their paramour.

Because it wasn't just sex, though it may have started that way. With Talia out of the picture, Townsend could finally relax, and she began to know him as more than just the monied playboy who sometimes snuck into her bed at night. As their relationship developed, their conversations deepened, broaching topics like Townsend's sick father and Amanda's dead parents, Townsend's fear of failure and Amanda's lack of direction. Intimacy had never looked like this in her past relationships, and she'd never realized that baring her soul could make her feel so much more vulnerable than baring her skin. The first time Townsend peed with the bathroom door left open, she nearly cried—how good it felt, to be let in, to be trusted. It didn't matter that Amanda wasn't a debutante like the girls Townsend was likely used to courting. He wanted her. Maybe even loved her.

Amanda only saw Talia at Raquel's Pilates class on one other occasion, a few weeks after she'd successfully stolen Townsend away. Late, as usual, Amanda set up her mat near the back of the studio, and she didn't approach Talia until later, in the locker room, where—this time—she was without her friend for protection.

First, Amanda stripped naked, wrapping herself loosely in a towel. Then she snuck up behind Talia and tapped her shoulder. When she turned around, Amanda thought she saw a flash of recognition in her eyes—but whether she was recognizing Amanda as the woman who'd once stepped on her Pilates mat or the woman she'd discovered in her ex's bed, or maybe even both, she couldn't be sure.

"I'm sorry," Amanda told her.

"You're sorry?"

"Yeah, I'm sorry," she repeated. "I'm sorry your boyfriend broke up with you before you could give him his Christmas present. I know you put a lot of thought into it."

She took a step back before she dropped her towel to the ground; she wanted Talia to see every inch of what Townsend had gotten instead. Where Talia was taut and toned, with her tiny, boyish breasts and skin stretched like Saran Wrap over sinewy muscles, Amanda was all youthful curves, all woman. She could see Talia taking note of her soft body—likely wondering, *Isn't Townsend disgusted by all that pinchable skin?*—and quietly understanding the truth: It didn't matter that she had sculpted her body into its most inoffensive shape. Talia's hunger could not compete with Amanda's well-fed form. At last, once it was clear that Talia had nothing to say back, Amanda turned—ever so slowly—and made her way to the shower stalls.

Scrubbing her skin under the hot water, Amanda felt so pleased with herself, so powerful. She'd pulled off some real Queen Guinevere shit. And at the time, she figured she'd never have to see Talia and her prissy little face ever again. She should have known it wouldn't be that easy. That girls like Talia are cockroaches. They keep coming back until you smash them under your heel.

Chapter Twelve

Townsend

Outside the window, Townsend can see it again: that dirty white Honda Accord with the cheap-looking Gemini-symbol decal, parked on the street across from his building. It's the third time he's seen it in as many weeks, and he feels certain now: Either he is losing his mind or Amanda is back in town. If she ever even left, that is.

Back when he was a portfolio manager at Bonnell Trust alongside his dad, Townsend could always manage to focus (though the steady stream of Adderall provided by his deskmate, Imran Patel, helped). But since leaving to dedicate himself to AutoInTune full time, his concentration has turned to shit. The silence in his home office is too loud. The walls? Too close. And the internet: too full of pornographic content he can't help but peruse during work hours. That's why Townsend tends to work on the sixth floor of his building, either in the library or in one of the executive meeting rooms. At least in these shared spaces he's forced to keep his hand off his dick and his eyes on his laptop screen. Except for those moments when they drift out the window and notice his ex-girlfriend's car parked outside, once again. Just sitting. Watching.

Work can't happen right now—at least not while Townsend feels like he's under surveillance—so instead, he types "Amanda Reade" into his search engine, curious what, if anything, he'll find. Along with her

Instagram (still untouched since March) and a press release about her disappearance from the Travis County Sheriff's Office website (brief and uninformative), Townsend notices a Reddit thread among the top results. He follows the link and is startled to find his own name on the screen in front of him.

There's a screenshot of an Instagram Story, seemingly written by Amanda's sister and posted from Amanda's account. He scans quickly through the message: . . . filed a police report . . . Amanda's most recent boyfriend, Townsend Fuller . . . involved in Amanda's disappearance . . . I have proof.

This is bad, he thinks numbly, his brain unable to compute much else. *Very, very, bad.* But what's worse is the parade of comments that follows.

The attacks on his appearance don't bother him much—though it creeps him out to see that someone has pulled an old photo of him from Google (was that taken at the St. Augustine holiday party, like, four years ago?) and cropped out the people on either side of him so it's just him, standing alone, grinning like an armless idiot. That's a punchable face if I've ever seen one, writes one commenter. Wouldn't leave my drink unattended around him, says another. And one person simply wrote, This guy 100% lies about his height on dating apps, which is almost funny to Townsend, because his above-average height has never been a source of insecurity, and it's sad that this internet troll can't even come up with a decent insult.

Honestly, the many commenters weighing in on his possible involvement in Amanda's disappearance don't irk him either. These people don't know him. They don't know anything about his relationship with Amanda. And they can write I bet he killed her as many times as they want, but that won't change the fact that Amanda is not dead or missing but is instead sitting outside his home—stalking *him*, threatening *him*—at this very moment. Accusations mean nothing when your innocence is indisputable and easily proven.

No, what really makes him sick to his stomach are the comments about AutoInTune—and though there are far fewer of them, these mentions seem far more pointed. One of the top comments, written by a user named LivingstonTheDream, even feels personal. I work in VC and he pitched his healthcare startup, AutoInTune, to us last week. It was kind of a shitshow TBH. Did Brett Livingston's brother Orson write that, that motherfucker? Are these comments questioning the legitimacy of his business just bullshit—the result of an indignant, indulgent internet pile on—or is someone actually out to get him?

It's still in its early stages, sure. But what these people don't realize is that Townsend has put more work into this company than anything he's ever done—and that includes his undergrad degree from Penn and the decade he spent toiling away at Bonnell Trust. Since launching to consumers earlier this year, AutoInTune has earned nothing but positive attention, including a spot on *Austin Incubator*'s "Top 25 HealthTech Start-ups to Watch." He has a staff of nine. He has an interdisciplinary team able to help patients with over forty different autoimmune diseases. He has a meeting tomorrow with telehealth giant Sage Clinic for an employer partnership. But he also has a problem: Fewer people are signing up than he'd anticipated. Like, *far* fewer people.

Is the $225-per-month membership fee too steep? It seems reasonable to him, considering everything AutoInTune has to offer. (Nutritional assessments! Curated content! Twenty-four seven access to a dedicated care team!) But he knows not everyone can afford it; he's aware of his financial privilege, despite what people may think. His hope is that he can secure the partnerships (and the funds) needed to lower out-of-pocket costs.

And if he has to inflate his membership numbers a bit to achieve those goals, then so be it.

Scrolling back to the top of the page, Townsend sees that the thread has generated nearly a hundred responses. His head pounds with red-hot fury tinged with a drop of anxiety. He hates to even entertain this possibility, but he wonders if this goddamn Reddit thread could be the reason why two separate venture capital firms canceled meetings with him. No one wants to deal with bad press. And speaking of bad press . . .

Townsend puts his fingertips to his temples and stifles a groan. Mother will absolutely shit if she gets word of any of this. The last thing he needs right now is to be accused of tarnishing the family name, especially if he wants access to his trust anytime soon.

Townsend's phone buzzes on the table next to him, and he jumps. But it's just the front desk calling.

"Ms. Danvers is here to see you," reports the doorman. Townsend recognizes the warbly, watery voice—it's the older dude with the limp whose time at the Austinite predates Townsend's but whose name he can never remember, if he ever learned it in the first place.

"Send her up," he says. It's growing dark, and there's no chance of him getting any more work done today, so he might as well meet Talia at his place. Gathering up his laptop, he takes one more glance outside. There it is, sitting just outside the yellowish orb cast by a nearby streetlight: that same fucking car. He flips the bird to the window (though who knows if she can see him; he certainly can't see her from here) and then heads to the elevator.

Talia is already outside his door, chewing on a thumbnail, when he arrives on the forty-eighth floor. The nail biting is strange, Townsend thinks. Talia isn't someone who's easily flustered.

"Hi there." He offers her a kiss on the cheek, which she accepts but doesn't quite acknowledge. "You okay? You seem upset."

As though remembering herself, Talia pulls her hand away from her mouth and uses it to tuck her hair behind her ear. Another nervous tic of hers. "I'm okay. But can we go inside? I need to talk to you about something."

Fuck. What now? Townsend wants to ask, but instead he says, "Of course."

He lets Talia ahead of him into his condo, where she kicks off her shoes and settles on the couch, her bare feet folded in her lap. He loves how comfortable she feels here, how well she complements his space. It reminds him that—no matter how shitty everything seems right now—he has at least one thing that's going right. He takes a seat next to her, and she hands him her phone.

"What am I looking at?"

"Just read it."

Townsend reads aloud the message that fills up her screen. "'I know you're with Townsend now, and I know it's not going to last.' Who sent you this?" He checks the sender before Talia can respond. "Who is Amy Stake?"

"A mistake," Talia corrects. "I think it's a pun." After a pause, she adds, "I think it's Amanda."

This he doesn't expect. "Amanda Reade? My Amanda?"

She flinches at these words—*my Amanda*—and he immediately wishes he could take them back. Instead, he presses on.

"Why would she know you? How would she know how to contact you?"

Avoiding Townsend's eyes, Talia slides her phone from his hands and places it on her lap. "I know she's been harassing you. And I think she's starting to come after me too."

"How—?"

Before he can form his question, Talia speaks in a rush. "It was stupid, and I told her not to do it, but Meera hacked into your Cuff messages. She found all these nasty threats from Amanda, going all the way back to when you first broke up."

Warmth floods his face and armpits. "Did you read everything?" he asks carefully. He thinks of the last message he sent her, the photo of the paintball gun on the dashboard. He knows just how bad it looks.

Talia nods. "But I don't judge you for anything you said," she adds. "It's obvious that she's obsessed with you. You said what you needed to say to get her to leave you alone."

Townsend's relief is so immense he's tempted to kiss Talia, right then and there. But then her phone vibrates on her lap, stealing her attention.

"Oh, my God."

"What?"

Once again, Talia hands him her phone. Another email from Amy Stake has appeared on her screen: Don't let your guard down. Remember I'm watching.

"Jesus Christ." Townsend thinks of that familiar Honda Accord, just idling on the curb across the street. Had she seen Talia enter his building? He's about to tell her to watch out for that car when Talia stands.

"We need to call the police, Townsend. This is serious."

"The police?" Townsend stands, too, his panic returning. "I don't think we should get them involved, Tal."

"Why not? They're already involved."

"And they're already suspicious of me. No, I don't think it's a good idea." He shakes his head. "I think you should just block her email. She'll get bored eventually and leave you alone. I know her."

Again, Talia blanches at this familiarity: *I know her*. He really needs to choose his words more carefully. "But what if she doesn't?"

"Please. Just give me a chance to handle it myself."

She studies him, and for a moment, he fears she can read his mind. He definitely can't tell her about Amanda's car now. "Okay," she says finally. "I trust you."

Townsend hugs her and buries his face in her dark hair. The familiar scent of her jasmine shampoo soothes him, and he tries to keep that feeling of calm with him, even after Talia goes to bed. Even after he closes himself in his office and returns to that Reddit thread.

Talia doesn't know the real reason why Townsend won't call the police; of this he feels pretty certain. But if these random trolls on the internet know what he's up to, then it's only a matter of time before Talia and the police do too.

Closing his eyes, Townsend repeats the mantra he's been saying to himself for weeks, the flimsy lie that's keeping him sane: *You didn't do anything wrong. Founders inflate their numbers all the time. All you need to do is find an enterprise partner—or get access to your trust—and everything will be okay.*

He hopes that if he repeats these words often enough, they'll finally start to feel true.

Chapter Thirteen

Kaitlyn

From Amanda's car, Kaitlyn watches as a dark-haired woman pushes through the revolving door of Townsend's building: Talia. She feels creepy knowing his girlfriend's name—and being able to recognize her, even from a distance—but she can't help it. When she's not at work, all she's done for the past few weeks is watch Townsend, waiting for him to slip up and reveal what he did to Amanda. Right now, knowing everything there is to know about the person responsible for her sister's disappearance is her priority.

Likely responsible, Kaitlyn reminds herself. She still doesn't know anything for sure. All she knows is Townsend rarely leaves his building and his new girlfriend basically seems to be living with him.

Kaitlyn figured out Talia's name the same way she found Townsend's: through a social media deep dive. Townsend's Instagram—deactivated weeks ago—was still no help, but she managed to find the profile of Will Dupont, the former classmate of Townsend's who she'd met for coffee. Then she scrolled through the accounts followed by Will until she found a familiar name: Brett Livingston, who was one of the guys posing with Townsend in that alumni-holiday-party snapshot she'd found on Google. From there, she went through Brett's grid until she stumbled upon a group photo, taken at what appeared to be Town Lake.

First Brotilla of the season, he'd captioned the photo, which showed him and a half dozen other friends, shirtless and sweating and swilling beers in kayaks. And there, in the middle of the chaos, was Townsend, looking not at the camera but instead at the dark-haired woman sitting in front of him in his boat. The same woman Kaitlyn had seen sitting in the passenger seat of Townsend's stupid little roadster a few weeks earlier, the first time she'd staked out his place.

She touched her finger to the screen. Sure enough, the woman in the photo was tagged: @taliadanvers. And though her profile was sparse—she hadn't posted a photo since 2017, and even that was a heavily filtered selfie—Kaitlyn at least had a name.

When she laid out all the steps she'd taken to find Townsend—and now his girlfriend—Kaitlyn knew it sounded a little unhinged. But she also knew that this kind of low-grade cyberstalking was a regular Tuesday afternoon for most Gen Zers. Her sister could be given a zodiac sign and a school mascot and turn up the entire life history of a friend's Cuff date in seconds. It wasn't so strange to have this skill. In fact, you could argue that it was dangerous *not* to do your research. You could end up with a weirdo, or a deviant, or a full-fledged psycho. You could end up dead.

Disappointingly, an extensive internet search turned up nothing about Talia's early life. It was as though she didn't exist—or, at least, didn't do anything worthy of leaving a digital footprint—before her time in college, when a Natalia Danvers started earning a spot on the dean's list every year at Auburn University. It surprised Kaitlyn to learn that Townsend's girlfriend attended a state school rather than an Ivy League university like him and seemingly all his friends. And even though Talia was a member of Zeta Tau Alpha (according to an article Kaitlyn found about a charity car wash), she didn't quite fit the mold of a sorority girl to Kaitlyn either. She wasn't blond, for one. And from what Kaitlyn could gather, Talia just seemed . . . *different*.

In her search, Kaitlyn found an *Inner Click* interview with Talia published three years earlier, not long after she was hired as a machine learning engineer at the dating app Cuff—and apparently sometime after she decided to start going by Talia rather than Natalia. Done as part of a Women in STEM series, the interviewer had asked Talia all about the challenges of working in a male-dominated field.

"I really hope that we can get to a point where we don't need communities just for women," Talia said at one point. "I want a future where women feel confident in communities for all people, where they can ask questions without hesitation and advocate for their own opportunities."

Dammit, Kaitlyn had thought. She'd been so prepared to dislike Talia—the woman who'd replaced her sister and tied herself to a man as dangerously arrogant as Townsend Fuller—but the more she read, the more she found herself charmed by this mysterious person. In another life, Talia was exactly the kind of person Kaitlyn would want as a friend: someone ambitious and articulate and put together. Someone so unlike the mess that Amanda is.

Or *was*. It still isn't clear if Kaitlyn should be thinking about her sister in the past tense. With each passing day, it feels less likely that Amanda will simply turn up in a whirlwind of tangled hair extensions and empty apologies. But still, Kaitlyn holds out hope. Because when she doesn't—when she acknowledges the possibility that her sister will never come back—it becomes difficult to catch her breath, her throat constricting like she's having an allergic reaction.

Before the accident that left her orphaned, Kaitlyn had friends. She got drinks with coworkers. She went on dates. Losing her parents as suddenly and dramatically as she did changed that—making relationships of any kind felt like a trap. According to her therapy chatbot on ShrinkGPT, grief can rewire the brain, effectively locking the mind in a permanent stress response. Kaitlyn liked this idea, that her amygdala and hippocampus and cortisol levels were responsible for her reluctance to socialize rather than some innate weirdness inside her. Would she have ever considered herself popular? Absolutely not (and Amanda, who was popular, often reminded her of this fact growing up). But she hadn't always felt this deeply alone, too afraid to even contact a human therapist for fear that they, too, would leave her. Amanda was the only person she had. Amanda was the only person who could even remotely understand what she'd been through.

Sitting now in her sister's car, outside her sister's ex-boyfriend's building, Kaitlyn knows she should leave. Now that Talia has arrived, it's unlikely that either she or Townsend will emerge again until morning. The idea of returning to her eerily quiet apartment, however, fills her with dread. No, she can't be alone, not right now. Instead, she puts the car into drive and heads to the shooting range.

The Range at Austin is about a twenty-minute drive from Downtown Austin, but over the past few weeks, it's become one of the only places where Kaitlyn feels like she can breathe. As a kid, she never understood her dad's love of the firing range, and she was never interested when he tried to give her lessons on properly handling firearms.

"A woman should know how to do three things," he told her once. "She should be able to change a tire, balance a checkbook, and handle a gun."

She laughed him off when he told her this. "I don't think anyone uses a checkbook anymore, Dad."

But he remained firm: "You're not like your sister, Kate. You'll never be happy with someone taking care of you."

Was this true? Kaitlyn was pretty sure that—if she had as many suitors as Amanda—she'd welcome a helping hand.

"I have no doubt that you'd be able to tackle anything on your own," he continued. "But it's a scary place out there, especially for a woman. I want to be sure you can support and protect yourself."

"I can," Kaitlyn promised him—though at the time, she never imagined that she'd be orphaned at twenty-four. She never imagined that her parents would just be gone one day, leaving her with only a fraction of their estate and the responsibility of looking after her eternally irresponsible younger sister.

It wasn't until the first time she visited the Range at Austin—not long after her parents passed—and felt the cold, unyielding pressure of a SIG Sauer P320 in her hand that it all finally made sense. Powerful didn't quite describe the way she felt. What she felt instead was a sense of release, like she'd overcome a long-held fear and could no longer remember why she'd been afraid in the first place.

Soon enough, she's standing on the firing line, pistol in hand, waiting for the cue from the range safety officer to commence firing. Downrange, she eyes the target: a faceless, genderless human silhouette that she initially thought of as a general threat but, over her past few visits, has begun thinking of as Townsend. When the range is declared hot, she aims and squeezes the trigger of her weapon. The first bullet clips the target's shoulder. The second hits close to his heart. She is still learning; she will improve. When Kaitlyn sets her mind to something, anything is possible.

Later—after making the trek back to her apartment and heating up a can of Chef Boyardee beef ravioli in the microwave—Kaitlyn checks her Reddit thread asking for information on Townsend. There isn't much new activity; after an initial spate of comments, it seems the internet sleuths have already moved on from Amanda's disappearance to a new case. The two new comments aren't of any use either; just one user writing So sad and another saying He looks like the kind of guy who'd call you "mommy" in bed.

Kaitlyn logs out of her burner account and back into her personal Reddit account. Then she posts a new comment as herself. It's time to stop hiding, she decides.

This is Kaitlyn, Amanda's sister, she types. I'm the OP of that message about Amanda's IG Story. I just wanted to say thank you to everyone who's taken the time to respond and offer any information you may have. Ever since losing our parents, Amanda and I have only had each other, and not knowing if she's okay has been unbearable. If you know anything about what happened to my sister, PLEASE reach out. It would mean the world to me.

After reading the message twice, Kaitlyn takes a deep breath and posts the comment. A little maudlin, perhaps, but why not tug at people's heartstrings? She doesn't have much left to lose.

She doesn't expect a response right away, but still, it would have been nice. She keeps her phone by her side with the volume turned up as she eats her ravioli, watches *The Real Housewives of Atlanta*, brushes her teeth, changes into an oversize Southwestern University T-shirt, and climbs into bed—and even though she refreshes the page every few minutes, no response appears. The only message she receives all night is from that chatty data science professor (who's been asking for a second date since May), and Kaitlyn is not in any sort of mood to arrange a date right now.

It's only as she's starting to fall asleep, imagining she's back on the range with her pistol in hand, when her phone beeps. She gropes for it in the dark, sensing it's a message that can't wait.

At first, she's disappointed. It appears she's merely been notified that someone upvoted her comment. But then she notices the username attached to the upvote: geminibaby530. It's Amanda's go-to password. The same one that had allowed Kaitlyn to hack her sister's Instagram. And while it could be a coincidence, something in the way her pulse races tells her that it's not.

Kaitlyn navigates to the profile associated with the username only to find no other activity. Could this be Amanda? Could this be her way of letting Kaitlyn know that she's okay? Her heart hammers in her chest as she simply thinks about the possibility. It doesn't explain where her sister has been—but the idea that she's somewhere and that she's safe makes Kaitlyn tingle all over with hope.

Of course, if this user *is* Amanda, that means Kaitlyn's second-worst fear could be true: that nothing nefarious happened to her sister at all. That her sister is just the unreliable, uncaring, unhinged mess Kaitlyn always thought she was.

Still on geminibaby530's profile, Kaitlyn clicks the chat icon in the upper right-hand corner. But all she receives is an error message—the user has already deleted their account.

Chapter Fourteen

Meera

"Explain to me again," Meera says, "why Townsend doesn't want to go to the police?"

It's Friday, and she has a shit ton of work to finish up before the weekend, not to mention an employee seminar about corporate policy to attend this afternoon. But she's finding it tough to concentrate, what with the news of Amanda's threats fresh in her mind. What's worse: Neither Talia nor Townsend seems to be doing anything about them.

Talia stands next to her in the Cuff office kitchenette, leaning against the counter as they wait for the coffee to finish brewing. "He doesn't want any more attention from the police." She shifts from one foot to the other, looking uncomfortable. "And he didn't say this, but I think he's a little afraid of them going through their messages and seeing that photo. The one with the gun on the dashboard."

There's no need for Talia to specify; Meera sees that photo every time she closes her eyes. It makes her queasy, thinking about her best friend sharing a bed with a man who not only owns a gun but isn't afraid to use it. Or, at least, *threaten* to use it.

Despite what Talia seems to believe, Meera isn't a bra-burning man-hater. Her failed marriage hasn't turned her against everyone with a Y chromosome or compelled her to write off half the population as chauvinist pigs. Even after being cheated on by Hari, Meera continues to date and enjoy the company of men (though admittedly, she's been doing very little of that as of late). Being male is not cause for disdain in her eyes. No, her problem is with the men who use their privileged status and leaner muscle mass to intimidate, and dominate, and inflict pain.

Meera has come to terms with Talia's boyfriend being an asshole. What she can't accept is the idea that Townsend could potentially be driven to kill.

"Did you ask him about that gun?" she asks Talia now. "Was it real?"

"I didn't. But even if the picture was real, I know his threat wasn't. He would never actually hurt someone."

"And did you show him all the messages you've gotten over the past few days?"

"Most of them, but not all. I don't want to freak him out."

"Are you freaked out?"

"Yes."

"Then he should know that," Meera insists. "It's weird, frankly, that he isn't more concerned. Between that and all the shady shit going on with his company—"

"Shady shit? What are you talking about? He just had a meeting with a major telehealth company for a potential partnership. He said it went really well."

Meera looks at Talia, who blinks back at her, genuinely confused. Of course, Meera reminds herself. As far as Talia knows, AutoInTune is going swimmingly. That's because Meera hasn't told her anything about the message she'd received yesterday on Reddit from LivingstonTheDream.

It took a few days, but eventually, Meera got her response, explaining what the user found suspicious about Townsend's company data. The numbers just seemed too good to be true, the message read. I'm pretty sure AutoInTune doesn't even get as many site visitors as he claimed to have as members.

Too good to be true—that's exactly what Talia said of Townsend when she first met him. If only she knew how right she was. But Meera knew she couldn't just take a stranger on the internet for their word. Do you have proof?

No proof, the person wrote. Just a hunch and years of experience doing this shit.

A hunch wasn't much, but it was something. And whoever LivingstonTheDream might be, Meera had to assume they didn't have a personal reason for wanting to see Townsend fail. Not like she did.

Meera can't get into AutoInTune with Talia, not now. She's already lost too much of her lunch break to parsing Townsend's idiotic behavior. "Point being, I don't think Amanda's threats should be taken lightly, by him or by you."

In the three days that have passed since that first "Amy Stake" email hit Talia's inbox, she's gotten at least a dozen more messages from Amanda, each one more disturbing than the last. On Wednesday, Amanda told Talia she still knew the key code for Townsend's condo. On Thursday, she threatened to use said key code when Talia least expected it. And just this morning, she told Talia to check behind the shower curtains and under the bed when she got to Townsend's place, because she could never know where Amanda might be hiding.

It's fucked up, these mind games, and looking at Amanda's photos online, you'd never guess such a pretty girl was capable of such fuckery. But apparently she is—and apparently Townsend is too concerned about his own reputation to ensure his girlfriend's safety.

Meera slaps her palm on the coffee machine, suddenly frustrated. "This piece of shit is taking forever. I'm just going to go out for lunch and get coffee there. Want to join?"

Talia shakes her head no. "I grabbed something earlier. Thanks, though."

"You did?" It has been a busy day, but still, Meera doesn't remember Talia stepping out. "When?"

"I don't know." Talia looks at her watch. "A little before noon? Does it matter?"

"No, I guess not." It bothers her that Talia disappeared from the office and Meera didn't even notice. Somehow, Meera feels responsible for Talia when they're at work, especially with Amanda ramping up her threats. Outside of work, she considers it Townsend's responsibility to protect Talia—though really, Meera isn't confident he's pulling his weight. Here, at least, it's on her to keep Talia safe.

"I'm walking to Mañana and getting something to go," says Meera. "You'll let me know if you get any messages from you-know-who in the meantime?"

"Sure," Talia says, but her thoughts seem to have already drifted elsewhere.

After work, she and Talia head to the parking lot. Meera's car is in the shop again—her check engine light keeps flashing, because that's just her fucking luck—and Talia promised to drive her home. Always a dependable friend, even while being harassed by a total psychopath.

"Did that seminar make you feel nervous at all?" Meera asks, referring to the end-of-day all-staff meeting. "Do you think the company is doing a security audit for a reason? Like, they know something?"

"Know something?"

"About"—Meera glances around the parking lot, then lowers her voice—"us reading Townsend's messages."

"Oh." Talia frowns, fishing her keys out of her purse. "I doubt it. Don't they do one every year?"

"I guess so. It's just something about the way the announcement was made. Like they expect to find something." Meera sighs. "I'm probably just feeling extra neurotic."

It isn't often that the Cuff staff is corralled into the auditorium. The last time was earlier in the year, after Cuff introduced an AI-based chat feature and company shares fell nearly 50 percent. During that meeting,

Cuff's COO, Betty Jeong—a pink-haired MIT grad with a penchant for colorful power suits—appeared jumpy, chastened; this time, she was as cool and commanding as a seasoned schoolteacher. And though Meera can't say for sure, she could have *sworn* that when Betty delivered her final warning ("Any breaches in security will be detected, and they will not be tolerated"), she looked Meera dead in the eye. As though she knew exactly what Meera had done.

Talia pats her shoulder. "I wouldn't stress about it."

"Right. Like you said, the security audit is probably just a routine thing." *You've been careful about using your credentials to hack Townsend's messages,* she tells herself. *You've covered your tracks. There's no reason you should be caught.* Still, the thought of the company unearthing her illicit activity makes her feel itchy all over.

"Oh, my God," Talia stops short. "Do you see that?"

"See what?"

"My car. Look at my car."

It takes Meera a moment to spot Talia's silver Volkswagen Jetta in the lot, but when she does, she lets out an involuntary gasp. All four tires have been slashed.

Talia approaches the car slowly, as though afraid it might detonate—or afraid someone is hiding behind it, waiting for her.

Meera follows close behind, noticing something as she nears. "Is that a note on the windshield?"

"Better than a parking ticket." Talia laughs, but the sound is hollow; she's clearly shaken.

Meera waits a moment, giving Talia a chance to grab the note, but when she doesn't, Meera picks it up instead. Trying to keep her voice steady—it feels important to be the strong one right now, for Talia's sake—she reads it out loud.

"'First your tires, next your throat.'"

Talia's hand flies to her neck, clutching it protectively. "Is it signed?"

"No, but I think we both know who wrote it." Meera folds the paper in half and hands it to her friend to see for herself.

Talia takes it without looking at it. "What should I do?"

"Tal, we don't have a choice here. We have to call the police."

"But Townsend—"

"—is being selfish," Meera finishes for her. "You two are out of your depth here. If he really cares about you, he will recognize that."

Talia considers this. "Okay," she says finally. "Let's call." She gestures to the car. "Doesn't seem like I'll be able to give you a ride home, though."

"That's the least of my concerns, Tal," says Meera. "My concern right now is getting this person to leave you the fuck alone."

Talia gives her a weak smile, and Meera feels a strange swell of pride. She knows she shouldn't think like this—she and Townsend are not competitors, vying for Talia's affection—but still, the thought bubbles up unprompted: *I've won this round.*

The Austin Police Department is too far from the Seaholm District to walk, so they take an Uber. On the ride there, Talia is silent, and Meera fears Talia might be resentful she's making her do this—but then she notices her friend picking at her cuticles. She's not angry; she's nervous. That's understandable. Meera sets her hand on top of Talia's, her way of saying *I'm here*. And when Talia takes her hand, giving it an appreciative squeeze, all the anxiety that's been fluttering in Meera's gut since the employee seminar ebbs away. Right now, she needs to be present, with Talia, not lost in her own worries.

Once inside, Meera feels less certain than she did in the parking lot, but she doesn't let Talia see her doubt. Instead, she charges ahead with conviction, like she's here every day reporting threats posed by an unhinged stalker.

"Can I help you?" The man behind the front desk seems bored with them already, though it's hard to read his tone through the thick layer of bulletproof glass that separates him from them. It's insulting, really, that glass. Like Meera and Talia are a threat to this man, rather than victims in need of an authority figure's help.

Talia speaks before Meera can. "Is Detective Harris available? Or Detective Burrows?"

"Are they—?"

Talia nods, somehow already anticipating what Meera is going to ask. "The officers who came to Townsend's place to ask about Amanda."

"I'll check." Without moving from behind his desk, the man speaks into his radio, his words mumbled and unintelligible. A moment later, a tall Black woman in a navy suit appears.

"Detective Harris, I don't know if you remember me, but I'm—"

"Townsend Fuller's girlfriend, correct?" Harris looks Talia up and down and then glances curiously at Meera. "I remember."

"Right. Talia Danvers. And this is my friend, Meera Ratnam."

Harris tilts her head, as though waiting for a punch line.

"You came to question Townsend after Amanda Reade's sister reported her as missing but . . ."

A beat passes. "But what?" Harris pushes.

Talia takes a deep breath and then pushes the words out all at once—and though she only says what Meera already suspects, Talia's confession still raises goose bumps on her skin.

"She's not missing, or dead. She's still alive, and I think she wants to kill me."

Chapter Fifteen

Talia

Talia is glad Meera pushed her to go to the police.

As much as Townsend doesn't want to involve them, Talia knows this is the appropriate next move. It's time for someone—besides Talia, Townsend, and Meera—to know what Amanda is up to. Alerting the authorities would only help protect her.

Once Detective Harris leads Talia and Meera back to her office, Talia recounts the series of threats: the emails from "Amy Stake," the slashed tires, the ominous note. She even hands over her phone so Harris can inspect all the evidence for herself, which she does in silence with a furrowed brow.

At last, Harris says, "I understand why you're shaken. But can I ask what makes you believe these messages are coming from Amanda Reade? Her sister hasn't heard from her in months. So why would she contact you?"

"She's sending threatening messages to Townsend too." Talia gestures to Meera. "We both saw them. They sound just like the emails I've received."

"She's been contacting Townsend through Cuff," Meera explains.

"Cuff?"

"It's a dating app," says Talia. "It's how they met. And it's how Townsend and I met." Though it doesn't really seem like Harris's business, Talia adds, "Meera and I work there as engineers." Perhaps it just feels good to mention this, that she's an engineer, a woman in STEM. Someone to be taken seriously.

Still Harris looks skeptical. "Townsend didn't mention these messages when we spoke to him."

The last thing Talia wants is to get Townsend in trouble, especially when he'd been so reluctant for her to approach the police. "He didn't want me to know about them. He thought he could handle her himself."

"Handle her?"

Shit. "Well, no, not handle her—that's not what I meant to say. He just wanted to ignore her, hoping she would leave us alone. But clearly that isn't working."

"And what are you hoping I can do?"

"Protect us!" Talia didn't mean to raise her voice, but she does, and she instantly regrets it. Seeing the look on Harris's face, she takes a deep breath before continuing. "She was outside my office. She slashed my tires . . ." Talia runs a hopeless hand through her hair. "I know her sister led you to believe that Amanda is in trouble, but I'm telling you: Amanda *is* trouble."

"All right." Harris nods. "We'll look into the vandalism charge. Please keep us updated. If you receive any more threats, you'll let us know, okay?"

"I will." Having gotten Harris on her side, Talia feels as she often does after sex: exposed and a little embarrassed, but too gratified to regret anything. Yes, she'd shouted. Yes, she'd made a scene. But in the end, she'd had her needs met, and is that such a bad thing?

Of course, she had Meera to thank for convincing her to go there in the first place. Meera is a good friend; she really is. Talia doesn't give her enough credit. She's the only person Talia has ever considered telling why she really moved to Austin—but as much as she values their friendship, she can't trust her with that. And unfortunately, it's not something she can share with Townsend either. To tell him would be to risk losing him, because he simply wouldn't understand.

Ever since the morning of Townsend's birthday brunch with his mother at the Verano Country Club, Talia hasn't stopped thinking about how things might have turned out for her, had she grown up with Townsend's privileges: private schools, etiquette lessons, a trust fund created to broaden her horizons and cushion her fall. Sure, his parents didn't seem like the warmest people, but they'd at least given him the assurance that only wealth can provide. Affection or affluence—if she could have experienced only one of these things in her formative years, she probably would have chosen the latter, to be honest. As it happened, she'd been given a family lacking in both love and funds.

While Townsend's family was a caricature of old Texan money, hers was an embarrassingly perfect representation of proud, provincial proletarians living just above the poverty line. Her parents weren't just uneducated—they were willfully ignorant, and they resented their bookish daughter for her ambition and dreams. Had she not met Malcolm Gray her junior year of high school, Talia wasn't sure she ever would have made it to college. Then again, Malcolm was also the reason she was forced from Alabama altogether. So it was hard to say whether she should be grateful for him or—as she has chosen to do—resent him with a white-hot passion, even after all these years.

But she can't waste time thinking about Malcolm now. Not with Amanda filling her inbox and taking a knife to her tires.

As they walk out of the police station together, Talia turns to Meera. "Hari has Grace this weekend, right?"

"Yup. He picked her up from school this afternoon."

"Would you want to have a sleepover at my place? Townsend is having dinner tonight with Sage Clinic executives to talk more about a potential partnership, and I really don't want to be alone right now."

Meera considers this for a moment. "Can we get drunk?"

"Absolutely."

"Then I'm in."

They take an Uber across the river from Downtown Austin to Talia's house in South Congress, a two-bedroom bungalow with vaulted ceilings, stainless steel appliances, and a sunny-yellow front door that makes her smile every time she pulls into the driveway. It isn't much, but it's hers, all hers, and no one can take that away from her. She almost wishes she could show it off to her parents, but she knows their reaction would only disappoint her—plus, she would have to tell them where she lives, which isn't an option.

Talia gives her friend some comfy clothes to wear as pajamas ("I think this is supposed to be oversize," Meera calls from the bathroom, "but it fits me like a baby tee"), and they settle on the living room couch with large glasses of red wine. Then they dance around the subject for a bit—discussing Gracie, Cuff, the approaching end of summer—before Meera asks what she's likely been dying to know for hours.

"Tal, do you really think Amanda is trying to kill you?"

Honestly, Talia isn't sure what she thinks; she was just as surprised when those words popped out of her mouth at the police station as Meera was. But when she said them, they felt right. Because even though Amanda *could* just be trying to scare her, the threat she posed seemed like more than that of a jealous ex. It seemed like that of . . . well, someone deeply unwell. Maybe even deadly. "I do," she says finally. "I really feel like I'm in danger right now."

Meera nods, taking this in. "I think it's impossible to say what she really wants or intends to do, but I'm just glad the police are involved."

The hint of doubt she hears in Meera's voice annoys her; isn't she the one who keeps insisting that Talia take Amanda's warnings seriously? But because she wants to have a good night tonight, she simply clinks her glass against Meera's and says, "I'll drink to that."

It isn't often that Talia has more than one drink in a sitting; there are few things she fears more than losing control. The stress of the day, however, has left her craving escape, and so one glass of wine turns into two and then into three. After a while, she isn't even sure whether Meera is keeping up with her—all she knows is that the inexhaustible voice in the back of her head has been dulled, almost silenced, and she can finally let herself relax.

She hadn't been planning on doing so, but by her third glass, Talia finds herself talking about her sister. She's been on Talia's mind recently, so it makes sense that—the minute she allowed her jaw to unclench—stories would come pouring out. Memories, blurred by time and pinot noir, but with pain and nostalgia still sharp as ever. She talks about the double-wide right off State Route 79 that they called home, and the shared bedroom where they traded books and secrets, and the playground down the street, where they would retreat whenever their dad returned from the butcher shop spoiling for a fight. She talks about coming home from school at fifteen to find her sister's half of the closet empty, about learning that Chelsea had been sent away to a home for unwed mothers and wouldn't be returning for months.

"Oh, my God, Talia," Meera says. "I never realized you didn't get a chance to say goodbye."

Talia refills her wineglass. Is this her fourth glass or her fifth? "I never got to meet her baby either."

"I know you don't have a relationship with her now, but do you know if she's okay? That maternity home must have been horrible."

"I don't know," admits Talia. She tells Meera about all the letters she wrote Chelsea, each one returned from Neveah's Oasis unopened. How alone she felt as she entered adolescence without a big sister to guide her. "Which is probably why I fell so hard for Malcolm."

Though she hasn't talked to Meera much about Chelsea, her friend is all too familiar with Malcolm, the promising football quarterback who, as a senior, saw something special in a mousy junior wearing secondhand jeans. Meera has heard all about Talia falling in love with Malcolm, losing her virginity to him in the back of his car, and eventually following him on a scholarship to Auburn, where he'd earned a full ride to play football. And Meera knows how he—like Chelsea—eventually shattered Talia's heart.

"Do you think that's why you've fallen so hard for Townsend too? Because of what happened with Chelsea?"

The room is spinning now. Clutching onto the couch doesn't help, but Talia does it anyway, hoping to ground herself. "Probably. And it's probably why I'm so afraid of losing him. Because I lose everybody."

"Well, you're never going to lose me. Remember that, okay?" Meera throws open her arms, offering a hug, and the unexpected movement stirs something in Talia. She thinks at first it is affection—but then her stomach is actually churning. She's going to be sick.

Hand clasped over her mouth, Talia runs to the bathroom, barely making it to the toilet before depositing everything she ate and drank that day into the bowl. Once she's finished, she sits back on her heels, feeling somehow cleansed. Almost good.

Washing her hands, she studies her face in the mirror above the sink. In her drunken state, it appears distorted and magnified, like a reflection she might see in a fun house: sunken eyes, thin lips, skin that looks drier and slacker than it had the day before. She stares for what feels like hours, so long her eyes cross and vision blurs. Then she reaches for a pen and the stack of sticky notes she keeps on the counter.

The idea came from the *Spot of Positivitea* podcast. Whenever she becomes fixated on her appearance, Talia tries to write down positive affirmations and stick them to the mirror so she can see them alongside her reflection. The affirmations are supposed to be about things that aren't necessarily physical ("You can use this exercise to remind yourself that you're a good friend, or a hard worker, or a thoughtful partner!" the podcast host said), but now that Talia's head is cloudy with wine, all she can think about is the physical, and nothing she can see is positive.

Flat chest, she writes on one sticky note.

Giant pores, she writes on another.

She writes and sticks until the whole mirror is filled, nearly blocking her reflection altogether, and then she steps back to admire her work. A voice that doesn't sound like her own laughs meanly in her head. *Now you'll never forget how unworthy you are,* it says.

Knowing she needs to return to Meera—too much time has passed, and her friend is no doubt wondering where she's gone—Talia scans through the collage of cruel messages one last time. That's when something catches her eye.

"Meera? Could you come here?"

"You okay?" Behind her, the bathroom door creaks open. "Jesus, what's going on with the Post-It Notes?"

"They're just . . . I was leaving reminders for myself." Talia quickly plucks them off the mirror and crumples them in her hand, leaving only the Post-It in the bottom right-hand corner of the mirror, the one she doesn't remember writing. "But I didn't leave this one."

"What do you mean?" Meera crosses the room to take a closer look.

"I wrote those other notes, but I didn't write this one. This is someone else's handwriting." Talia peels it off the mirror and hands it to her friend. "Was this here when you were in the bathroom changing earlier?"

"No, it wasn't." Silently, Meera reads it, and then in a low voice says, "Oh, God."

Meera squats down and holds the note in front of Talia's face so she can read it for herself: *Think the police can protect you? Think again.*

"She was here." Talia's stomach gurgles angrily; she's going to be sick again. "Amanda came into my house. She left this message for me. She—"

"How is that possible?" Meera asks. "We would have heard her if she broke in, right?"

"Apparently, we don't know what she's capable of doing." Talia snatches the note back. "I need to call the police. I mean, what if she's still here?"

"We'll have them come here and search." Meera's face swims before her eyes, sliding out of focus, but her voice is steady and reassuring. "And I'm here. She can't hurt you while I'm here. Okay?"

"Okay," Talia agrees. "I'll be right out. Just give me a minute."

Once Meera returns to the living room, Talia shreds the crumpled collection of notes in her hand, sprinkles them into the toilet, and flushes them away. The police don't need to see those; Talia doesn't need them thinking that *she's* crazy.

Chapter Sixteen

Townsend

Townsend didn't think Mother would be up for it this year, but he was wrong. His family's annual Fourth of July party is still happening, his dad's death be damned. It's only noon on a Thursday, and already more than one hundred guests are milling around his parents' Tuscan-style estate on Verano Drive, sipping spicy palomas and snatching hors d'oeuvres from the trays of uniformed servers. Townsend chugs his own cocktail miserably and attempts to ignore the newest addition to Mother's art collection: an oil portrait of his father, sitting behind his desk and glowering at everyone below him. *Either I'm drunk,* Townsend thinks, *or those fucking eyes are following me.*

Usually, he doesn't mind this yearly fete. Of course, he isn't usually being stalked by a vindictive ex while internet trolls attempt to take down his company. At least he can feel safe for a bit within the barriers of his parents' gated community. And he has a win to celebrate, since Sage Clinic agreed to a collaboration with AutoInTune on Monday, just a few days earlier. Sure, he still needs the money to officially launch his enterprise solution (and hopefully boost his pitiful membership), but it's the start of something promising.

If only the day got off to a better start.

He and Talia had a fight that morning while getting ready for the party. He told her he didn't understand why she'd gone to the police about Amanda, even after he'd asked her not to. "She's not a real threat," he said. "She's looking for attention. And you're giving that to her."

"It was one thing when she was just sending me messages," Talia replied. "But then she stabbed my tires and somehow snuck into my bathroom while I was home. I consider that a threat."

Townsend knew she was right, but still, anger coursed through him. "You should have told me about it before going to see those detectives. I am still your boyfriend, right? Not Meera?" He wasn't trying to control Talia, obviously. It just irked him that someone had more influence over her decisions than he did.

"She was just being a good friend. She didn't force me to go to the police."

"Right. And she just happened to be with you when you discovered both your busted tires and the note on your bathroom mirror."

Talia gave him a strange look. "What are you suggesting?"

"Nothing," Townsend said, because he really wasn't sure himself. "Let's just get through this fucking party."

Talia nudged his shoulder, always eager to lighten the mood. "That's the spirit."

Next to him now, Talia inspects the six-burner Wolf range and double ovens in the kitchen with childlike wonder. "I can't believe there's a home theater in here," she murmurs. "And nine bathrooms."

"Eight bathrooms," Townsend corrects. "And this is nothing. You should see my friend Jackson's house." He knows it's not nothing—this 7,500-square-foot home—but it's all he's ever known, so nothing about it feels extraordinary. It does feel good, however, to see Talia—who usually does a good impression of someone accustomed to wealth—slip and expose her greed. She can pretend to be unfazed by his building's luxury amenities—which include a private spa and wine cellar—but on occasion, he still catches whiffs of it, like an inoffensive but potent odor: hunger. And he is more than happy to keep her fed.

He likes giving her a taste of this world, and her gratitude reminds him that he should feel more thankful himself. Not everyone has his status and privilege. A memory comes to mind of Amanda holding up one of his vintage Patek Philippe watches—inherited from his father and made almost entirely from 18-karat yellow gold—and asking, "Don't you feel like an asshole owning a golden watch when there are people in your own country starving?"

"It was a gift," Townsend said. "Am I supposed to donate it to an orphanage?"

She grinned in response, showing off the dimple in her right cheek that he loved. "Or you can donate it to me. I'll make sure it goes to a good cause."

Nope. He's not thinking about Amanda today. Townsend takes another sip of his drink, washing away all thoughts of her.

"I can't believe how many people are here," Talia continues. "My parents don't know this many people."

Her parents. Townsend hasn't heard Talia mention her estranged family since the birthday brunch with Mother at the club. He's tempted to follow up with a question, but when he turns, he finds her gaze directed at the floor—her way of saying *I don't want to talk about it,* as he's learned. It's time to change the subject. "Sure I can't get you a drink?"

Talia shakes her head no. "I feel like I've just recovered from all that wine I had last Friday with Meera."

Fucking Meera again. Townsend bites his tongue. He doesn't want to start another fight, so instead, he takes her by the hand. "Let me introduce you around."

For the next hour, he leads Talia around the party, stopping every few feet to present her to a new family member or friend. She meets Townsend's little sister Blake and her giggly friends, his racist aunt Ruth with the botched fillers, his childhood T-ball coach, the lesbian neighbors his mom considers herself very progressive for inviting, and—of course—the old St. Augustine gang.

"Y'all remember Talia, right? And Tal, this is Brett, Warren, and Jackson." Townsend points to each guy as he names them, feeling slightly guilty that he's avoided them all summer so far. But they must understand: They're still doing the same old shit (drinking, dating around, going to Party Island) while he's grown up.

"Nice to see you all again." Talia smiles brightly, and he can feel his friends' envy; she may not have the pedigree, but damn, does she have a nice smile.

"Nicole is somewhere around here too," Brett says. Townsend didn't think they'd last through the summer, but apparently Nicole and Brett are still going strong. "She's probably out back smoking with my brother and hoping your mom doesn't catch them."

"We're not in high school anymore, dude. My mom doesn't care if you smoke." Townsend isn't sure he believes this even as he says it. Then something occurs to him. "Wait, your brother is here?"

"Yeah. Like I said, you'll probably find him out by the pool."

As discreetly as he can, Townsend brings his mouth to Talia's ear. "Babe, will you be okay if I leave you here for a minute? I just want to have a word with Orson."

"Sure," Talia says, though her eyes betray her nervousness. He's thankful that she knows enough not to cling to him. Few things are less attractive in a woman than clinginess.

As Brett suspected, Orson is by the pool with Nicole, a glass of whiskey in one hand and the other wrapped around the waist of Nicole's friend Chrissy. Are they an item now? Townsend really is out of the loop.

"Ladies." He nods to Nicole and Chrissy. "Long time no see."

"Look who it is." Nicole gives him a clownish grin. "We haven't seen you all summer. That lady friend of yours really has you pussy whipped."

Townsend cringes at this. "I've actually been busy expanding my company's platform. Speaking of which"—he turns to Orson and offers his hand—"thanks again for taking that meeting with me, man."

Orson removes his hand from Chrissy's hip to shake. "Of course, dude."

"Any word yet from the team at Silicon Hills? I've pitched a few VC firms, but I'm still waiting to find the right match." Townsend thinks again of that mortifying Reddit comment, which has been haunting him since he first read it: *He pitched his healthcare startup, AutoInTune, to us last week. It was kind of a shitshow TBH.* If Orson really wrote that, Townsend is going to get him to admit it.

"Oh, c'mon." Orson takes a swig of his whiskey, his discomfort palpable. "It's a party. Let's not talk shop here."

"It's been weeks. I'd love to just get some feedback." He's pushing too hard, Townsend knows this, but he can't seem to stop himself. Those spicy palomas must be heavy on the tequila.

"We'll talk soon, okay? Soon." Orson pats him on the shoulder and then points back into the house. "Right now, I think someone else may need your attention."

It doesn't take Townsend long to find who Orson is referencing. There, in the sitting room, he sees his worst nightmare: Mother talking to Talia, their faces too close. As if on cue, Talia turns to look at him, her eyes panicked.

"Dammit." Townsend grabs another paloma from a passing tray and hurries inside.

By the time he pushes his way through the kitchen and into the sitting room—it seems the party has doubled in size in the past hour—Talia's head is bobbing rhythmically, the clear sign of a person who has stopped listening and started planning their escape. Townsend touches the small of her back, and she turns.

"All good over here? What are you two talking about?"

"Nothing much." Talia smiles tightly. "I'm just going to use the restroom to freshen up. Which of the nine—?"

"Eight," Townsend corrects her again. "And the closest one is through the kitchen down the hall. Want me to take you?"

"I think I can handle it. Excuse me." She smiles—a little more warmly this time—and heads off to the bathroom. Then Townsend turns his attention to Mother.

"What was that about? She seemed upset."

"What?" Mother puts one hand on her hip, the other gripping a shrimp cocktail that she probably won't eat. "I can't have a chat with your girlfriend?"

Townsend feels the eyes from his father's portrait watching him again, but he ignores them. "Not if that chat is an inquisition."

"I was just asking her more about her people."

"Her people?"

"I think it's strange," Mother continues, "that you don't share any mutuals or connections."

"What's so bad about being from different backgrounds?"

His mom gestures to the guests around them. "I know these people. I know where they golf, where they vacation, where they went to school, and where they're going to send their children to school. I don't know anything about your girlfriend's people, and because of that, I can't trust her."

"C'mon, Mom. You can't trust her because she doesn't have a chalet in Aspen or a degree from an Ivy League school? Doesn't that seem a bit elitist to you?" He's getting heated now. "It seems like no one I date is good enough for you."

"That's not true."

"Remember Heather, who you said had cheap shoes? Or Dahlia, whose teeth you didn't like? You practically ran them both out of town. And now Talia—"

"I can't trust Talia," Mother interrupts in a stage whisper, "because she is hiding something."

"That's ridiculous. You don't even know her."

"Do you? What kind of young woman doesn't speak to her family? It just isn't right, if you ask me."

Townsend tries to keep from rolling his eyes. His mom must also be feeling the effects of the strong palomas. "Right. Well. While we're on the subject of trust"—he checks the hallway behind her to see if Talia has reappeared yet—"have you given any more thought to me accessing my trust?"

"Whatever for?"

"I told you, Mom. I need funding for my company."

Mother looks unsurprised, maybe even amused, by this news. "What happened to those meetings you've had with investors? All that talk about partnerships?"

"I have a partnership lined up—a big one, actually." Townsend waits for his mom to offer praise (or any sort of reaction, really), and when she doesn't, he continues. "But I still need money. I need to expand. I need to grow."

"Townsend." Her sigh reminds him of Orson's reaction when Townsend had asked about the pitch meeting. "I cannot get into this with you right now." She gestures grandly again. "I have a party of people to entertain. This is neither the time nor the place."

"But when will be?" he asks, his voice dangerously close to a whine.

"We'll talk." Mother makes eye contact with someone over his shoulder and nods, and when he turns, he finds Talia, anxiously tucking her hair behind one ear.

He leans in close to her. "Let's get out of here soon, yeah?"

Talia grins, visibly relieved.

"But first . . ." Townsend runs his hand along the back pocket of his chinos, feeling for his keys. "Stay here for a second, will you? I'm just going to see if my car is blocked in."

Outside, the air is stifling, but it's still a relief, being out of that house. As he starts down the street toward the car, loafers smacking on the pavement, it occurs to him that he's drunker than he realized, because he *swears* he can see that fucking filthy white Honda Accord, double-parked right alongside his roadster. But that would be impossible, because his parents' house is in a gated neighborhood. An unregistered visitor would never be able to get in. Right?

As he approaches, the Honda suddenly roars to life. It is her. And she's going to try and drive away. He can't let her keep running.

"Stop." Townsend spreads his arms wide, trying to make himself appear bigger. He heard this is what you're supposed to do if you encounter a bear. Maybe the same logic applies to this scenario. "Hey, stop."

The Honda pulls away from the curb, undeterred.

Scaring her isn't working; he needs to attack. "Stop!" Before the car can make any more progress, he runs forward, throwing his hands down onto the hood. "Fucking stop!"

After so many sightings, he's finally close enough to the windshield to get a look inside. And when his eyes meet those of the woman staring back at him, he sees someone he doesn't even recognize.

Chapter Seventeen

Kaitlyn

It feels a little surreal that—after nearly a month of researching him, following him, tracking his every move both online and in real life—Townsend now sits next to Kaitlyn in her car. Or, rather, her sister's car. That was the first bit of information they needed to clear up.

Once he blocked her vehicle, rendering her unable to escape, she stepped out of the car and put her hands in the air. As though she were the culpable one. Then again, she had slipped into the gated neighborhood by following closely behind the car in front of her, so she was technically trespassing. He had the upper hand.

"You're not Amanda," he said, sounding perplexed.

Equally confused, she replied, "Of course I'm not."

"Then why do you have Amanda's car? And why have you been following me?"

"I'm Amanda's sister. I've been trying to figure out what happened to her."

"Nothing happened to her." He said this coolly, factually. It pissed her off.

"She's been missing for months, dude. Did you not know that?"

"She's not missing. She broke into my girlfriend's house last week."

Kaitlyn felt suddenly woozy, a combination of the heat and this new information, which wasn't making any sense. "Do you think we can go inside and talk for a minute?"

"You're not coming into my house."

"Can we at least sit in the car?"

Townsend looked at her carefully, as though trying to decide if she was a threat.

"I just want to sit in the AC and talk. It seems like you have as many questions as I do."

"Fine," Townsend agreed at last. "Just for a minute."

Now they sit side by side in Amanda's car, the AC spitting out cold air and a thousand unanswered questions lingering between them. This close, Kaitlyn can smell his sweat, see every pore on his face, watch his chest rise and fall. She's spent so long fixated on the idea of him that she's forgotten that he's real, made of tendons and muscles and occupying space. He scares her and fascinates her in equal parts, but it's hard to summon the hatred she's felt toward him for weeks now that he's here and next to her. And though Kaitlyn has preferred girls to boys since the sixth grade, there's no denying it: Townsend is handsome, albeit in a generic, forgettable way.

I should let someone know where I am, Kaitlyn thinks, *just in case this doesn't end well.* But the only other person she's spoken to all day—other than her ShrinkGPT therapy chatbot—is the persistent data science professor, with whom she had a brief text exchange earlier that day. To ask her for help would only send the wrong message, and she doesn't need any more drama in her life right now. She could use a few more friends, though.

"What makes you think Amanda broke into Talia's house?" Kaitlyn finally asks.

Townsend pauses, seeming to clock the use of his girlfriend's name but ultimately letting it go. "She was hanging out with a friend, and Amanda left a note on her bathroom mirror without Talia even realizing she was there."

"What did the note say?"

"'The police won't protect you from me' or something like that. I can't remember exactly."

"Why the fuck would she say that?"

Townsend blinks, taken aback by Kaitlyn's outburst. "Because your sister has been saying shit like that to me and to my girlfriend for a while now. And I thought she'd been following me, too, but"—he gestures to the car—"apparently that's been you."

Kaitlyn feels her unwavering conviction—the only thing that's been keeping her steady and, frankly, sane since she determined that her sister was missing—slowly start to crumble. "I thought you did something to her. I reached out to you. You wouldn't return my messages."

"So you decided to stalk me?"

The word makes her uneasy, *stalk*. "I wouldn't say I was stalking . . ."

"And go to the police about me? And write shit on the internet about me?"

The more he says, the worse her crimes sound. Kaitlyn could have never imagined that Townsend Fuller, of all people, would be able to convince her that *she* was in the wrong.

"You and your sister are both fucking psychos, you know that? She's harassing me, you're stalking me . . ." Townsend sighs deeply, and the smell of tequila fills the car. "I'm powerful," he adds. "I could easily make you both go away." It occurs to Kaitlyn that he's been drinking and that it may have been foolish to invite him into an enclosed space, where no one can witness what he might do. Which is probably what compels her to tell him what she does next.

"I have a gun."

"What?"

"I have a gun," she repeats, less certain this time. "In the trunk of my car."

Townsend gawks at her. "Are you threatening me?"

It was a stupid thing to say—especially to a man who, to his credit, is likely pretty powerful—but Kaitlyn can't back down now. "I'm just stating a fact."

For a moment, they simply stare each other down, Townsend's face contorted with rage. Kaitlyn needs to distract him, get the conversation off herself and back on Amanda.

"You said my sister has been harassing you and your girlfriend. Do you have any proof of that? Any messages?"

"Every last fucking one."

"Could I see some of them?"

He scrolls through his phone and then presents her with the screen. Kaitlyn leans across the center console to read the message.

Don't think I forgot about you bxtch. I know your with Townsend now and I know it's not going to last. Watch your fxcking back. As soon as it falls apart I'm coming for you both.

A chill runs down Kaitlyn's back. She turns off the AC. "She sent this to Talia?"

It's a mistake to use Talia's name again, because Townsend's face instantly darkens. "How do you even know my girlfriend's name? Or where my parents live? Or where I live?"

"I—"

"How do I know it's not you who's sending these crazy messages rather than your sister?"

Now Kaitlyn feels like she can't breathe. She turns the AC back on. "It's not me, I promise. But Amanda would never threaten someone like that either. That isn't like her at all."

"If she's not like that," Townsend says, his face closer to hers than she would like, "then why did she kill your parents?"

This question is so outlandish, so unexpected, that Kaitlyn wonders if she's heard him wrong. "What?"

Before he can answer, Townsend's phone vibrates in his hand. A picture of Talia fills the screen. Kaitlyn only gets a glimpse of it, but she sees Talia smiling sweetly and holding a glass of wine up to the camera. So unassuming, so effortless. So unlike Amanda in every way.

"Shit. I need to go." Townsend reaches for the door handle.

"Wait!" Moments before, Kaitlyn couldn't wait to be away from him, but now, she desperately needs him to stay. "What do you mean she killed our parents?"

He doesn't answer. Instead, he steps out the door and—just before he can close it—leans in again, eyes narrowed into angry slits. "Leave me and my girlfriend the fuck alone. You and Amanda both. Okay?"

"Okay," she agrees, because what else can she say? And then Townsend is gone, running back to his girlfriend and leaving Kaitlyn more confused than ever.

Back home, she checks Reddit, just to see if geminibaby530 has reappeared. No luck. Her thread does, however, have a new comment from a user named t_fuller90. She reads it, feeling more ashamed than angry.

> Amanda Reade is NOT missing. She is a bitter ex obsessed with revenge, and she's ruining people's lives. Do not listen to her sister's claims. These bitches are in on something together and not to be trusted.

After all the time and energy Kaitlyn has spent looking for Amanda, it doesn't seem possible that she could have been right here all along. Her apartment is still untouched. Her Instagram is still inactive. Neither her landlord nor her boss at the cocktail club where she most recently worked has seen her since March, and now it's July. And up until an hour ago, she never believed Amanda capable of such treachery.

But Kaitlyn saw Townsend's face when she stepped out of the car—it seemed like he genuinely expected to see Amanda instead. There's also the matter of that message he showed Kaitlyn, containing Amanda's trademark of swear words censored with *x*'s. ("It's considered not social media friendly to have obscenities in your captions," she once explained to Kaitlyn. "I have to keep my shit clean.") That doesn't necessarily mean her sister is guilty, of course. It just means that things look really, really bad for her right now.

She can't stop thinking about what Townsend said, when he claimed Amanda was responsible for their parents' deaths. They died in a car accident, and she knew this as a fact—she saw the pictures, surveyed the wreckage. How could Amanda possibly have been involved? Of course, Kaitlyn can't exactly contact him to ask what he meant; Townsend has made it clear he wants nothing to do with her. Living with this accusation and not getting any answers, however, is not an option. Whether her sister is an innocent victim or a deeply troubled psychopath, Kaitlyn needs to know for sure. For what feels like the millionth time in the past few months, she thinks about just what she would do if given the chance to speak with Amanda for ten minutes and get her side of the story.

A memory comes to mind. She's eleven, and Amanda is nine. She's just returned from soccer practice when Amanda beckons her into their shared bedroom, her eyes wide with worry.

"Kate," she whispers. "You need to help me. I've messed up."

Taking her hand, Amanda leads Kaitlyn over to her bed and then points beneath it. "What's under there?"

"Just look."

"Is it bad?"

"You'll see."

When Kaitlyn gets onto her knees and lifts the bed skirt, the stench hits her first. Like a rotting body—or what she imagines a rotting body to smell like. Then she sees the brown paper bags—dozens of them, damp looking and carpeted with fuzzy, bruise-colored growths—and throws a hand over her mouth and nose.

"What have you done?" Kaitlyn asks, her voice muffled behind her fingers.

"I didn't mean to," Amanda says. "But no one brings lunch from home anymore."

In a rush of tears, her sister explains how everyone in the third grade buys lunch from school, and she didn't have the heart to tell their mother. Instead, she'd borrow a dollar and a quarter from the office to buy pizza and then bring her bagged lunch home, where she'd hide it beneath her bed. She always meant to throw them away, but as her collection grew, so did the task of destroying the evidence.

"It's too big now," Amanda tells her. "Mom and Dad are going to find out. They're going to kill me."

But Kaitlyn won't allow that to happen. They wait until their parents go to bed before transferring the mess of moldy sandwiches into the trash bag Kaitlyn snagged from the kitchen earlier that night. Then they creep out to the woods behind their house, where they bury Amanda's secret beneath a tree. Before they return inside, Kaitlyn asks Amanda to make a promise: Tell Mom no more bagged lunches.

"I will," Amanda says, and Kaitlyn believes her. She helped her sister clean up her mess and did so without judgment; telling the truth is the least Amanda can do.

A loud pop shakes her out of her reverie. Then another. And another.

Gunfire, she thinks. But then she sees the explosion of color out her window. Fireworks. Of course. It's the Fourth of July, and most people are celebrating. Then again, most people aren't trying to decide whether their sister is missing or out of her fucking mind.

Kaitlyn grabs her keys and heads for the door. Though not actually gunfire, the noise outside has stirred a desire in her. She needs a pistol in her hand and a room full of people who don't know the first thing about Amanda Reade. Kaitlyn will fit right in, since apparently, she doesn't know her sister either. At least, not as well as she thought she did.

In the car, she fires off a question to her therapy chatbot on ShrinkGPT. "What should I do," she asks, "when I feel like I'm losing control?"

"Identify controllable elements in your life," the chatbot tells her in its resonant baritone—a voice she chose because it reminded her of

Morgan Freeman. "Make a list of stressors and determine which sources of stress can be reduced or even eliminated. I'll set a timer and give you one minute to list those stressors out loud. Ready? Let's begin."

Fuck lists, she thinks. What she wants to know is whether Townsend actually did something to her sister. And if not? If Amanda is out there messing with him, not caring about the grief she's putting her sister through? Then Kaitlyn might just kill Amanda herself.

Chapter Eighteen

Amanda

Opening up to others was something Amanda rarely did. Opening up to a man she was screwing was something she *never* did. But just a few weeks into her relationship with Townsend, Amanda found she wanted this person to know her, really know her, both inside and out. A stupid mistake, of course. She'd gleaned enough experience with men to know that few—if any—were worthy of trust. Still, at the time, she felt sure: This man didn't just have the means to offer her financial security; he would keep her secrets safe too.

It's hard to say what made her trust Townsend, exactly. After all, this was a man who'd cheated, deceiving both his girlfriend and his paramour in the process. But something about the way he focused when she spoke, eyes never straying to his phone screen or some other more interesting distraction—it was new yet comforting. Good breeding had made him this way, yes, and maybe some good acting. Still, Amanda had never felt more interesting. She would have told Townsend anything, if only to bask in the glow of his attention for another minute.

That's probably why she told him what she did, that night they drank too many prickly pear margaritas at De Nada Cantina. It was late January, about a month after Talia caught her and Townsend in bed together, and Amanda felt certain that she'd never been happier. Too drunk to make it all the way back to Townsend's condo, they decided to crash at Amanda's East Austin apartment, where they had sex, smoked, and then had sex again. It was only then—only when Amanda's guard was completely down—that she decided to tell Townsend the story. Such a stupid fucking mistake.

They had been on her mind a lot, her parents. The two-year anniversary of their death was in February, a few days before her sister's birthday. And because she was feeling unsteady and sentimental and emboldened by the intensity of Townsend's stare as they lay in bed together, she told him what happened the night her parents died. The night her parents were killed, more accurately.

At the time, Amanda didn't have a car, because after her parents moved to East Austin postretirement, she didn't need one; she could always borrow theirs. She tried to be respectful of it—cleaning up her take-out bags, filling the gas tank when it was low, replacing the windshield wiper fluid every once in a while—but sometimes, she was thoughtless. And that's exactly what she was when she drove home drunk one night after partying with coworkers. It was less than a ten-minute drive. She'd driven drunk before; she thought she'd be fine. Even after she drove up onto that curb, the car miraculously looked okay—no scratches or dents, nothing to indicate what had happened. According to her outgoing calls, she'd apparently reached out to her sister at three a.m.—a foolish move—but as long as Kaitlyn didn't tattle, Amanda thought their mom and dad would never be the wiser about her drunken joyride. And unfortunately, she was right.

Steering failure was the cause of her parents' crash.

Both her parents were in the car, and they both died instantly—or, at least, that's what the police claimed, so that's what Amanda chose to believe. The alternative—that they'd survived the initial impact and suffered several minutes in the smashed-up vehicle, terrified and in pain—was too unbearable to contemplate.

Over the next two years, she asked herself the same question hundreds, if not thousands, of times: Had she somehow fucked up the wheel when she hit that curb? Would her parents still be alive if she had just told them about the accident instead of returning their car the next day like nothing had happened? Would she ever feel peace, knowing she could have possibly prevented her parents' death, or would she live with this guilt until the day she died herself?

But still, she never told a single soul the truth, not even her sister Kaitlyn, who deserved the truth more than anyone. No, she kept it all locked in, letting it eat her alive—until Townsend put her at ease enough to confess.

"It's not your fault," he said over and over again, rubbing circles on her back. "You didn't know. You couldn't have known."

It wasn't true, what he said, but it was exactly what she needed to hear. So she just held him and cried, feeling that, if this were the closest she ever came to peace, she would be okay.

The peace didn't last. A few weeks later, when Townsend started to pull away, she thought it was, once again, her fault. Maybe she'd said too much. Maybe he'd decided that, yes, she *was* to blame for her parents' fatal crash and he no longer wanted anything to do with someone like her. But when she confronted him, asking why he'd grown so distant, he just claimed he was tired, or busy with work, or distracted by his dad's failing health, or in need of a little space. And when he finally broke up with her, just days after the anniversary of her parents' death, he even had the audacity to say this: "It's not you. It's me."

"That's bullshit," she replied, "and you know it."

It took a little coaxing, but eventually, she got him to admit what had really changed his mind about her. "You're just coming on a little strong. Your messages . . . They're intense."

"What are you talking about?" Amanda hopped off the bed—where she'd just given Townsend a fantastic blow job for nothing—and retrieved her phone so she could rattle off her last few texts to him. "'Let's hang later.' 'I'm horny.' 'Want pizza?' What about these messages is intense?"

"Obviously not those," said Townsend.

She paused. "Are you referring to the thing I sent a few weeks ago? After I told you about my parents' accident?" Her face grew hot just thinking about the uncharacteristically sappy message she'd written to him, her head still fuzzy with after-sex bliss and the tangible relief of having finally unloaded her sob story: I can't tell you how good it feels to have finally met someone I can trust . . . He'd never replied, and she'd been stewing in regret for having sent it ever since.

"All of this is just too much," Townsend continued. "You're too much."

Amanda didn't even bother to defend herself, because it was over, and what was the point? Instead, she bid adieu to his slightly smaller-than-average prick and made her way home.

Before deleting the Cuff app from her phone, she'd scrolled through her messages with Townsend one last time, not so much out of nostalgia but for closure. His double entendres and flirty come-ons—which had once charmed her—now seemed immature, gross. But what really made her squirm was the smattering of over-the-top effusive messages she'd sent to him, many of which she didn't even remember composing.

This feels like the beginning of forever.

Your my missing puzzle piece.

I want to have five kids and I want them all to have your eyes.

Jesus. Apparently, she'd blacked out and let her fingers loose on more than one occasion. The cringe-worthy missives just felt like further proof that she wasn't cut out for this kind of vulnerability. Who was this person, who'd been so enamored that she'd written words that she now couldn't even recognize? If this is what being in a committed relationship did to her, then Amanda didn't want any part of it, not again.

This is what she was going to do: She would quit her job. She would sublet her apartment. And then she would buy a one-way ticket to Paris, or Barcelona, or Rome, where she would have such a fabulous time that she'd entirely forget the name Townsend Fuller. If living well was the best revenge, then she wasn't going to just live well—she was going to live exceptionally. And she wasn't going to let anyone—certainly not Townsend Fuller—stand in her way.

Chapter Nineteen

Meera

Though they live closer to Tarrytown Park, Gracie favors the Alliance Children's Garden—not because of the many slides and climbing walls or even the splash pad but because of the tunnels. Meera's daughter loves navigating the network of blue child-size tubes that meander through the park, so Meera is willing to drive the extra few minutes to the farther playground. Plus, Gracie's dad always takes her to the Alliance Children's Garden during his weekends with her, and there's no way she's letting her ex win best parent for something she can easily do herself.

From her favorite bench under a shady grove of trees, Meera can watch Gracie duck in and out of the turf hills, chatting happily with everyone she encounters along the way. This chattiness must have come from Hari; while Meera is fine making small talk with any parents who happen to plant themselves next to her, she's relieved to find her bench empty this Saturday. It's not even ten a.m., but it's the peak of summer, and it's mercilessly hot. Meera just wants to watch her kid play and read her book—*Meat Cute* by Kennedy J. Abbott, which she took from Talia's bookshelf after her friend insisted that she give romance a chance.

But just a few pages in, Meera's attention starts to drift. Talia has been evasive ever since they discovered the Post-it Note in her bathroom, as though she wants to forget everything about the night—Meera included. It doesn't make sense to her, but really, nothing about this situation does.

As drunk as Talia was that night, Meera agreed when she suggested they call the police. Yes, it seemed a bit implausible that someone could have snuck into the house without either of them noticing, but Talia was insistent: She did not write that note, and it did not appear there on its own. The station then sent a pair of rookie cops to walk through Talia's home, where they looked in closets and under beds, like participants in a reluctant game of hide-and-seek. Talia seemed almost disappointed when—after their brief inspection—they determined the house was all clear.

"What happens if she comes back?" she asked.

"Just call the station," one of the cops replied. "We'll be here as soon as possible."

Sensing Talia's distress, Meera added, "And I'm not going anywhere." That still didn't seem to put her at ease, but eventually, she crashed on the couch, and Meera stayed up, watching over her friend's sleeping form like a sentry. And when Talia woke—rumpled and hungover but smiling—she simply asked Meera if she wanted coffee to go, as though the whole home invasion had just been a bad dream.

Sweat beads up on Meera's hairline and trickles down her back. Fuck this heat, fuck this book, and fuck this Amanda chick for ruining the life of the sweetest person Meera knows. She stands from the bench and quickly surveys the area, hand shielding her eyes, until she spots Gracie giggling alongside a girl with chin-length microbraids.

"Babe," she yells, "I'm going to the car to get water. Do you need more sunscreen?"

"Sunscreen is stupid," Gracie yells back, which sends her and her new friend into another round of giggles.

Whatever. Meera will lecture her daughter about the use of the word *stupid* again later. Right now, she just wants to sit in her car, blast the AC for five minutes, and then get through the rest of this playground visit like the dutiful caretaker she is.

In the car, Meera reclines her seat all the way back. Gracie will be eight years old in a month; she's old enough now that Meera doesn't always need to watch her to know she's okay. Even after bringing her car to the shop, the AC still makes an annoying rattling sound, but it feels so good that Meera doesn't mind. She'll just sit here for a moment or two, or at least until she's no longer actively sweating. Gracie won't miss her.

With her few minutes of peace, Meera returns to her current project: trying to figure out the identity of LivingstonTheDream from Reddit, who sent her the message about Townsend's potentially fishy company. Based on the other subreddit pages contributed to by the mystery user (r/Yale, r/VentureCapital, and r/MaleEquestrian), as well as the username itself, Meera has decided that LivingstonTheDream is most likely Orson Livingston: graduate of Yale University, vice president at Silicon Hills Venture Partners, and—according to his bio on the company website—avid horse rider. But she's not 100 percent certain, especially after discovering that Orson graduated from the same school as Townsend just a few years earlier. Why would he out a former classmate on such a public forum? Weren't these cis white men with trust funds supposed to protect one another?

Today is not the day to make sense of this. It's too damn hot, and Meera is too damn tired. She's just closed her eyes when her phone vibrates on the center console. Maybe it's Talia, finally explaining why she's been holding Meera at arm's length. Meera opens her messages and is confused to find—instead of a text from Talia—a snapshot of her daughter, ducking into a tunnel. It's the kind of picture Hari would send her, along with the caption Having tons of fun, just to rub in her face what a good dad he is. But Hari isn't here. And the person who sent this picture isn't saved in Meera's contacts.

A short text message follows the picture: Probably shouldn't leave your kid alone. You never know whose watching.

Who's, not whose, Meera thinks. Then, just as quickly: *Gracie.*

She leaps from the car without turning it off, her heart pounding so loudly she can barely hear her flip-flops slapping on the red-hot asphalt of the parking lot. When she reaches the tunnels and turf hills, her daughter is nowhere to be seen, though she does see the little girl with the braids, collecting blades of grass.

"Where did your friend go?" Meera asks the girl. "The one with the ponytail and the pink Roblox T-shirt?" She feels like she's giving a description to the police, and her eyes tear up involuntarily.

"I'm not supposed to talk to strangers," the girl informs her.

"But I'm a mom." The tears start to flow, and the girl skips off, no longer wanting to be part of this drama.

Frantically, Meera sprints from tunnel to tunnel, peeking in each tube and desperate to find her daughter's face inside. But every tunnel she checks is empty, empty, empty. Meera is crying hard now, her shoulders shaking and vision blurred. Hari will never forgive her. She will never forgive herself. Her daughter is gone.

"Mom?" At the sound of Gracie's voice, Meera turns—and there her daughter stands, head tilted to one side but totally unharmed. "Mom, why are you crying?"

"Oh, my God." Meera runs and scoops her up, not caring that Gracie is almost eight and wriggling to get out of her grasp, too old for public hugs from her mother. All Meera cares about is the fact that her daughter is safe. Though apparently Meera isn't as safe as she thought she was.

Meera waits until she's driven Gracie home and plopped her in front of the TV before she calls Talia; she doesn't want her daughter to hear what she's going to say.

"I was just going to call you," Talia answers. "I was thinking again about the Post-it Note in my bathroom and—"

Before Talia can finish, Meera chokes out a sob.

"Meer, what's going on? Are you okay?"

Leaning against her kitchen wall, trying to keep her voice low, Meera quickly tells her friend about the park, the picture, the foreboding piece of advice. "I think it was Amanda," she concludes. "I think she's after me now too."

Talia takes a moment to answer. "What makes you think that?"

"She spelled 'who's' wrong. And who else could it be?"

"But why would she threaten you? How would she even know who you are?"

"I don't know," Meera says, louder than she intended, "but she is. Maybe she knows I pushed you to talk to the police. Or maybe she's going after everyone in your orbit, just to fuck with you." It pisses her off, really, that Talia seems almost skeptical, especially after everything Meera has done to protect her. She risked her job for Talia. And apparently she's endangered her seven-year-old daughter in the process.

"That's possible," says Talia. Her voice sounds far away, already distracted by another matter.

Before she can say something that she'll regret, Meera wraps up the call and collapses at her kitchen table. Amanda isn't just after Talia and Townsend anymore; it's clear that Meera's involvement has made her a target as well. And while Amanda could have easily figured out that Talia and Meera are friends (like she said, she's always watching), Meera can't help but think that she's landed on Amanda's radar for another reason. Perhaps Amanda knows something. Something that Talia doesn't. Maybe she knows the truth about Meera's history with Townsend.

It kills her to do this, but Meera has no choice: She needs to let Hari take Gracie, at least until she feels she's safe again.

"You really can't tell me what's going on?" Hari asks, not for the first time. They stand in his kitchen, where Gracie cannot hear them over the sound of the music in her bedroom. Meera recognizes the song—it's from the *Wicked* soundtrack, Gracie's favorite. Her eyes well up at the thought of leaving her here and going home alone. It's the best solution, but it still feels wrong.

"It's nothing," Meera says. "It's just something I have going on for work."

Hari looks at her, and because they were together for over a decade, Meera knows just what he's thinking: *I don't believe you.* And he shouldn't believe her either. Because it's not nothing.

In the two days that have passed since the incident at the park, Meera has received another three messages from the number she's convinced belongs to Amanda, each one more menacing than the last. The first one, after a trip to the grocery store: That's a lot of wine. Having a dinner party? The second one, late on Sunday evening: Don't forget to turn off the kitchen light before you go to bed. And the last one, the one that made her decide Gracie wasn't safe with her anymore: a picture of her daughter waiting at the school bus stop. No text accompanied the photo, and Meera found the silence even more terrifying than anything Amanda could have said.

"When I spoke to Gracie on the phone a few days ago, she said you've been upset," Hari pushes.

"I've been stressed, not upset." Meera hates hearing this, that her anxiety has become evident to her seven-year-old. She really did try to hide it.

"I don't think this just has to do with work."

"It's complicated, but I'm taking care of it. You won't have to watch Gracie for long."

"Gracie is not the problem. You know that Jessica and I"—Meera represses a groan at the mention of the new girlfriend—"are always happy to have her here. As is Marty, of course." Hari gestures down to the dachshund puppy, who's busy chewing on the shoelace of Meera's Nikes. "I just want to make sure you're okay."

The softness of his voice breaks her. She loved him for so long, and sometimes, she can imagine loving him again, despite what he did to their family. But she can't think about that now; instead, she needs to tell him enough to assuage his curiosity and not so much that he panics. "You know my friend Talia from work?"

"Sure." After the few occasions the two met, Hari wasn't impressed with Talia—he dubbed her a people pleaser who couldn't express an opinion if it killed her.

"It has something to do with her." Cautiously, Meera adds, "She's gotten herself into some trouble, and I want to be free of distractions while I help her out."

"Do you need to get involved at all?"

"I do, unfortunately."

"Why?"

Meera sighs. He isn't making this as easy as she'd hoped. "Because I might be in trouble now too."

"Is this work trouble you're talking about or"—Hari lowers his voice—"legal trouble?"

"Work," Meera says, because it's not exactly a lie.

"Jesus, Meera." Hari shakes his head. "I don't know why you still work at that place. After the shitty way they treated you when you were first diagnosed . . ."

"It's not Cuff's fault I have Hashimoto's."

"But the company is at fault for not doing more to accommodate you."

And what did you do to accommodate me? Meera wants to ask, but it wouldn't be fair; Hari did do a lot to help her out, just as he's helping her now. He isn't the enemy, she reminds herself. For as long as they live, they'll be tied by Gracie, to whom he's always been a good father. He just didn't happen to be a good husband.

"I just think you'd be so much better off doing your own thing, Meer. You're so brilliant, and your talent is wasted at Cuff."

Meera leans against his kitchen counter, already tired of this conversation. "Says the guy doing backend engineering for a telehealth giant. What makes you think I'd want to do my own thing anyway?"

"Oh, c'mon. You've always wanted to do your own thing. Remember at NYU, when you wanted to develop that app connecting mothers to milk banks?"

"I forgot about that," Meera admits.

"Or what about that idea you told me about a year or so ago, right after you got diagnosed?"

Meera's stomach clenches. She'd rather not talk about that idea. "It was a dark time for me. I wouldn't trust anything I said around then."

"No, it was great." Hari is insistent now. "Remember? You'd wanted to create a platform offering holistic autoimmune care to people like yourself. Why didn't you ever move forward with that?"

"Because I've been too busy raising the child you only have to deal with every other weekend." Meera regrets the words as soon as they're out of her mouth, but it's too late. The damage is done.

"I don't *deal* with Gracie," Hari says, his voice icy. "I live for my weekends with her. And you know I would do anything to have more time with her."

"I'm sorry. I shouldn't have said that. I didn't mean it. I just . . ." Meera shakes her head. "I don't want to discuss my lack of ambition right now, if that's all right with you."

"For what it's worth, I think you're plenty ambitious. I think you're just stuck right now."

"Maybe I am."

"And it's probably not any consolation, but . . ." A strange look crosses Hari's face, and he trails off.

"But what?"

"Someone did end up creating a virtual platform for autoimmune care. Sage is in the process of establishing an employer partnership right now."

Meera's blood runs cold. "Your company is working with AutoInTune?"

"You've heard of it?"

"I have, unfortunately." She digs her fingernails into her hand. She must control her anger, at least until she gets home. Hari just won't understand.

And luckily, her ex doesn't seem to notice the shift. "Well, I'm always here if you need help getting unstuck." Lowering his voice again, he adds, "Or if you want to tell me what's really going on here."

Meera ignores this last part. "I appreciate it. And I appreciate you helping me out with Gracie until I get things resolved."

"Want to stay for dinner? Jessica will be here soon. We're making black bean burgers."

I'd rather die, Meera thinks. She says thanks, but no thanks and gives Hari a friendly, perfunctory hug. Then she heads to Gracie's room, where she finds her daughter performing "Popular" for the mirror above her dresser.

"Did Dad say he's making black bean burgers for dinner?"

"I'm afraid so."

Gracie sticks out her tongue. "Yuck."

Meera squats down and wraps her arms around her. "I hear they taste just like real burgers if you put enough ketchup on them. And hold your nose when you take a bite."

Her daughter pulls back and gives her a serious look. "You'll come back for me soon?"

"Cross my heart," Meera says. "As soon as I get things straightened out."

"You mean once that lady stops following us?"

For a second time that night, Meera's stomach tightens like a fist. "Did you see her?"

"No. I overheard you on the phone with Aunt Talia." Gracie lowers her eyes. "I didn't mean to snoop."

"You don't have to be sorry. I'm the one who's sorry." Meera knows for sure now that she's making the right decision, leaving her daughter here.

"You'll be careful?"

Meera touches her finger to Gracie's perfect button nose. "You don't worry about me. I'm the mom. Let me worry about you."

"'Kay."

As she does every time they part, Meera says, "You'll be the last person I see when I close my eyes."

"And you'll be the first person I think about when I wake up," Gracie finishes.

But that night, as she lies restless in bed—her lights off, her windows locked, her curtains drawn, her phone in her hand—Gracie's face isn't what she sees. Instead, she sees Townsend's, with his fastidious coif and smug fucking grin. Even the generous glass of wine she had before bed can't dull her rage, which has been brewing since Hari mentioned her start-up idea in his kitchen.

Because the truth is this: Townsend stole her start-up idea to create AutoInTune, and she let him get away with it.

And every time she's reminded, she feels angry enough to lose all control.

Chapter Twenty

Townsend

The email arrives without warning on a Tuesday morning, perfectly polite but as foreboding as a death sentence: Sage Clinic wants to look at his books.

Townsend skims through the message once, twice, and then a third time, just to make sure he's not overreacting . . . want to perform due diligence as part of our new partnership and potential equity investment . . . preliminary list of documents and information needed for review . . . includes, but is not limited to, user metrics data such as monthly recurring revenue per user, customer lifetime value, retention rate, origination sources . . . please provide at your earliest convenience.

Sage Clinic isn't accusing him of anything, Townsend tells himself. In fact, the company is offering to invest in AutoInTune, to help it grow for their mutual benefit. He's merely being asked to hand over some documents. The problem, of course, is that the real documents will demonstrate that he's been providing false information about the size of his company's user base. And if he doesn't start increasing membership (and stop inflating his numbers in the meantime), he's going to be in deep shit . . . if he isn't already.

Sage Clinic could rescind its offer. Worse than that: He could go to fucking prison.

As reluctant as he is to do so, he knows who he must call. He sighs, thumbs through his contacts, and then selects the name of his dad's old college roommate, Carter Bonier.

He answers after the first ring. "You got Carter."

"Carter, hi." Townsend forces a smile, hoping it may inject some more enthusiasm into his voice. "This is Townsend, Randolph Fuller's kid."

A phlegmy cough erupts in Townsend's ear, likely the result of those Nicaraguan cigars that he and Townsend's dad used to smoke like fiends. "Of course, of course. It's been too long. How are you holding up, son?"

"I'm good." Townsend pauses, reconsidering his lie. If Carter—a former federal prosecutor turned partner at Rutland & Wiles—is going to help him, then he should probably start with the truth. "I'm okay. I'm in a bit of trouble, actually."

"Ho, boy." Carter chuckles, probably expecting Townsend to regale him with tales of some low-stakes boyish antics—hitting a mailbox with his car or knocking up a girlfriend, perhaps.

"Like, *legal* trouble."

Too long of a lull follows. "I'm free after four," Carter says at last. "Come by the office."

Townsend hasn't been to Frost Bank Tower in months, not since Dad died and he quit his job at Bonnell Trust—where he'd worked alongside his father—to dedicate more time to AutoInTune. The old office is only a few floors below Carter's, and Townsend thinks about stopping by, but instead, he rides the elevator straight up to the Rutland office. Surely there aren't many people (if any) who miss him at Bonnell, if he's honest with himself. It's tough to make friends when you're the boss's son.

After weaving through a maze of beige cubicles and closed office doors (including the office of someone named William Dupont—why does that name sound familiar to him?), Townsend finally happens upon Carter Bonier's corner office. Then he wipes his sweaty hands on his chinos and knocks with as much authority as he can muster. When the door swings open to reveal his dad's old friend—just as pear shaped, ruddy faced, and beady eyed as Townsend remembers—he plasters a shit-eating grin on his face and offers his hand.

"Carter, thank you for—"

Before he can finish, Carter clasps his hand and pulls him into a bone-crushing embrace. "Nonsense, nonsense. Anything for Randy's boy. So sorry I couldn't make the funeral, by the way. You know how it is."

Townsend didn't even notice Carter's absence from his dad's funeral; the whole day was a blur, made blurrier by the bottle of scotch he downed to self-medicate.

Once Carter settles behind his desk—and Townsend in the much smaller chair facing it—he gets right to business. "Who's the trouble with, son? A girl?"

If only a girl were his main issue. "No. It's with some documents requested by a potential investor."

"Ah, shit." Carter cranes back in his chair. "What's going on?"

Making sure to give no more information than he needs to, Townsend tells Carter about his new partnership with Sage Clinic and its due diligence request. "Financials, audits, prospectuses, investor presentations, communications—they want everything." Townsend runs a hand through his hair. "And I have to give it to them, right? Including user metrics?"

Carter gives him a cryptic look. "Is there a reason you wouldn't want to?"

Is he really going to make him say it? Carter isn't representing him yet; he has no idea whether there's any attorney-client privilege at work here. But surely his father's memory will at least grant him Carter's discretion. "I used synthetic data to get the offer."

Apparently, this isn't the right thing to say. Carter groans. "Synthetic data? You mean fake data?"

"The data makes it appear as though my company has over two hundred thousand members. In reality, I have fewer than twenty-five thousand." Saying it out loud makes it seem so much worse than it does on paper.

"Have you talked to your CFO about the request?"

"I . . ." Townsend's face burns. "I don't have a CFO."

"How about a CIO?"

"I plan on hiring those roles once I secure more funding."

"You're telling me AutoInTune is just you?"

"I have a team of nine. But they're all software engineers and graphic designers, except for my clinic ops lead. And my director of engineering."

"Is that who you asked to generate the false data?"

"No, of course not. I paid a data science professor to manufacture it."

Townsend can still recall nearly every word of his conversation with Dr. Eileen Drew when they first met at a coffee shop back in early May. She was in her mid-thirties—young for a professor—and saddled with student loans. She had experience generating synthetic data like this, she told him, and the opportunity to make some easy cash was too good to pass up. (*Synthetic data*—that's the term she kept using, and Townsend liked how professional it sounded.) She could contact an external data compiler and make it appear as though AutoInTune boasted ten times the number of registered users that it actually had, complete with identifying information and unique IDs. It would cost him, of course, but she promised it would look legit.

She made it seem simple—harmless, even. She made it seem as though this was done all the time. So Townsend shook her hand and wired her the money. A few weeks later, he had his list of over two hundred thousand synthetically generated AutoInTune members, ready to impress anyone who may ask to see it.

For a little while, Townsend thought he would get away with it . . . so long as no one tried to audit him. That no longer seems to be a reasonable expectation.

It's one thing to present those falsified numbers to potential investors, to feel as confident as possible selling a company he genuinely believes in and wants to see reach its full potential. But to hand over manufactured documents to an actual committed investor and pass them off as real—*that* is a step too far for Townsend's comfort. He's a salesman, not a criminal.

Not to mention that anyone who looks too closely at the data may just see through the smoke and mirrors.

Sitting across from him now, Dad's old friend doesn't have to say a word for Townsend to know what he's thinking: *What an amateur. What a fool.* At the risk of sounding even more foolish (but unable to stop himself), he asks, "What could happen if they figure out what I've done?"

"Well." Heaving another heavy sigh, Carter interlaces his sausage-like fingers on top of his desk and leans forward. "If this due diligence uncovers any fraud—and it sounds like it will—Sage is going to pull the plug on your partnership, but that's the least of your worries. They could take this to the Securities and Exchange Commission. Then you're probably looking at a monetary penalty. A substantial one. You could also be barred from serving as an officer or director of a public company."

"But will I get"—the words catch in Townsend's throat, forcing him to sputter them out—"prison time?"

"That wouldn't come from the SEC. It's when the DOJ, USAO, and FBI come knocking that you should be worried."

"And will that happen?"

Carter shrugs. "It's possible."

"Fuck." Townsend presses his fingertips to his temples. He will not cry. He will handle this like a man, like his father would.

"Who else knows?"

The question doesn't compute; Townsend is too busy picturing himself in an orange prison jumpsuit. "Knows what?"

"Knows that . . ." His lips pulling into a tight line, Carter makes a vague gesture with one hand.

"That I committed fraud?" It seems silly, at this point, not to openly acknowledge what he's done.

"I just want to know who else is aware of this 'synthetic data'"—Carter adds emphasis to the words with air quotes here—"other than that data science professor."

His mind immediately goes to Orson Livingston, who's treated Townsend like persona non grata ever since his investor presentation. "There's a VC who didn't seem to buy my numbers. He may have done a little digging, but he's my buddy's brother. I don't think he would say anything to either Sage or the feds."

"What about a girlfriend?"

"No. I mean, I have one. But she doesn't know anything." He pictures Talia's pretty face then, imagines her brows creasing with concern as he describes the depth of the shit he's in. Yes, he knows honesty is important to her (especially considering his past infidelity), but he's been careful not to involve her in any of his company's less savory dealings. It's nice, having her believe he's some entrepreneurial wunderkind.

"An ex?"

Now this is a possibility Townsend hasn't considered. Could Amanda be responsible for this too? There were some vulnerable postcoital moments when—emboldened by her willingness to share dark parts of her past—Townsend reciprocated, spilling his guts about the struggles of starting a company, of convincing investors and partners to share his vision. He doesn't remember exactly what he revealed in those early-morning hours spent wrapped around her in bed, but chances are he said more than he should have.

Wait. No. *Fuck.* How could he have forgotten? Amanda was the one to suggest he use that data science professor in the first place. She even gave Townsend Eileen's name; they'd briefly worked together at a sushi restaurant when Eileen was between jobs.

They may have been broken up by the time Townsend approached Eileen, but Amanda still knew exactly what he intended to do. And chances were she'd jump at the first opportunity to fuck him with that information.

Carter clearly interprets Townsend's silence as a yes. "I see. Well. My advice is to provide Sage with the documents requested. The *real* documents."

This isn't what Townsend hoped to hear. "And admit what I've done?"

"I'm afraid so. The cover-up is worse than the crime. Present Sage with fake documents, and you're only compounding your fraud."

"But . . ." There has to be a way out of this. If Townsend learned anything from his father, it's that powerful men always find a way out. "How would Sage even know the documents are fake? All I need to do is close this partnership, and my user numbers are bound to increase. It won't matter where my numbers started as long as they get where they need to be, right?"

"Except you hired that data science professor. And they could talk. They could even testify against you."

"She wouldn't," Townsend says. He doesn't know this for sure, of course, but that's too humiliating to admit. His father never would have worked with anyone he didn't trust with his life.

Carter stands; it seems Townsend's time is up. "Just promise me you'll come clean before this gets worse for you, all right? Oh, and tell your mother that I have a name for her."

"A name?"

"Just tell her I'll give her a call later."

"Okay." Townsend already feels stupid; it doesn't seem worth it to ask any more questions and further demonstrate his idiocy.

The short walk home is spent in a daze; all Townsend can think about are penalties and prosecution and prison time. When he approached that data science professor, hoping to give his numbers a little boost, he wasn't driven by greed or a desire to deceive; that's not the kind of man he is. All he wanted was to prove himself to his mother, to show her he was deserving of both her respect and the money in his trust. He wanted to make her proud, and he wanted to make his father proud too. And he's worked way too goddamn hard preserving his father's legacy for shit to end like this.

He's so distracted that it takes him a moment to register the sight of a figure stretched out on his couch—smiling eagerly at him—when he opens his door.

"There you are." Talia gestures to the plastic containers she's spread out on the coffee table. "I picked up dinner from Uchibā. Your favorite."

Still standing at the door, he pauses, suspended in time. He takes in her bare feet curled up beneath her, toenails painted purple; her dark hair pulled back into a short ponytail at the nape of her neck; her lithe frame swallowed by his old Penn crewneck. How lucky he is, to have this gorgeous girl waiting for him, somehow able to anticipate his every need. How nice it would be, to come home to this every day, to have this person who's fully committed to him for life no matter what kind of shit he faces.

"You okay?" Talia tilts her head to one side, a gesture he finds unexpectedly charming. She may be a woman in STEM, but he likes these reminders that she's still a babe in arms at heart.

"I'm just amazed you knew I was craving sushi when I didn't even know it myself."

"What can I say? I'm all-knowing." Talia breaks her chopsticks apart with a splintering crack that makes Townsend flinch. "You sure you're all right?"

"Just had a weird day," he says, which isn't a lie. "But you're here, so it's better now." Wherever Amanda is hiding, he's going to find her, he decides. He won't let her reveal what she knows. He won't let her take everything he's earned away from him.

"I'm glad you're better." Talia hands him a pair of chopsticks. "Now stop being weird and let's eat."

Chapter Twenty-One

Talia

Waiting for her iced coffee at Jo's on Wednesday, Talia does what she often does to fill unstructured time: She opens Instagram.

She scrolls past a post from her boss Betty, celebrating her twenty-year reunion at MIT. Another from Townsend's buddy Brett, sailing around the Balearic Islands with his girlfriend Nicole. Then she pauses on a post from her favorite author, Kennedy J. Abbott—a dewy-skinned selfie in which she's holding up a mug. *POV: Hubby knows exactly how you like your morning matcha*, the text at the bottom of the image reads.

Matcha. Of course she drinks matcha. Talia glances up to see if her order is ready yet; perhaps it's not too late to change her coffee to an iced matcha.

On her phone screen, a second Story from Kennedy appears. It's a professional portrait: Kennedy and her husband Thad and their identical twin girls, all dressed in white and huddled together in a field on a red gingham blanket. Looking like characters Kennedy had conjured up for one of her novels. *One year ago today*, she captioned the photo, *and feeling just as immeasurably blessed.*

Scrolling through Kennedy's photos—seeing her house and spouse and pink-cheeked babies—used to be a painful experience for Talia.

A reminder of all the things she'd yet to accomplish. But then she reconnected with Townsend, and now the fairy tale that is Kennedy's Instagram grid feels less like an aspirational mood board and more like a glimpse into Talia's possible future. The future she and Townsend could share together.

Despite all the factors conspiring to tear them apart, Talia and Townsend have never been more in sync; Talia is sure of this, and she feels sure that Townsend would agree. Nearly every time she grabs her phone to text him throughout the day—just a heart emoji or a quick *I miss you*—she finds a message already waiting from him, because he'd been missing her too. And despite her spending nearly every night at his place, he still lights up when he sees her at his door and wakes her every morning with a kiss. Just last night, she brought him take-out sushi after work on a whim, and he looked at her as though she were a mind reader, the answer to his prayers. Just as he is the answer to hers.

Yes, he cheated, as Meera never tired of reminding her. What Talia can't get her to understand is that he's changed. He's more industrious than the man he was last year, and more thoughtful too—the kind of guy who can remember her coffee order at Jo's (a large Iced Turbo with sugar-free vanilla syrup and an extra shot of espresso) and will surprise her with one when she needs it most.

And of course, she can't get Meera to understand what it felt like to be in his family home for the Fourth of July party, to wash her hands with a bar of soap shaped like a seashell and scented like a summer peach, to have someone whisk away her dirty plate before she even noticed or could thank them. The life Townsend offers is as plush and comfortable as the half dozen goose-down pillows stacked on his bed, the ones he kicks onto the floor during the night without a second thought, and while she would love him no matter where he came from, the fact that he came from a lot . . . well, it makes Talia more forgiving. Not a lot, but a little.

With Townsend, she feels secure in a way she never felt with Malcolm—more secure than she feels even with Meera, who's been cagey and strange ever since Talia got back together with Townsend. At first, she thought Meera was jealous, but more recently, she's become convinced that her friend is keeping something from her. It would be insane for Meera to lie about receiving that photo of Gracie playing in the park, but Talia can't stop thinking about it. The way Meera seemed so convinced, so sure she was now a target of Amanda's wrath, just like Talia—it isn't sitting right with her. What reason would Amanda have to go after Meera? Of course, Meera did encourage Talia to report Amanda's harassment to the police. Is that why Meera thinks Amanda is after her now? Or is there some other reason—some connection between the two women that Talia isn't aware of? The thought would be laughable if it weren't so disturbing.

"Large Iced Turbo with sugar-free vanilla and an extra shot?"

Talia looks up from her phone to see a barista brandishing her coffee and scurries over to grab it.

A line from Kennedy J. Abbott's novel *Right on Track* pops into her head: *Emmeline tends to get tangled up in narratives that only exist in her own head.* The same could be said for Talia, who'd be the first to admit she has an overactive imagination. She'd never want to jeopardize her friendship with Meera over an imagined betrayal, and she's just about to text Meera, to ask to clear the air—until she steps into the parking lot and sees a matte black Ford Taurus has sidled in right next to her car. This normally wouldn't set off alarm bells in her head, except the parking lot is otherwise empty, and it seems strange for this car to choose a space directly beside the only other car in the lot. Plus, both the windshield and front side windows are tinted, which she doesn't think is allowed in Texas—at least not *this* dark.

Whether or not a person sits inside the vehicle is impossible to tell. Still, she feels sure that someone is in there. Waiting for her.

Instinctively, her eyes drop to her new tires. No slashes, thank God. But still . . .

Amanda isn't the only one conspiring to tear them apart. After the Fourth of July party, Townsend told Talia all about the strange conversation he had with Amanda's sister, Kaitlyn—the one who kept insisting that Amanda was missing and that Townsend had something to do with it. "She told me she had a gun in her trunk," said Townsend. "She's lucky I didn't call the police."

"Maybe you should have." Talia paused and then added, "Did she say anything about me?"

Townsend shook his head no. "She didn't," he said, "but if she comes anywhere near you, tell me, because I'll fucking kill her."

Standing outside Jo's now, Talia is tempted to turn around and go right back inside—at least until she can identify the owner of this Ford Taurus with its blacked-out windows, sitting close enough to her car to feel like a threat. But she doesn't. It's broad daylight, and there is no reason for her to be afraid. Just because something is unfamiliar doesn't mean it's a threat, she reminds herself. Some things are outside her control; that's okay. She's probably getting tangled up in a narrative that only exists in her own head.

Steeling herself, she starts toward her Volkswagen Jetta, and as she nears, she hears a gentle hum, which grows steadily louder. The car next to hers isn't just parked; it's on and idling, ready to peel away at any moment.

Inside her purse, her fingers fumble for her keys. Then, as discreetly as she can, she slides a key between each knuckle, squeezing her hand into a fist. She can't remember where she saw this self-defense tip—an Instagram video probably. Something she would have watched during her infinite scrolling in bed, never expecting she'd ever actually put it to use.

The walk seems endless, but eventually, she makes it to the driver's side door. Once there, she has no choice but to turn her back to the mysterious vehicle to get into her own. The beep of the car lock remote is deafening in the nearly empty lot, like a scream. She's just about to close the door behind her, finally safe, when she hears it: a soft click. A camera shutter?

Talia doesn't want to hang around to find out. She hightails it out of the parking lot and off to the Cuff office, the conversation she hoped to have with Meera already forgotten.

Chapter Twenty-Two

Kaitlyn

As soon as she steps into the police station, Kaitlyn wonders if she's doing the right thing. Just being here makes her feel complicit, like someone is going to come up behind her and put her in cuffs simply for knowing too much. But really, the problem is that she doesn't know enough. She's here because she's ready to start learning the truth.

Grief, Kaitlyn always believed, was something felt by everyone and best felt together. What she didn't realize: just how differently shared grief could manifest itself. Following their parents' death, Kaitlyn pushed away everyone except Amanda, while it seemed Kaitlyn was the sole person Amanda didn't want to see. Even more painful than the pictures—an endless parade of them on Instagram, showing parties and trips with people Kaitlyn had never seen in her life—was the silence. Amanda didn't need her; that much was made clear. She began to wonder if anyone did.

For a while, Kaitlyn simply went through the motions of daily life, feeling like she was playing a losing game (and a boring one at that). Sleep, eat, work, repeat. Lying on her couch, scrolling through pictures of her sister on yet another jaunt to Nashville or New York City, she'd wonder whether all the rituals required of a functional adult—all the scrubbing and shaving and brushing and buffing and folding and flossing—were worth the trouble. She would only have to do them all again the next day. How much easier it would be to just sleep and let the filth consume her.

Things improved eventually. Even while Amanda continued to keep her at arm's length, Kaitlyn found solace in the shooting range and ShrinkGPT. And strangely, these past few months spent investigating the mystery of her sister made her feel more alive than she had in a long, long time—even before her parents' passing. It was kind of nice, finally feeling needed.

While Kaitlyn stands in the lobby of the police station, hesitating, a behemoth of an officer brushes past her, so close she can smell his woody aftershave. Detective Burrows, his badge reads, and instantly, the name triggers a memory: He was one of the two officers Kaitlyn spoke to back in June, when she first reported Amanda as missing. Chances are he wouldn't recognize her, but still, Kaitlyn ducks her head until he pushes through the doors. It would be difficult to explain why the person she claimed was in danger is now the person she's here to investigate.

At the front desk, a woman attempts to give her a smile that ends up looking more like a grimace. "You need something?"

"I do," Kaitlyn says, summoning confidence. In moments like these, when a self-esteem boost is needed, Kaitlyn used to ask herself, *What would Amanda do?* Now—after learning about her sister's recent behavior from Townsend—she's a little afraid to ask that question. "I'd like to request a copy of an accident report."

The receptionist snaps her gum. "Names of involved drivers and passengers?"

"Martin and Josephine Reade," she says, and though it isn't necessary, she can't help but explain: "My parents."

The woman glances up at her through the thick glass separating them. Kaitlyn thinks she's going to apologize for her loss, as so many others already have, but instead, she turns her attention back to her computer screen. It's impossible to say whether Kaitlyn feels relief for escaping this empty, obligatory exchange or a little disappointed. Maybe it would have been nice, having the enormity of what she's about to do be acknowledged.

Nearly two and a half years have passed, and still Kaitlyn has never tried to find out exactly what caused her parents' death. A car accident was enough for her; she didn't need to hear the gory details. But ever since Townsend planted the stupid idea in her head that Amanda was somehow involved, Kaitlyn can't help thinking there's more to the story than she realized.

Six dollars and an hour later, she sits on her couch, reading through the report but not quite absorbing the words. *Erratic steering result of suspected wheel misalignment; indications of prior frame damage.* As far as Kaitlyn knew, her parents had never gotten into so much as a minor fender bender before the accident that claimed their lives; they were steady, careful, hands-at-ten-and-two drivers. How had their car's frame become damaged? And did that frame damage later cause them to go careening off the road?

A memory comes back to Kaitlyn then, so sharp and urgent that she wonders if it's an invention of her own mind: a chilly night in late February, not long before their parents' death. A three a.m. phone call from Amanda. She's sobbing, howling, saying she didn't mean to hit the curb; she didn't think she was that drunk, and she thought she could make it home without an issue. Kaitlyn, still fuzzy with sleep, telling her sister to go to bed, check out the damage in the morning, tell their parents the truth, don't do it again.

She wonders: Was it possible Amanda's careless driving that night damaged the frame and caused the wheel to become misaligned? Was it possible Amanda never told their parents the truth, so they proceeded to get into their car, totally unaware they could lose control at any moment?

When Townsend first accused Amanda of killing their mom and dad, Kaitlyn's mind immediately leaped to clichés. Agatha Christie–like motivations. Maybe Amanda knew the bulk of the estate would be left to her. Maybe she killed them on purpose to get the money.

But if anything, this revelation is more sinister, because it's at once so mundane and so much more real. It's classic Amanda, Kaitlyn thinks coldly. Killing their parents in the laziest way possible. All she had to do was tell their parents the truth about damaging their car, and she could have saved them. This tragedy could have been avoided.

Instead, her selfish sister cared more about covering her ass than facing the consequences of her actions. Bitterness lurches inside her like some untamed beast, clawing to escape. Sure, Amanda has never been afraid of telling a lie, but Kaitlyn never imagined her sister would be capable of a deceit like *this*. And now, Amanda is somewhere out there, firing off unhinged missives to her ex without a single thought to the mess she's left in her wake.

She doesn't know what she hopes to accomplish, exactly, but for some reason, Kaitlyn finds herself driving to Amanda's empty apartment, which she hasn't visited since June. Stepping through the threshold, she notices that the stench of bleach—so strong it stung her nostrils the first time she broke in over a month ago—has since dissipated; the unshakable feeling that something bad occurred in this place has not. A thin layer of dust coats the side table by her sister's front door, and Kaitlyn runs her finger through it, leaving a long streak.

If you're not here, she thinks, *then where the fuck are you, Amanda?*

The last time she was here, Kaitlyn found that gold class ring, which ultimately led her to Townsend. Tracking him down may have been a bust, but perhaps there is something else in this apartment that can offer Kaitlyn clarity about where Amanda is hiding—or who she even is.

Just like the first time she ransacked this place, she starts with the drawers, working her way from the tiny kitchen over to the bed, which is sectioned off from the rest of the studio with a bookcase. Lifting up the bedsheets, she sees nothing out of place, and peeking under the bed, she finds only dust bunnies. No notes, no fingerprints, no stray hairs, no blood stains. Not a single clue to indicate where Amanda went and whether she went there willingly. The only new item Kaitlyn finds is a flyer advertising a protest of the polarizing I-35 expansion. Strange—she never once thought of her sister as an activist. Perhaps this is yet another facet of Amanda's personality that Kaitlyn never witnessed for herself.

She is just about to leave when she notices a nail hammered into an otherwise empty wall in the kitchen, one she could have *sworn* used to hold a piece of art. It takes her a moment before she remembers: A topless black-and-white modeling shot of her sister used to hang there, and now it's gone. Though it feels odd to take a picture of something that *isn't* there, Kaitlyn pulls out her phone and snaps a photo of the bare wall. That's when a text message bubbles up on her screen.

Hi Kaitlyn. It's Will Dupont, the text says. Hope you're doing okay. Just wanted to let you know that I saw our buddy Townsend Fuller yesterday, and it made me think of you.

Her curiosity is piqued. Where did you see Townsend?

His response comes almost instantly. He came into the Rutland office and met with one of our partners. I was going to say hi, but he looked stressed AF, so I left him alone.

A tingle of suspicion creeps up Kaitlyn's spine at the thought of Townsend speaking to a lawyer. Could he have done something to Amanda after all? But that couldn't be. Townsend had shown Kaitlyn all those threatening messages from her sister. If anything, he's probably seeking legal action *against* Amanda, a thought that makes Kaitlyn feel too ashamed to keep the conversation going.

Strangely enough, this is the second time someone has brought up Townsend to her this week. After much cajoling, Kaitlyn had finally agreed to a second date with the data science professor last Saturday night, if only for the distraction. Once the drinks started flowing, her guard fell away, and she even handed the professor her phone to scroll through pictures of her windowsill herb garden. But her date swiped one image too far, coming across a screenshot she'd taken a month earlier of Townsend at his alumni holiday party.

"Wait, I know this guy," she told Kaitlyn, tapping her finger on the screen.

"You do?"

"Yeah. Small world. He hired me to do a project for him."

"What kind of project?" Kaitlyn asked, but Eileen wouldn't elaborate; apparently she'd signed an NDA.

Figures, Kaitlyn thought. Even if Townsend wasn't guilty of hurting her sister, he was surely guilty of *something*.

The lobby was miraculously empty when Kaitlyn first entered Amanda's building, and though she hoped to have the same luck when exiting, she instead finds the landlord waiting for her at the bottom of the steps, idly sweeping the floor.

"I thought I heard someone up there." The man squints, as though trying to place her. "You new here?"

He doesn't recognize her from the last time she was here. This doesn't surprise her; Kaitlyn is used to being forgotten. She considers lying, but she just doesn't have her sister's gift for it. "My sister lives in 3C. Amanda Reade." She hesitates, and then—before this man can lecture her—adds, "I know she's so behind on rent but—"

"Nah. She's good." The landlord shakes his head, his wispy gray ponytail flapping behind him.

"What do you mean?" Her sister is attractive, yes, but is she really hot enough to get herself excused from several months' worth of rent?

"The woman has been coming by to pay it."

This Kaitlyn didn't expect. "The woman?"

"She comes by once a month to drop off cash. Said she works with Amanda."

Her pulse quickens. Someone is paying Amanda's rent? She can't think of any reason why someone would be so generous . . . unless . . . "Who is this woman?"

"I don't know. Just some lady."

"Can you describe her?" Kaitlyn pushes.

The landlord sighs, clearly bored with this line of questioning. "Youngish. Dark hair. Good looking. I'm getting paid, so I don't really care who she is."

"Okay." It doesn't seem like she's going to get anything else from this man, so Kaitlyn reaches into her bag with sweaty palms and pulls out a crumpled receipt and a pen. Just moments before, she was ready to write her sister off as the worst kind of fuckup, but now, she once again—perhaps foolishly—feels a flicker of uncertainty.

Maybe Amanda is not off on a bender after all. Maybe Kaitlyn has been on this wild-goose chase for good reason.

"I'm going to write down my number," she tells him. "Do you think you could call me the next time she comes by? Maybe even get a picture?"

Heaving another sigh, the man accepts the slip of paper. "Sure. If I remember."

That isn't good enough. This is finally a lead; Kaitlyn can sense it. "Please. It's important."

Her desperation must be palpable, because the landlord says, slightly more convincingly, "Okay. Yes. I will."

"Thank you."

Kaitlyn takes a deep breath, feeling—for the first time in days—like she might actually be close to some answers.

Chapter Twenty-Three

Meera

Meera is angry, and not for any one reason or at any one person.

Her focus has simply been hijacked by pulsating, unrelenting resentment—at Townsend, at her failing body, at the fact that she cannot tuck her daughter in at night. Maybe even at Talia, for making her feel like she's simultaneously doing too much and not nearly enough to help her.

Sitting at her desk, she tries to channel that fury into productivity, but it's no use. Her mind keeps slipping off her screen and out the door, hoping to find an answer for why Talia hasn't arrived yet, and why Talia didn't let her know she was running late, and why Meera spends more time worrying about Talia than her own kid.

Meera could probably use a hobby or a few more friends; she knows this. But she's gotten herself too deep into this mess with Talia and Townsend and Amanda to back out now. She's part of it, whether she likes it or not.

Her computer chirps, signaling a new email. Meera opens it, eager to busy herself, but her heart sinks as she reads the message. It's a follow-up from the employee seminar about corporate policy a few weeks back, during which Cuff announced an impending security audit. From the audit, it seems the company determined that some customer reports aren't getting through to the right teams. So now, they're going to conduct a comprehensive examination of Cuff's systems and practices to mitigate potential risks, such as privacy breaches, malicious activity, identity theft . . .

This isn't about you, Meera assures herself, closing the email. All she did was look at a few messages; she didn't do anything wrong. And while she genuinely believes this to be true, that doesn't stop her palms from sweating.

Just as Meera starts to feel her anxiety overwhelm her, Talia flies through the door of the ML-team office, harried and panting. Their coworkers barely glance up from their keyboards, but Meera immediately stands from her desk and leads Talia to the bathroom, sensing they need a private space to talk.

"What's going on?" Meera asks. "Is it Amanda?"

"I don't know." Talia drops her bag to the tile floor and leans against the sink. "I don't know who they were, but I'm pretty sure they were taking pictures of me."

Using the same tone she always employs when Gracie is frustrated or upset, Meera says, "How about you start from the beginning and tell me what happened."

"Okay." Talia takes a deep breath. "I was leaving Jo's this morning—"

"You got Jo's this morning?" Meera doesn't mean to interrupt but can't help herself. "I would have met you there. Why didn't you tell me?"

Talia gives her a strange look. "I didn't realize I needed to."

"Right." The words hurt more than they should.

"Anyway. I was leaving Jo's, and I saw this car with blacked-out windows parked next to mine. And as I was getting into my car, I could swear someone took a picture of me."

"You think they were waiting for you?"

"I don't know what to think," Talia says. "I'm just . . ."

"Angry?" Meera wonders if her friend feels the way she does, like her overwhelming rage might come spilling out of her at any moment, burning everything in its path.

Talia shakes her head no. "I'm just tired." Next to her on the counter, her phone vibrates, and they both look at it with apprehension, as though it has suddenly sprung to life. Cautiously, Talia picks it up and checks the screen.

"It's not *her*, is it?"

"No." Talia shows her the screen. "It's you." And she's right—on the screen is Meera's weekly performance-optimization email, identifying bottlenecks in the ML pipeline for Talia to tackle.

"Oh, right. I forgot I'd scheduled that to send at ten a.m. I didn't want to bug you with it earlier because"—Meera shrugs and tries to keep the bitterness out of her voice—"I wasn't sure where you were."

Talia misses this dig. "It's already ten? I've got to get to work."

Meera waves her off. "I'll be right behind you. I just have to pee first."

She waits as Talia gathers up her bag and phone and pushes through the door. Then she locks herself in a stall and sinks down onto the closed toilet seat, cradling her head in her hands. It's so tempting to fall apart right now, but she can't allow it. *Stay strong,* she tells herself. *Gracie needs you. Talia needs you.*

Heading back to the ML-team mod pod, Meera gives herself a pep talk: She's going to get through her inbox, make it through the day, and not give Amanda another thought until she's home and free to let her mind wander. But on her way back to her desk, she spots Talia sitting motionless in front of her own computer, something clamped between her hands.

"What is that?" Meera asks. Then the stink hits her. She backs up, shielding her nose with both hands. "Jesus, Talia, it smells like death."

This gets the attention of the whole ML team, who crowd around and watch as Talia opens her clasped hands to reveal the crumpled mess of fur and cartilage inside them.

Meera peers over to get a better look, hands still over her face. "Is that—?"

"It's a bat," Talia finishes for her. "A dead bat."

Most of the team scatters then, dousing their hands in sanitizer and shouting warnings of rabies to Talia.

"They're right, you know," Meera says. "You'll need to get the rabies vaccine." Noticing that her friend still hasn't moved, she approaches. It's possible Talia is in shock. "Are you all right?"

"There's a note." Talia nods to her top desk drawer, which she has left open. "I found it under the bat. I haven't read it yet."

Meera snags a tissue from the box on Talia's desk and reaches for the paper. "May I?"

Talia nods.

Grabbing just the tip of the note between her tissue-covered fingers, Meera reads the message out loud. "'Remember the night he took you to Congress Avenue Bridge to see the bats fly? Remember this instead: I'm going to kill all nice memories you two have together, and when I'm done, I'm going to kill you.'" She drops the note, letting it flutter to the floor. "Okay, this is fucked up, even for Amanda."

"Don't throw that away," Talia says, gesturing at the letter. "We'll need that for evidence."

"And what about that?" Meera points to the carcass still held aloft in Talia's hands. "How long do you think that thing has been in your drawer?"

"It wasn't here yesterday, I know that. We would have smelled it."

"Do you think . . . ?" Meera hesitates. "Could Amanda have snuck into the office overnight to plant it?"

"Is that even possible?"

Meera shrugs. "Probably. Should I grab a bag or something to . . . ?" Meera inclines her head to the bat. "You can't keep holding that thing, Tal."

"But we need to keep it for evidence." Still her friend seems to be in some kind of trance. Meera needs to snap her out of it.

"Well, we can keep it in a garbage bag. I'm going to get one from the kitchen, you're going to put the bat inside of it, and then you're going to scrub the shit out of your hands."

"And then what?"

"I will help." The unexpected male voice makes both women jump. Meera whirls around to find Aarav the custodian, likely sent over by one of their coworkers.

"Aarav, hi."

"Vanakkam, Meera," he greets her warmly. Then he turns to Talia and gives her a shy nod. "Morning."

"You're not giving him the bat, are you?" Talia hisses in her ear.

"No, of course not," Meera says back.

"Will you ask him?"

"Ask him what?"

"Whether it's possible for someone to break into the building."

Aarav looks at her curiously, waiting for a translation.

"How would he know that?" Meera asks.

"He's here all the time," says Talia. "He would know whether Amanda could have snuck in last night."

Meera relents. "Fine." In Tamil, she briefly explains the situation to Aarav, saying they think someone snuck into the office last night after closing and left something in Talia's desk. "I just want to know, is there any way for someone to get into the building overnight? You spend more time at this place than anyone—would it ever be possible for someone to trespass?"

"Absolutely not." Aarav shakes his head firmly. "Not without a key card, no."

"No?" His insistence surprises her. "Well, did you happen to see anyone unfamiliar in the office this morning?"

"No. You were the first person to arrive after me."

"What did he say?" Talia asks.

Aarav turns to her and, in English, says, "No key card, no entry."

"You're sure?"

"I'm sure," Aarav says, switching back to Tamil. "Someone would either have to steal a key card or know someone on the inside to help them."

"What did he say?" Talia asks again.

"Nothing." Meera watches as Talia deposits the bat into the plastic bag Aarav holds open for her. Then she smiles and nods at Aarav, dismissing him. "Now can you please go wash the disease off your hands?"

After work, Meera and Talia visit Goldie's at the Austin Proper, because they both agree that a dead bat in a desk drawer calls for a drink or two. With its rose-printed wallpaper and plush velvet seating, the space is an Instagram influencer's dream, and cocktails are stupid expensive—Meera shouldn't be spending twenty-six dollars on a truffle old-fashioned right now—but she orders one anyway. This is where Talia wanted to go, and Meera wants to be a good sport. Her friend has had a shitty day, after all—though you wouldn't know it to look at her. Talia seems strangely calm, really, as she repositions the mint-leaf garnish in her coupe glass before snapping a pic.

"You've been posting a lot more often on Instagram," Meera says, an observation that comes out sounding more judgmental than she intends.

Talia doesn't seem to notice. "Have I?" Eyes still glued to her phone, she adds, "Gracie would love this place. You should take her here for afternoon tea."

"She would." Meera's heart hurts just thinking about Gracie.

"Is she still at Hari's?"

"She is."

Tucking her phone away, Talia gives her a sad smile. "I'm sorry, Meer. You must miss her like crazy."

"You have no idea."

"How long is she going to stay there?"

"Until Amanda is caught, I guess." Meera stares into her overpriced cocktail, willing herself not to cry. "Do I have any other option? I need to keep her safe." Since that night at Talia's place, when they found the note in the bathroom, Meera hasn't even spoken to the cops—though she was tempted to after the incident in the park with Gracie. With Amanda after her daughter now, it made sense to involve herself in this mess as little as possible. And that meant no police.

Talia deflates, sinking back into her velvet club chair. "I'm sorry, Meer," she says again. "Really, I am. You didn't ask for any of this, and yet you've found yourself in the middle of everything."

"It's not your fault," says Meera, before adding under her breath, "It's Townsend who should be sorry."

"What about Townsend?"

"Forget it." Meera shakes her head. She's not looking to start an argument. "How are you two doing?"

"We're good. Really good, actually." Lips curling into a grin, Talia leans forward conspiringly. "Can I tell you a secret?"

"Always."

"I think he's going to propose soon."

The admission hits her like a punch to the throat. Meera lets out an involuntary gasp. "Already?"

"I saw a text conversation between him and his sister pop up on his phone the other day. He was asking her about their grandmother's engagement ring." Talia pauses, as though just hearing Meera's response. "Wait, what do you mean by 'already'?"

"It just seems kind of soon, don't you think?" Hoping to defuse the tension, Meera adds, "But remember, this is coming from the divorcée. I'm a bit jaded."

Talia's eyes narrow. "A bit? You might be the most jaded person I know."

The hostility in Talia's voice surprises Meera. "I'm just saying, this is all happening kind of fast. How well do you even know Townsend?"

"I know him better than anyone. Certainly better than you, who does nothing but judge him."

"Did you ever consider that I might have reason to judge him?"

"Because he made one mistake?"

"I'm not talking about him cheating on you." Meera pauses. She hadn't meant to let the conversation get this far. Talia blinks at her, clearly wondering where she's going with this. Meera doesn't have to tell her friend everything, she decides. She can tell Talia just enough to plant a seed of doubt. "Two summers ago, before you ever met him, Townsend and I took an entrepreneurship course at UT together. I told him about an idea I had for a health care start-up, and he took it from me."

"Wait—what? You two knew each other? Why wouldn't you tell me?" The expression on Talia's face isn't one of betrayal so much as confusion.

"That's not the point, Tal. The point is that he's a thief. He stole the idea for AutoInTune from me."

Talia hesitates, then asks, "Did you have articles of incorporation?"

"What? No, I—"

"Did you file for a patent? A copyright? Because it sounds to me like you're just bitter that Townsend was actually able to make something happen. You can't blame him for your failures."

Meera flinches. "I'm not blaming him for—"

"You've always been so territorial. I mean, you have one fleeting idea, and so no one else is ever allowed to pursue something similar?" Talia scoffs. "And you probably think he stole me from you too."

It's true; she does feel like Townsend snatched her best friend away. But she's not going to give Talia the satisfaction of knowing she's right. "Fine. Even if you ignore the fact that he took my idea, he created a company that's not even legitimate, Talia. This VC at Silicon Hills thinks he's inflating his user metrics. And you know the telehealth company that wants to partner with him? Hari works there, and I'm thinking about telling him—"

"You just hate to see me happy with someone else," Talia interrupts. She doesn't seem to have heard Meera at all. "You loved it when Townsend left me, because it meant we could be miserable old spinsters together forever. I ruined your plan, and now you have no choice but to admit how empty your life is."

It no longer matters that Meera paid twenty-six dollars for her stupid drink; she downs the rest of it in one gulp. "I don't have to be in a romantic relationship for my life to have meaning. I'd much rather be a miserable old spinster forever than stake my self-worth on a man, like you've done time and time again."

"That's not true."

"Isn't it, though? You followed your ex to college. You told me you only moved to Austin because he broke your heart and you needed to distance yourself. It seems like every major life decision you've ever made has had to do with a guy."

A server comes by the table, eyeing their drained glasses. "Can I get you ladies another round?"

Meera and Talia answer in unison: "No."

Once the server retreats, Meera takes thirty dollars from her wallet, drops it on the table, and stands. "If you'll excuse me," she says icily, "I have an empty house to return to."

Talia stays seated. "You're wrong about Townsend, and you're wrong about me."

Meera takes a final look at her friend, pretty and doe-eyed and filled with more animus than she ever realized. She wonders when they'll speak again, if ever. "I hope I'm wrong," she tells Talia. "But I don't think I am."

As soon as she leaves the bar, she shoots a quick message to Hari.

I need you to do me a favor.

Chapter Twenty-Four

Talia

Talia is leaving her early bird Pilates class on Monday when she sees it for the sixth time since last week: the matte black Ford Taurus with the darkly tinted windows, parked—as always—right alongside her Volkswagen Jetta.

After that first time outside Jo's, Talia was able to convince herself she imagined it. No one took her photo, she told herself, and that car being parked next to hers had been just that: another car, belonging to someone who didn't care who Talia was or where she was going. It was important to be vigilant, especially as a woman living in a city. But after all the Amanda stuff, Talia was bordering on neurotic. And that wasn't healthy.

But then she saw the Ford Taurus the next morning, parked outside her house in South Congress. And then again, the day after that, in the Cuff parking lot, where she'd stepped out during her lunch break to run errands. Twice over the weekend she'd spotted the car again—always idling eerily by, never with a driver in sight—and now, as she stares the car down in the Pilates parking lot, she can no longer pretend otherwise: She's being followed.

Nearly a week has passed since her fight with Meera, but Talia still feels keyed up and querulous in a way she can't shake, and being pursued by a stranger isn't helping. What's worse: She can't confide in Meera about this relentless stalking, because the two aren't speaking. Every time Talia glances over at her former friend—just a few desks away in their compact ML-team mod pod—she rehashes their argument on repeat in her head until her blood boils. The heightened tension would be enough to make anyone snap.

Talia is powerless to stop it.

Judgment clouded by rage, she stomps over to the vehicle, her rolled-up Pilates mat thwacking against her back with each step. She squeezes between their two cars and knocks on the blacked-out driver's side window—gently at first, and then with her whole fist. "Come out," she says. "Show yourself."

A few of the women leaving the studio shoot her curious looks, but she doesn't care. If only Talia could explain to them that she's just an ordinary person—a good person, at that—trying to enjoy her ordinary life without constant surveillance. Then they'd understand.

Suddenly, with a loud whining sound, the window retracts into the door. Talia jumps back; she didn't actually expect him to acknowledge her. A man with weathered skin and aviator sunglasses sits on the other side, his expression unreadable.

"Can I help you?" he asks, and for an unsettling moment, Talia wonders if she did, in fact, imagine this whole thing. Perhaps she's now the one harassing an ordinary person.

She's tempted to retreat, but instead, she stands her ground. "You've been following me."

"Yes." The man says this matter-of-factly and without apology, as though she'd asked whether it was Monday.

"Why?"

"Because I was hired to do so." Again, his tone is completely devoid of remorse. This is quickly turning into one of the strangest interactions Talia has ever had.

"By whom?"

He laughs, showing off the gold fillings on his back teeth. "You know I can't tell you that." She hates that she can't see the eyes behind those sunglass lenses, which are as dark as the windows on his car.

"Can you tell whoever it is that I have nothing to hide? That I'm not doing anything wrong? That I'm just grocery shopping and working and"—she gestures to the Pilates mat strapped to her back—"trying to fucking exercise in peace?"

"I don't get paid to talk," he says, an obnoxious smirk still plastered to his face. "I get paid to watch."

"Well, watch this." Talia takes a step back and shows him her middle finger, a crass gesture that she never imagined feeling motivated to use herself.

The man turns then and reaches for something on his passenger seat—*oh, my God, he has a gun,* Talia thinks—but when he turns back to the window, he's holding not a gun but a compact Nikon D3500. "Say 'cheese,'" he says before snapping a picture. And then, just as quickly, he peels out of the parking lot and out of sight.

She needs to get to work, but after climbing into her car, Talia finds herself paralyzed. Someone has paid this man to stalk her, and she cannot move—cannot think about anything else, really—until she finds a reasonable explanation for who that someone could be. A running list starts to form in her head. Amanda Reade's nosy sister, the one who reported Townsend to the police? What about her own sister, who she hasn't seen in years? Or her estranged parents? Or even Meera, her supposed best friend, who seems to trust Talia less and less by the minute? Her head aches, so she slumps forward, letting her forehead rest on the steering wheel. Though she isn't convinced that any of these suspects would actually hire a private investigator to follow her, the thought alone is enough to send her reeling.

Another possibility crosses her mind. It pains her to consider it—like poking an unhealed wound—but still, it makes too much sense *not* to take into consideration: Malcolm's family. Perhaps they are the ones who sent this man with a camera after her. Perhaps they still believe, even all these years later, that Talia is somehow responsible for what happened to Malcolm.

They weren't officially together during her senior year of high school; Malcolm's football practice schedule at Auburn kept him too busy to maintain a relationship. Arriving at Auburn for her freshman year, Talia felt sure things would go back to the way they were in the beginning, when they first fell in love. She'd spent her entire senior year dreaming of how things would be, the life they would have together. Unfortunately, Malcolm didn't share her vision.

It was the same cycle over and over: They'd hook up, she'd get her hopes up, he'd let her down, rinse and repeat. By her senior year (during which time he was still at Auburn, working as an assistant football coach), it seemed increasingly unlikely that she would be receiving a ring before spring, as nearly every girl in Zeta Tau Alpha was expected to. But the biggest shock came right before her graduation, when Malcolm did propose . . . to someone who wasn't her.

She didn't blame Malcolm for meeting Clara Belle Linhart. He wasn't doing anything malicious when he fell in love and decided to start a life with her. But still, Talia couldn't deny that it hurt.

For years, Talia followed Malcolm and Clara Belle's love story through her phone screen as they exchanged vows on a farm, and then bought a home in Opelika, and then adopted a Labrador named Scratchy. Watching someone else live out her happily ever after was painful.

Talia knew the only way she would ever be able to fully move on would be to leave. So, she did. She moved away, began working at Cuff. She started a new life, and most days, she could let herself pretend that Malcolm Gray had never existed.

That's why it didn't make any sense when Malcolm's parents pointed a finger at her after his accident. By then, she hadn't spoken to him in years. But as she knew all too well, trauma can rob people of their senses. Perhaps his parents' way of dealing with the guilt and grief—of getting a semblance of closure, even if they can't get answers—is passing the buck to her. It isn't fair, but Talia understands; the best way to avoid becoming a scapegoat, after all, is to find one.

Enough about Malcolm, enough about his parents, enough about the Ford Taurus with the blacked-out windows and the camera-wielding loser driving it. Talia needs to get to work and invest her energy elsewhere. And while she's eager to put this morning behind her (and still pissed from last week's argument), she has a strange urge to tell Meera about flipping that PI the bird. Talia has a feeling she would be proud.

But when she gets to the ML-team mod pod, she finds Aarav the custodian, rather than her coworker, at Meera's desk, packing Meera's half-alive succulent into a cardboard box.

Immediately, Talia's mind goes to the worst possibility: Meera is having a Hashimoto's flare-up and had to take a leave of absence from work. Talia knows stress can trigger flare-ups in autoimmune conditions like Meera's; perhaps their horrible fight at Goldie's sent her over the edge.

"Good morning, Aarav. Do you know where Meera is?"

The older man continues to clean Meera's desk, as though Talia hasn't spoken. She knows Meera has a soft spot for him, what with their shared understanding of Tamil, but something about Aarav has always given Talia the creeps. She watches as he picks up the framed school photo of Gracie from Meera's desk and stares at it for a beat too long before packing it in the box with the plant.

"Aarav?"

"She has let go," he says, still avoiding her eye.

"She what?" For an awful moment, Talia thinks the custodian is telling her that Meera is dead, and the large Iced Turbo she chugged before Pilates churns sickeningly in her stomach.

"She *was* let go." This comes from David, whose desk is to the left of Meera's. Talia neither dislikes nor particularly likes David, who's efficient and competent but has a habit of crunching on pistachios all day and leaving the shells stacked on his desk.

Talia whirls to face him. "How do you know that?"

"I ran into her as she was leaving Betty's office. She didn't tell me much, other than the fact that she got suspended, but rumor has it she was misusing her access to customer data." David raises his eyebrows. "I bet you know what happened."

"I don't," she lies. The floor tilts beneath her, and she steadies herself on Meera's desk. For all the nasty things Meera said to her during their argument last week, Talia knows she was just as cruel, if not crueler. This is worse than a Hashimoto's flare-up; this is all her fault.

"For Meera." From the corner of her eye, Talia sees Aarav offering her a folded piece of paper.

"This is for Meera? Did you find it on her desk?" Her brain pulses with a single thought, a reflex at this point: *Amanda*.

Aarav nods. Talia unfolds the paper slowly only to find that the note inside is written in what must be Tamil script. The letter is from Aarav, not Amanda, and Talia feels foolish for letting her neuroses get the better of her, if only for a second.

"For give to her," Aarav says.

"Forgive her?" Talia wonders how Aarav could possibly know about their fight. Had he noticed the friction between them in the office? Then she repeats the sentence back to herself. "For give to her. You want me to give this to her."

He nods again.

"I will," she says. "I promise." But as soon as Aarav returns to his office, Talia deposits the note in the box with the rest of Meera's belongings. Meera isn't going to want to see her, not after this. No doubt she's going to cast blame on Talia, just as Malcolm Gray's parents have done. And perhaps this time Talia deserves it.

Still, she can't help but think, *I never asked Meera to retrieve those messages. I never asked Meera to misuse her access to customer data.*

Talia may look like the bad guy here, but one could argue that Meera brought this all upon herself.

Chapter Twenty-Five

Townsend

At Foothill Grille, the hostess leads him to Mother's usual table, the same one she requested for his thirty-fourth birthday brunch. He finds her drinking a Tito's greyhound, the Greek salad she'd ordered untouched.

"Mom." He kisses her lightly on the cheek, which feels powdery and dry. "You're looking well."

Mother waves his compliment off and takes a sip of her drink. "You want something. That's the only reason I hear from you. So what is it?"

It stings, hearing this from his mom. Not because it's not true, but because he thought himself more artful than that. "I want to ask about Grandma Birdy's ring. Her engagement ring."

"Oh?"

"I want to know if I can have it."

"And what are you going to do with it?"

Townsend grits his teeth. "I want to give it to Talia, Mom. I'm going to propose to her."

"Did it occur to you that your sister might want Birdy's ring?"

"I already talked to Blake. She doesn't want it. She said she hates a marquise cut."

Drawing her lips into a thin line, Mother says, "What a shame. I was hoping the ring would stay in the family."

"It's going to stay in the family."

"Townsend, sweetheart." Mother gives a withering smile. "That woman is not family."

Townsend feels a sudden urge to overturn the table, run out of the restaurant, drive his car into the pool. He looks around for a waiter he can flag down instead. A drink will calm his nerves. "Okay, well, maybe not yet. But she will be after I ask her to marry me."

"No, dear. She won't."

A server finally appears. Townsend orders a glass of top-shelf Macallan as a satisfying sort of "fuck you" to his mom, who will later have to foot the bill. He's ready for a fight. "Can you just tell me what your problem is with her?"

"I don't have a problem with her."

"You clearly do."

"I don't. Really." Mother shrugs. "I just think marrying her would be a mistake."

"Which would imply you have a problem."

"It's just . . ." Mother purses her lips, looking regretful for ever having agreed to meet Townsend here. "Like I said before, she comes from a different—"

"A different world, I know," he finishes for her.

A beat of silence follows; Mother seems to be deciding whether to confess something. Honesty wins out. "I'm having her followed."

"You're what?"

"I hired someone to follow her. A private investigator."

"Why the fuck would you do that?"

His mom glares at him; the waiter has just arrived with his drink and no doubt heard Townsend's expletive.

"Pardon my language," he mutters to them both.

Once the waiter has shuffled off, Mother clears her throat. "Like I told you, I do not trust her. I feel like she's hiding something. And so I decided to have someone look into her."

"Is this what Carter Bonier was talking about when he told me he had a name for you?"

Mother's brow twitches; her Botox must prevent her from being able to properly arch it. "When did you speak to Carter?"

No way is Townsend getting into his legal troubles now, especially since (as far as he knows) he has no troubles. He sent Sage Clinic the falsified documents. He heard nothing but "thank you" in return—and so far, he's heard nothing from Amanda either. While his ex continues to harass his girlfriend, Amanda seems content to leave him be, though the fact remains that she knows more than she should. Perhaps he should give that private investigator a call himself.

He ignores Mother's question, instead telling her, "This is insane, Mom. Seriously." He pauses to take a swig of his whisky, and then adds, "Did you even find anything?" A tiny bit of curiosity edges into his voice; he hopes his mom doesn't hear it.

"It's just . . ."

Clearly Mother is dying to share something. "What?"

"She is perhaps a little more . . . *fragile* than you may realize."

"What do you mean by 'fragile'?"

His mom runs a polished nail around the edge of her glass. She's loving his eagerness. "How much has she told you about her life before moving here?"

"I mean, I know where she's from. I know where she went to college. What else is there to know?"

"Do you know that her real name is Natalia?"

Townsend did not know this. "Plenty of people use nicknames."

"Do plenty of people change their legal name to their nickname right before moving out of the state?" His mom smirks, as though this is some kind of smoking gun. "And did you know about her sister?"

Townsend feels a surge of smug satisfaction. "Yes, as matter of fact, I did know. Are you trying to suggest that having a sister who got pregnant out of wedlock makes Talia unmarriable?"

At this, Mother's smirk disappears. Apparently, her PI had failed to turn up this particular detail; he must have found some other bit of unsavory info about Talia's sister that Mother hoped to use as ammo instead.

"That's not—"

"Look," he says, "you don't have to give me Birdy's ring, but I'm going to propose to Talia, whether I have your blessing or not." It occurs to him, a moment too late, that he can't possibly afford a decent ring on his own right now. But there's no taking his words back.

Mother sniffs, her expression suddenly more hurt than annoyed. "It's your funeral."

That's all he needs to hear. Pushing back from the table, Townsend stands. "I need some air."

Out in the parking lot, Townsend paces, mind racing. Maybe he should have heard his mom out. What could be so damning that she'd try to prevent her only son from finally settling down, as she'd been begging him to do for the past decade? Was there even anything she could tell him that would change his mind about Talia? And did Talia really change her name?

He's about to return inside—maybe try to convince Mother one more time to let him have Birdy's ring—when the sound of shattering glass rings out like a shot. A deafening howl follows: a car alarm. No, not just a car alarm; *his* alarm. Someone is breaking into his car, and he would bet anything that it's Amanda.

As he's weaving through cars, making his way toward his roadster, Townsend can think of little else; he's already picturing the damage his beloved car may have incurred. That's probably why he runs headlong into another body—though when he steps back to apologize, he doesn't see some random country-club guest. He sees his girlfriend, who looks just as stunned to see him.

"Tal, what are you doing here?"

She furrows her brows, confused. "You told me you were having dinner with your mom here. I was waiting in the parking lot for you to be done."

Townsend doesn't remember making this plan, but his mind is too jumbled to question it. "Well, I'm pretty sure that's my car alarm going off. And I'm pretty sure Amanda is responsible."

Together, they beeline for his car, which he can see—even from a distance—is fucked. Shards of glass decorate the pavement around what used to be his back window, which is now just a gaping void. "Jesus," he mutters.

Talia points through the jagged opening. "What is that in there?"

"Probably whatever was lobbed through my fucking window." Townsend is about to open the side door to investigate when Talia reaches right through the broken glass. "Tal, be careful."

"I am." When she straightens up, he sees that she now has a brick in hand. She holds it up to examine—impressively, she can hold it in one hand without her arm even shaking—which is when he notices something written on its surface in white paint.

Townsend takes the brick from Talia's hand and holds it close enough to read in the dim light of the parking lot. "'Thief,'" he reads.

"What does that mean?" He can hear in her voice that she's reluctant—maybe even afraid—to hear the answer.

"I don't know," he answers honestly. Is it possible Amanda knows that AutoInTune isn't entirely his own creation? The thought unnerves Townsend; the last thing he needs is for Amanda to have more dirt. Looking up from the brick, he notices the trail of blood dripping from Talia's elbow down to her wrist. "Are you okay, babe? You're bleeding."

"It's okay." Without even looking at her elbow, Talia wipes it on her shirt. "It doesn't hurt."

"Still, we should get that cleaned out." He pulls out his phone. "I'm going to get my car towed, and then I'll drive yours back to my place, okay?"

"What about your mom?"

"I'll let her know I'm heading out. This is more important."

Talia flashes a sweet, grateful smile, and Townsend feels relief over never having learned whatever Mother was trying to tell him earlier.

The Talia he knows and loves—his future wife!—is right here in front of him, and whatever happened before him doesn't matter.

Chapter Twenty-Six

Talia

Another morning at Jo's, waiting for her caffeine fix, another compulsory check of Instagram.

Kennedy J. Abbott, as usual, has posted a new Story (this time showing the heart-shaped pancakes prepared for her by her husband), and for once, Talia doesn't feel that heavy thud of longing. She feels hope because—for the first time in what feels like a long time—the fairy tale that is Kennedy's life feels attainable. Talia smiles down at her left hand, which grips the phone. That telltale finger is still bare—but it won't be for long.

As Talia scrolls, she's taken right back to last Saturday: to herself and Townsend in a boat on Town Lake, going for the first time since May to see the bats fly.

"Just like our first date," Townsend told her as he rowed toward Congress Avenue Bridge.

"Our second first date," corrected Talia. "Our unofficial second first date."

"Semantics." Townsend smiled goofily, and Talia just knew. It was happening tonight. It was finally happening.

He waited until they were under the bridge, minutes before the bats would emerge and right as the sun began to dip in the sky. When he tucked his oar under his seat and took her hands, any doubt she had floated away with the breeze. This was it.

"Talia," he started, a slight quiver in his voice. "I'm the world's luckiest man to have met you, and I upended the rules of luck when I got a second chance with you. Luckily, I don't plan on ever losing you again."

A nervous giggle escaped from her, and she was relieved when he laughed too.

"Sorry. Not my best work. This is my first time, you know."

Talia squeezed his hands. "I'll be gentle with you."

"Do you promise? Because I'm about to ask you something, and it's kind of scary for me."

It was happening, it was happening, it was happening. "I do."

Getting down on one knee proved difficult in a canoe. After nearly tipping the boat twice (which sent them both into a fit of nervous giggles), Townsend said "Fuck it" and cupped her chin in his hand instead. "Talia Danvers, will you marry me?"

The bats burst from under the bridge just as she said yes, swirling dizzily around them in a cloud of beating wings and jubilant squeaks. And when she kissed him, it felt at once like the first time and the thousandth time. Like she was finally home.

"Large iced matcha with oat milk?"

"That's me." Talia steps forward to claim her drink and then heads out to her car.

After getting home on Saturday night, Townsend showed her a picture of the diamond: a four-carat marquise cut. It was getting resized, he said. She was going to love it, he said. And she did, just as much as she loved him. In the face of all the drama (the private investigator, the creepy Post-it Note, the dead bat in her desk drawer, the brick thrown through Townsend's car window, and even the fight with Meera, when she made those insane accusations about Townsend's company), everything was now falling into place.

Bridal gowns and floral arrangements could replace thoughts of break-ins and threats. She was engaged! She was happy! And she deserved to enjoy it.

Outside Jo's, the black Ford Taurus isn't waiting for her, thank God—but still, her body feels stiff with unease. It isn't until she pulls into the Cuff parking lot that Talia pinpoints the root of her discontent: Meera. She's missing her friend, and she really wishes she could share the news of her engagement with her.

But she can't. She has no choice but to swallow her sadness and start her day.

It's been over a week since she was unceremoniously escorted from the office, but still, it seems all anyone can talk about is Meera and her suspension.

"Hey, Talia," Meera's deskmate David calls as soon as she enters the ML-team office. "Is it true that Meera hacked Cuff profiles to send random messages?" Curious, their other coworkers look up from their screens, awaiting Talia's response.

"No," she answers before correcting herself. "I don't know."

"Sure." David crunches noisily on a pistachio, adding another shell to the precarious stack on his desk.

"No, really. I don't know anything. Honest." This doesn't feel like a lie, since she doesn't know what happened, not really. She's texted and called Meera a dozen times since finding out about her suspension only to hear nothing in return. She'd be happy to set her coworkers straight, but clearly, Meera wants to keep Talia as in the dark as everyone else.

Plus, she doesn't have the time to defend her former friend. In Meera's absence, Talia's workload has nearly doubled. Meera's weekly performance-optimization audit has now become Talia's responsibility in addition to her own tasks, and she has to get it all done while her coworkers continue to gossip around her.

"I heard Meera tried to expense an office chair with a built-in massager," David says at one point. "Apparently, she has the same disease as Gigi Hadid."

"Lyme disease?" This is asked by Otto, who sits across from Talia and who earned the nickname Mercury for routinely microwaving tuna in the office kitchenette. (In fact, if Talia recalls correctly, it was Meera who gave him this nickname.)

"No, that's Bella. Gigi has some thyroid disorder. And apparently, Meera thought she needed a two-thousand-dollar chair because of it."

Galina, whose desk is to the right of Otto's, also pipes in. "Does this thyroid disorder also make you rude and chronically tardy? Because that would explain a lot." It's well known around the office that Galina hasn't liked Meera ever since she refused to buy Girl Scout cookies from Galina's niece.

Otto sniffs. "She drank my last Diet Dr Pepper once, even though I'd written my name on every can. She said she didn't see the label because she didn't have her glasses on. I don't think she even wears glasses."

"That wouldn't be the first lie she's told," says David. "I've heard her use the excuse that her car is in the shop at least four times this year alone. No one's car breaks down that frequently."

Though she doesn't say a word, Talia has to agree: Meera's car *does* break down suspiciously often.

"I just don't think she gave a shit," Galina concludes. "Not about this job and certainly not about any of us. Except for . . ."

Three pairs of eyes shift over to her at once. Talia pretends not to feel the stares. She should be defending Meera right now; she knows that. But frankly, she's still pretty pissed at Meera herself and doesn't feel like coming—yet again—to her rescue.

"Oh, holy shit, guys." Out of the corner of her eye, Talia sees David squinting at his computer screen. "Check your email."

Silence fills the mod pod for the first time that day as they all turn to their screens, Talia included. A message from Cuff's COO,

Betty Jeong, has just appeared in her inbox with the subject line "Team Update." Before Talia can even open the message, Galina spoils the punch line:

"Wow. She's been fired. Meera actually got fired."

Shit. Talia's mind immediately goes to Gracie. Without a job, how is Meera supposed to support a seven-year-old who plays a new sport every season? Talia may not be responsible for Meera's actions, but she feels guilty all the same—especially now that a child's livelihood is at stake. She has to say something. Even if Meera blows her off again, Talia wants to at least say she tried.

That's how she finds herself outside Meera's Tarrytown condo after work, a place she's visited dozens of times but where she now feels unwelcome, like a door-to-door salesman or a home invader. The windows are dark, and when Talia knocks, she's surprised (as well as a little relieved) to find that Meera isn't home.

She's tempted to leave, sparing herself any awkwardness rather than waiting for Meera to return, but then she remembers: A spare key that Meera gave her ages ago is still in her work bag. Perhaps it's wrong to use it without permission, especially following their big argument. But Talia just wants to leave a little gift, to let Meera know that she's thinking of her, even if they aren't on good terms. She doesn't see the harm in popping in for a minute. After this, Talia has one more errand to run, and then she can return home to her fiancé.

Fiancé. As she steps into Meera's empty condo, Talia grins to herself. She could get used to saying that.

Chapter Twenty-Seven

Meera

It's official: She's fired.

Just a few weeks ago, her ex suggested that Meera was too good for Cuff, that she should quit and move on to bigger and better things—and though she didn't admit it, she agreed with Hari. And now she's been terminated without pay. It's humbling, really. Humbling and maddening.

What's worse is that Meera felt hopeful when she was called into the Cuff office yesterday for an early-morning meeting. Just over a week had passed since her initial suspension, which (according to her boss, Betty) was due to the company's belief that Meera was misusing her access to privileged data. Per the COO, Meera would be put on leave until a full investigation had been conducted—and apparently they'd come to a decision.

Unfortunately, from the moment Betty opened her office door, Meera could tell her news wasn't good. The pink-haired executive wasn't much of a smiler to begin with, but her expression was particularly dour as she ushered Meera into her office, located right across from the ML-team mod pod. Before stepping inside, Meera took one last look, just to confirm it: The office was still empty. She wouldn't have to face Talia, at least not that morning.

After exchanging a few obligatory pleasantries (Betty even had the gall to ask Meera "How have you been feeling?" as though she cared), she finally dropped the bomb: "We're going to have to let you go, Meera."

The words didn't click right away. "You mean . . . permanently?"

"I'm afraid so," Betty said, not looking the least bit afraid. But perhaps she should have been. As the COO droned on about the terms of her dismissal ("You will not be eligible for unemployment insurance. You will not receive severance pay. Your health benefits will end immediately."), Meera could feel anger rising like steam inside her, starting in her chest and radiating through her skull. Her teeth clenched. Her hands shook. It wasn't fair; she didn't deserve any of this. And she was ready to make someone fucking pay.

When Betty handed Meera her parting gift—a stack of termination paperwork outlining the findings from the security audit—Meera was too pissed to give it much more than a glance before shoving it into her work bag, almost instantly forgotten.

That night, she stopped by Hari's place to fill him in. She cried, embarrassingly, because even though she was—as Hari had pointed out—probably too smart for the job, it was a job nevertheless, and now she had nothing. Too young to understand why her mom was so upset, Gracie simply sat beside her on the couch and stroked her hair, a gesture so pure and sweet it only served to make Meera cry harder. She was a good girl, the best girl. Meera would do anything to get her back.

When Hari stepped into the kitchen to check on dinner, Gracie put her mouth to her mother's ear. "I love Daddy," she whispered, "but I want to come home with you."

"I want you to come home with me too," Meera told her.

"So can I?"

"Soon," promised Meera. "Not yet, but really, really soon."

It wasn't until Gracie was put to bed that Hari finally confronted her, as Meera knew he would. "Is your friend Talia the reason you were fired?" he asked.

Meera had expected her ex to have questions, but she hadn't expected this. "Why would you say that?"

"When you first brought Gracie here, you said you were in trouble at work, and it had something to do with Talia. Now you're out of a job while she—I assume—is still employed." Hari threw his arms out. "Explain that to me."

"I wish I could, but it's complicated," she said. "All I can tell you is that it's not Talia's fault."

And it's true: It was Meera's idea to peek into the company database. It was Meera who took the risk. It was Meera who probably would have lost her job long ago had it not been for Talia, who covered for her those times she was too sick to work. But what she didn't tell Hari is that—irrationally or not—she's livid with her former friend.

And of course, none of this would be happening if it wasn't for Townsend fucking Fuller.

It was just over two years ago—not long after her divorce from Hari was finalized—that Meera decided to take that entrepreneurship summer intensive through the UT Austin McCombs School of Business. With many of her weekends now free, she needed ways to fill her time that didn't involve moping and drinking. Plus, as Hari always reminded her, she *did* have an entrepreneurial spirit. And when a tall, handsome man chose the seat next to hers on the first day of class, it felt like a sign: Her life wasn't over. She could still have a second act.

"Is it just me," the man said to her, "or do you feel like you missed a memo about this intensive only being for undergrads?"

Meera looked around the room, noticing for the first time just how young the class skewed. She decided not to let it bother her. "Are you worried they're going to kick you out?"

"No, I was just relieved to see you and know that I'm not the only thirtysomething . . ." He trailed off, catching himself.

"How do you know I'm not an undergrad too?"

Confusion crossed his face. "I mean, I don't mean to assume—"

"Relax." Meera swatted his arm. "You assumed correctly, and you're in good company. If we lay low, I bet no one will find us out."

His features relaxed again. "I'm Townsend, by the way."

"Meera." She extended her hand, and they shook. "I'm here because I just got divorced and am apparently having an early midlife crisis. What brings you here?"

Seemingly taken aback by her bluntness, Townsend spat out, "I'm here because I want to do something on my own for once after a lifetime of having everything handed to me."

He was rich. This intrigued Meera, but it also affirmed what she'd already expected: Men like him were very much not her type. Still, he was handsome and—as he'd correctly pointed out—they did seem to have a good decade on everyone else in the room. So she asked, "Do you want to grab lunch later?"

"Sure," he said.

Over the course of the next eight weeks, Meera and Townsend developed a strange, tenuous bond, the kind she used to form at summer camp when she knew the stakes were low and the time was limited, so why not put everything out there? Chances were that she and Townsend would never make an effort to meet up again after the intensive ended, and that was perfectly fine with her. In fact, it became preferable around the fifth week of the program, when they started sleeping together.

The first time was fueled by booze, as—in Meera's experience—these things often are. The program hosted a happy hour with several kegs and nothing to eat aside from a single plate of cheese and crackers, and afterward, Meera suggested that she and Townsend keep the party going. She wouldn't have admitted it at the time, but she knew what she was doing: She was newly single, and she wanted to feel good. They went to a nearby dive bar, tossed down a few more drinks, and then took an Uber back to his place, where they spent the whole ride kissing.

Though she'd prepared herself for the possibility of it being a one-time thing, Townsend made it clear he was down for a repeat performance—and even while sober too. A few nights a week, after Gracie was tucked into bed, Townsend would visit her Tarrytown condo, and they'd hook up, all without rules, or expectations, or (ugh) *feelings*. Sometimes she feared he was just doing it for the novelty, especially when he would make comments like "I can only imagine introducing you to my mom. She would absolutely shit herself." But she knew who she was: a divorcée living in a cramped condo with her kid. And she knew he—a ne'er-do-well born with a silver spoon in his mouth—wasn't her type either. What should it matter if she wasn't his?

This relationship (if you could even call it that) had an expiration date from the very beginning, as well as a clear objective: to fuck and to forget.

After the sex, they would chat—just as she and Hari used to do back in grad school—about their future aspirations and what they hoped to create. She described to him the platform offering holistic autoimmune care that she hoped to design (though she didn't tell him about her recent doctor's appointment, where the word *hypothyroidism* had been used for the first time). He told her that he had a knack for marketing and sales but just couldn't find a strong vision—and she actually consoled him, saying, "The right idea will come to you when it's supposed to. I know it." If only she knew then what she knows now. Perhaps she wouldn't have been such a fucking fool.

As she predicted, they didn't talk much after the summer intensive ended, and then not at all. Just about a year later, she saw him post about his holistic health care start-up, AutoInTune, on LinkedIn. Not long after that, Talia was twirling around Meera's kitchen, gushing about how she'd met the man of her dreams on Cuff. By the time Meera found out that man was Townsend, it was too late to say anything.

She could forget that they'd slept together—but stealing her idea? That was something she just couldn't forgive.

Lying prone in bed now, attempting to read *Meat Cute* (that Kennedy J. Abbott book she borrowed from Talia's place), Meera feels strangely grateful—at least in this moment—that Gracie is at her father's. She would hate for her daughter to see her like this, still in bed at noon with muscle aches and brain fog. It's impossible to say whether she's depressed, or experiencing a Hashimoto's flare-up, or a combination of both. All she knows is that she's never felt more resentful, and she can think of little else besides Talia and Townsend, who are seemingly conspiring to ruin her.

She wonders: *Is there any chance Townsend sought Talia out on purpose?* Maybe he somehow put together that she and Talia were friends—*best* friends at that—and thought *Now this will* really *piss Meera off.* But what did she ever do to him, aside from befriend him, and sleep with him, and unwittingly hand him the idea he needed for his stupid start-up?

Perhaps it was the other way around. Perhaps Talia learned of their summer fling and pursued Townsend, effectively avenging some crime Meera hadn't even known she'd committed. This doesn't make any sense to Meera, either, but what's the alternative? Could this really all just be some cosmic coincidence, yet another *fuck you* from the universe?

Since her diagnosis, Meera has spent more time than she probably should researching Hashimoto's disease, so she knows the effect it can have on brain function. Her doctor has never mentioned Hashimoto's encephalopathy by name, but he has expressed concern about her recent episodes of memory loss and confusion—and after she told him about the threats from Amanda (he wanted to know if she was experiencing any undue stress), he even suggested that she may be suffering from hallucinations.

"I'm not crazy," she told him. "What's happening to me is real. These threats from Amanda are real."

He replied, "I don't doubt that," but in a way that made Meera believe he did, in fact, doubt it.

Above her, the ceiling fan spins dizzily. *Maybe I am losing it,* she thinks. *Maybe I'm losing everything.* She's already lost her job; it's probably only a matter of time before she loses her kid and then her mind. But she can't lie here having a one-woman pity party forever.

Plus, this book is beyond stupid. A butcher's daughter falling in love with a vegan? She could possibly get on board if it weren't for the thinly veiled pro-life subplot with the sister who gets knocked up at sixteen and decides to keep the baby, thanks to some sweet-talking nuns.

In the kitchen, Meera puts on a pot of coffee and leans back against her counter. That's when she sees it: a basket sitting on her table, which hadn't been there when she left for Hari's the night before. Did someone drop it off while she was out? A note is folded beside it, and Meera picks it up with shaky hands.

Sorry to let myself in, but you weren't here when I stopped by, it reads. *Thinking about you and hope you're doing okay.* It isn't signed, but Meera would recognize Talia's loopy scrawl anywhere.

Normally, she'd be touched by a surprise like this. The basket is filled with all her favorite things: a bag of beans from Summer Moon Coffee, a six-pack of chocolate chip cookies from Teddy V., an expensive-looking bottle of Cabernet Sauvignon. But instead of appreciative, Meera feels violated and almost violently angry. She lost her job, and Talia thought she could make up for it with cookies? Un-fucking-believable.

Fortunately, before she left last night, Hari sent Meera off with a much better gift.

"I looked into the documents provided by AutoInTune like you asked," he told her.

"And? Did you see anything that looked off?"

"I'm an engineer, Meera, not a data analyst. I have no idea what I was looking at." Hari paused. "But I can tell you something."

"What?"

"Today I was asked to work on a test marketing campaign, which Sage plans to send to AutoInTune's customers via email ahead of the official partnership announcement."

"And?" Meera wasn't seeing the point.

"And if only a fraction of those marketing emails is actually opened, then Sage might start to question whether the list of users provided by AutoInTune is legitimate."

So delighted was she by this news that Meera kissed Hari right on the lips for the first time in years, taking them both by surprise.

"What was that for?" he asked.

"For giving me hope," she answered.

Enough moping, enough hesitating. Pouring herself a scalding-hot cup of coffee, Meera makes a decision.

It's time for her to get what she's owed.

Chapter Twenty-Eight

Kaitlyn

By the time the phone call comes, Kaitlyn had nearly forgotten she requested it.

But still, when she sees the unknown number pop up on her phone, she answers it. She has no leads on where Amanda may be, no hope of her sister contacting her, and no faith that—when and if she does turn up—she'll even be the least bit sorry. She has nothing to lose aside from a minute of her time, and her time doesn't feel all that valuable these days anyway.

"It's Roger," says the voice on the other end of the phone.

"I'm sorry, who?"

"Your sister's landlord."

"Roger, hi." Kaitlyn feels confident he never mentioned his name before, even when she handed over her number. Her phone screen feels suddenly clammy against her cheek. "Is everything all right?"

"Sure. I just wanted to let you know that lady came by again today."

"The lady . . . ?"

"The one who's been paying your sister's rent. She brought me cash today to cover the month of August."

Kaitlyn lets out an involuntary little gasp. "Did you get a picture?"

"She was in and out. I didn't get the chance. Sorry."

Her heart sinks. "Did you at least get a better look at her? See any noticeable features?"

"I can do you one better. I have her on video."

Once again, her heart pounds madly; this back-and-forth can't be great for Kaitlyn's cardiovascular health. "How?"

"I recently installed a security camera in the lobby. The police have been sniffing around, and it's making residents uneasy. They think something shady went down that I'm not telling them."

"Why have the police been around? How recently?"

Roger's voice becomes defiant. "Listen, this shit has got nothing to do with me. I run a clean, respectable property. I'm not in the business of getting into people's business, you know what I'm saying? But it's got nothing to do with me."

Kaitlyn needs to de-escalate the situation or risk losing his help. "I didn't mean any offense. I imagine this has been a stressful time for you."

Roger grunts.

"If you're willing, I'd love to come by and watch any security footage you might have caught of the woman who drops off the rent. Whenever you're free, of course."

A beat passes. Finally, Roger says, "I have some shit to do today, but I'll be around tomorrow. Come by then."

"I will. Thank you."

Another grunt is offered in lieu of a goodbye, and then the call ends.

Kaitlyn sets her phone down and is looking around her small, stale, suffocating apartment—wondering how she's going to possibly keep herself sane until tomorrow—when the phone rings. Once again, it's an unknown number, and once again, she answers it.

"Is this Ms. Reade?" The voice on the other end this time is stern, authoritative.

"Speaking."

"Ms. Reade, this is the Austin Police Department."

"Oh." A dozen thoughts race through her head: Townsend reported her. Talia reported her. The police think she's a stalker. The police want to know why she requested her parents' accident report. They found Amanda, and she's alive. They found Amanda, and she's dead.

"We're going to need you to come down to the station."

"Now?"

"If you're able."

It's a Friday, and though Kaitlyn is technically working remotely today, her calendar is clear; the day stretches ahead of her without motive or agenda. Whether it's good news or bad that awaits her, it's almost a relief either way, just having something to do with herself.

"I'll be there as soon as possible," she says.

"We don't know how to tell you this," Detective Burrows says. He sits across a table from Kaitlyn in a drab office, with Detective Harris—the other officer Kaitlyn spoke to in June, back when she first reported her sister's disappearance—at his side.

"Okay." Kaitlyn remembers hearing these same words when she received a phone call two and a half years earlier, informing her that her parents were dead.

"It's seeming more and more likely that your sister, Amanda, is not missing, as we'd initially believed. Now that it's been nearly five months without contact, we've begun exploring the possibility that she is deceased." Burrows pauses and then, almost seeming to mean it, he adds, "I'm sorry."

Kaitlyn shakes her head. "That can't be right. I spoke to her ex-boyfriend, Townsend Fuller. He said he's been in contact with Amanda." She reminds herself not to reveal *too* much; she doesn't want to incriminate her sister if she's been sending Townsend threatening messages, as he claimed.

"He shared those messages with us," Harris says, "and we have reason to believe Amanda wasn't the one who wrote them."

"You think someone was"—Kaitlyn grapples for the right word—"I don't know, posing as her?"

Burrows nods solemnly. "We do. And we think the same person may have hurt her."

"Who would do that?"

The detectives exchange a look. "The investigation is ongoing, so we aren't able to discuss names just yet," Harris says. "But we wanted to do you the courtesy of letting you know that this missing person case is now being investigated as a potential homicide."

Kaitlyn's thoughts feel slow, sludgy. "You're not looking for my sister anymore. You're looking for her body."

"I'm afraid so," says Harris. And then, echoing her partner's words from earlier: "I'm sorry."

For months, Kaitlyn hoped against hope that her sister—her feckless, freewheeling, free-spirited sister—was still out there. Getting by on cash and car rides and getting off on ignoring Kaitlyn's messages. But somehow, this news doesn't feel like a surprise to her. It feels like confirmation of something she already knew to be true but wasn't ready to accept.

Kaitlyn thinks of the words her therapy chatbot had her repeat during one of their first sessions together: "Everyone will leave me. Everyone will leave me. Everyone will leave me." The hope was that—upon hearing the phrase over and over—the words would lose meaning and her fear would seem irrational. Silly, even. But instead, Kaitlyn found that the exercise just imbued the words with power, made her dread feel less like generalized anxiety and more like an active threat. And now that horrible prophecy had come true yet again. *Everyone always leaves her.*

The tears will come later, she knows that. Right now, it's anger she feels. Anger that makes her want to hurt someone else the way she's hurting.

"Amanda's landlord called me," she tells the officers. "A woman has been paying her rent. She delivers cash once a month. According to the landlord, she claimed to work with my sister."

This intrigues them. "Could he describe her?" Burrows asks.

"Not really. But . . ." Kaitlyn hesitates. Even though she knows it will only benefit her to offer up any information she has, she's tempted to keep this last piece to herself. How satisfying it would be to watch the footage, identify that woman, hunt her down, avenge her sister.

"But what?"

She knows how to shoot a gun. She knows how to do it without leaving a mess too.

"Can you tell us the landlord's name?"

Her anger has shifted, becoming something she doesn't recognize and turning her into someone unrecognizable too. She thinks, *You know what? Fuck these police officers.* Kaitlyn doesn't want to be a team player; she wants revenge, which means seeing that footage before the detectives can. "Roger something. I'm not sure."

"Okay. Could you share his number at least?"

"I don't have it."

"You said he called you."

"The number was blocked." Kaitlyn stands. "Look, I need to go. I need to get out of here."

"Wait." Harris holds out a hand. "Please, just another minute."

Kaitlyn sinks cautiously back into her chair as Harris produces a photo from the folder in her hand.

"Do you know her?"

Leaning forward, she studies the photo, a corporate headshot showing a dark-haired woman in a navy blue suit. She looks familiar—broad shoulders, small hoop nose ring, thick brows, possibly Indian—but Kaitlyn can't quite place her. Didn't Roger mention that the woman paying her sister's rent had dark hair? Maybe this is her. But who is she? "No. Sorry."

Harris tucks the photo back into her folder. "If you come across any useful information, you'll call us, yes?"

"Sure," Kaitlyn says, not yet convinced that she means it.

Walking out of the police station, Kaitlyn feels as though the ground is shifting and tilting beneath her. She needs to get to Roger to watch the footage. No, she needs to tell the police the truth. No, she needs to plan a funeral, because her sister is dead. Oh, God, her sister is dead. Her sister is dead.

Her arms tingle with restless energy; maybe a trip to the shooting range will help her focus. She always feels calmer after firing off a few rounds—not to mention that it'll give her a chance to decide what to do next. Her brain on autopilot, Kaitlyn makes the twenty-minute drive to the Range at Austin. Once there, she pops open the trunk to retrieve her SIG Sauer P320, which she always keeps handy in its black leather-trimmed hard-shell case. Except . . .

This can't be. Kaitlyn shifts around the tangle of jumper cables and spare indicator bulbs and reusable shopping bags—carefully at first, and then with an urgency bordering on frantic. It's no use; the case is nowhere to be seen.

She may have a penchant for jumping to conclusions, but this time, Kaitlyn feels sure her gut is right: Someone has stolen her gun.

And the only person she ever told about that gun? Townsend Fuller.

Chapter Twenty-Nine

AMANDA

The first thing Amanda did after Townsend broke up with her was text her sister. There were a dozen things she wanted to say—*I'm sorry for how our brunch ended,* and *You were right about Townsend,* and *I could use a friend right now*—but she didn't say any of them. Some small, petty part of her was annoyed that Kaitlyn had been right, because Kaitlyn was always right. Instead, she merely wished her sister a happy birthday and promised herself that tomorrow, when she was feeling less resentful, she would fix things.

Instead, she woke up the next morning feeling more bitter than ever—not toward Kaitlyn, or even Townsend, but toward the person she allowed herself to become around Townsend. Someone who was whiny, needy, vulnerable. No more of that; her new life would begin today. Her first move: redownloading the Cuff app and changing her location to Paris, France, where she planned to begin her Euro trip. It made sense to scope out the dating scene ahead of time, she figured. Then she'd waste no time when she finally arrived.

However, when she attempted to shoot her shot with a twenty-two-year-old philosophy student at the Sorbonne (she thought she'd open with a simple "Voulez-vous coucher avec moi?"), an error code popped up on her screen. "Message not sent," it read. Because of course she would be cockblocked by technology, right when she was on the cusp of reclaiming herself.

A quick check of her outgoing messages confirmed that her latest missive had failed to send. But strangely enough, it seemed several other messages had been sent from her account over the past couple of days . . . even though she'd deleted the Cuff app from her phone. What was even more concerning was that they'd all been directed to Townsend. Head pounding, Amanda quickly scrolled through the messages, each one crazier than the last.

Your going to be so fxcking sorry, one message read, sent the same night she and Townsend split.

Sleep with one eye open motherfxcker, read another, supposedly sent the next day.

Yet another message, sent a few hours later: I'm gonna make you wish you never met me.

Amanda may have lost herself in her relationship with Townsend, but she knew this much to be true: No amount of tequila could have compelled her to fire off these insane threats.

Scrolling back further, she reread the messages exchanged before her breakup with Townsend, which had struck her as uncharacteristically sappy when she first saw them (likely sent in a stupid post-sex fog, she'd figured) but now seemed entirely foreign. I want to have five kids and I want them all to have your eyes? There was no way she would write that shit to a man, no matter how infatuated she was. Not even on ketamine. Not in a million years.

It became clear to her now what should have been obvious to her before: Someone was messing with her account.

On the app, Amanda navigated to the "Troubleshooting" tab and selected "Trouble with Messaging." When asked to describe her issue in detail, she wrote, Someone hacked my account and wrote a bunch of weird shit to fuck with my relationship. Then, thinking better of it, she pressed backspace until the words disappeared, and she rewrote her complaint: I believe someone has gotten access to my account because I'm seeing outgoing messages I didn't write myself. As Kaitlyn always reminded her, you catch more flies with honey than with vinegar.

After receiving the standard "thank you for your inquiry" autoreply, promising help from a member of Cuff's support staff within twenty-four hours, Amanda waited. No response ever came, so the next day, she submitted another complaint: Someone is sending messages from my account. Please advise.

Another twenty-four hours passed. Still no response.

After sending her third complaint (Someone has stolen my identity. Is this not a violation of Cuff's terms?), Amanda decided that honey was too sweet for her taste anyway. She scrolled through her camera roll until she found the picture she had in mind—a racy shot of herself taken with a self-timer in Townsend's room one day while he was in the shower—and posted it to Instagram along with the caption He's in your head but I'm in his bed. So what if she and Townsend were broken up? This would annoy the fuck out of whoever was messing with her account—and that was all that really mattered.

Plus, there were her followers, who were better than any man, or drug, or even designer bag. Watching those likes and comments pour in, Amanda flopped onto her couch and luxuriated in the familiar dopamine rush, that addictive tingle brought on by the soft pings of her phone and the steady stream of praise that accompanied it.

> Literal dream girl.
>
> Your body is unreal, my God.
>
> Just saying, whoever is sleeping next to you in that bed is the luckiest man alive.

The comments were so different from the ones she received on dating apps, where men—emboldened by the unspoken agreement that they were all looking for someone to fuck—felt welcome to thrust their tawdry fantasies upon her. That never happened here, in the safe space that was her comments section. Here, she was seen, *really* seen, by men and women alike, and loved for what she had to offer.

But as she watched comment after glowing comment appear under her photo, an eerie one materialized: You're not done paying for your actions. It was written by a user with the handle @geminibaby530—which wouldn't have caught her eye if not for the fact that geminibaby530 was her password for everything, from her Instagram to her Cuff account.

She clicked on the username, but it led nowhere; the profile associated with the handle had somehow already been deleted. Could this be the same person who'd sent those unhinged messages to Townsend on Cuff? The thought made her uneasy. After a moment of hesitation, Amanda deleted the comment as well. She didn't need this kind of negativity in her life, not when it was finally about to get good again.

For the rest of the day, Amanda tried to block it out of her mind: the breakup, the Cuff impostor, the creepy Instagram comment. Still, a sense of unease followed her, like an intruder lurking out of sight. It was almost a relief to go to work, where she'd be too busy to even sit down, much less think about herself. She put on the tight black T-shirt that always earned her extra tips, and by the time she got back from the cocktail club at two a.m.—tired, sticky, and slightly tipsy from taking shots with customers—the day's anxiety was already a distant memory.

Then she noticed the light on in her bathroom. She never left the light on in her bathroom.

Still standing in the doorframe of her apartment, Amanda tried to rationalize the situation. She'd been distracted all day. She'd gotten ready for work in a rush. It was entirely possible she forgot to hit the switch before heading out.

But then she heard a cough. And there was no denying it: A stranger had broken into her home.

Slowly, quietly, Amanda crept from the front door of the studio toward the bathroom. The door was slightly ajar, and she could see a pair of hands rifling through the medicine cabinet above her sink. Her heart hammered in her chest so violently, she was surprised her unexpected visitor couldn't hear it. But the intruder was too busy rattling her pill bottles and inspecting her toothbrush to notice she'd returned.

This was her chance. She could turn around, creep back out the door, and call the police without the trespasser being any the wiser.

Except that's the moment the intruder chose to close the medicine cabinet, revealing the mirror on the other side. And in its reflection, a pair of eyes landed on Amanda, caught halfway between the front door and the bathroom.

Then came a command, delivered by a shaky voice: "Don't move. We need to talk."

Chapter Thirty

Townsend

When Townsend hears the knock on his door Friday evening, he assumes it's Talia, hands too full to punch in the key code. But when he opens the door, her friend Meera Ratnam—a woman he has not seen or spoken to in over two years—is waiting on the other side.

"Hi," he says, too perplexed to say much else.

"May I come in?" Without waiting for permission, Meera slips past him into his condo.

"It's been a while." Townsend watches as Meera walks a slow circle around his living room. She only ever visited his place once or twice during their . . . whatever it was, but still, having her here feels like a violation of some sort, like a glitch in the matrix.

She nods without looking at him. "Two years."

"Is Talia okay?" Only two ties bind Townsend and Meera together, and he can't imagine that she's here about the one that doesn't involve his girlfriend.

"She's fine," Meera says, "other than . . . you know."

"Right." Even after years with no contact, so much unspoken information exists between them, all thanks to their shared connection. Not for the first time, Townsend wonders if Meera is bitter that he ended up with her friend—a total coincidence, but probably a tough pill to swallow nevertheless. As far as he knows, Meera has never mentioned their prior relationship to Talia, so perhaps she thinks of Townsend as little as he thinks of her. That's the beauty of summer flings: You fuck, and then you forget (unless, of course, someone makes the mistake of catching feelings).

"I'm not here about Talia." Meera flops down onto his sectional, making what sounds like a small groan of pain as she does so.

"Okay." He joins her on the couch, because continuing to stand feels silly.

"I'm here for a job."

"A job where?"

"A job with your company," she says, as though this were the most obvious thing in the world. Then she stares him down, daring him to choose his answer carefully.

Townsend wasn't sure what to expect from this visit when he let Meera into his home, but it certainly wasn't this. "Don't you work at Cuff with Talia?"

"Not anymore."

"What happened?"

"Cuff performed a security audit and accused me of misusing my access to privileged data." She pauses and then adds, without apology, "I used my credentials to look up your past conversations with Amanda. A few times, actually."

Talia has already told him as much, but Townsend still takes the opportunity to act indignant. He knows he probably won't have the upper hand for long—at least, not if this conversation goes the way he suspects it will. "That's a violation of my privacy."

"I know. That's why I was fired. And that's why I need you to hire me."

"But . . ." Is she really going to make him say it? "Why would you want to work for me, given our history?"

Meera blinks at him, her expression betraying nothing. "I need to have health insurance. I don't know if you know this, but I have an autoimmune disease. It's what inspired this idea I had for a holistic autoimmune-care platform. But I never could come up with a name for it." She waggles her finger at him, like he's a naughty schoolboy. "AutoInTune. A little gimmicky, but cute."

After two years of waiting for the other shoe to drop, it's almost a relief, having this accusation out in the open. Plus, Meera has nothing to back up her claims, save for a few private conversations shared beneath her sheets in the early hours of the morning. She has a flimsy anecdote; he has plausible deniability. "You're not seriously suggesting what I think you are, are you?"

"You built your start-up off of my idea, Townsend."

He summons a laugh. *Make her feel small,* he coaches himself. *Make her feel stupid.* "Actually, my start-up was inspired by my father's rheumatoid arthritis, which caused him to develop heart disease and die."

"I'm sorry for your loss," she says, the empty platitude sounding even more hollow than usual coming from her mouth. "But that doesn't change the fact that you stole your idea from me."

"Even if what you're saying were true, you can't prove anything."

"It is true, and I can prove you're a thief."

Thief. Why did that word feel so familiar? "As much as I'd love to have you join the team, we aren't hiring right now."

Meera raises an eyebrow. "You're not hiring? How big is your team?"

"I'm hiring to scale at the moment."

"Do you plan to expand your budget for new hires?"

"Eventually."

"I guess that should be expected," she says, "given that AutoInTune is currently hemorrhaging money." Then she shoots him a withering smile, as though to say *Gotcha.*

Except he isn't convinced that she has him beat. "My company's finances aren't a matter of public record, so you might want to check your sources."

"Well, you might want to check Reddit, because your company's finances are a hot topic."

Dammit. He needs someone to scrub that goddamn Reddit thread from the internet. "You work for a dating app. You of all people should know better than to believe everything you read online."

"I believe Orson Livingston, who commented on the thread and basically called you a sham. He's a VC at Silicon Hills, right? Where you tried to get more funding?"

Townsend's face must betray his surprise, because Meera grins again, encouraged.

"I talked to him a few days ago. I sent him a message, asking why he would call you out so publicly, considering you grew up together. He told me some story about a party you and your friends threw at his parents' house in high school. You fired a paintball gun at one of their neighbors and fucked up his eye. And you never got in trouble for it."

Townsend remembers that party, that neighbor, that horrible mistake. He's tried to put that night out of his head, but he still remembers. He was young and stupid. Remembering what he did is punishment enough.

"Orson said he's tired of watching assholes and liars win," Meera continues. "And I have to say that I agree with him."

"Who says I'm a liar?"

"Sage Clinic might, after they investigate those user metrics you provided for your company."

"How—?" Townsend hasn't told anyone except for his dad's buddy, Carter Bonier, about the due diligence request and what it may potentially uncover. Not even Talia. The only person who could possibly know . . . "Are you working with Amanda?"

The glint in Meera's eyes is positively gleeful now, almost crazed. "All this time you thought you should be scared of Amanda," she says, "but really, you should be afraid of me."

Is this really the same woman he met through that entrepreneurship intensive at UT Austin a couple summers earlier? The chill, self-deprecating divorcée with the wrinkled T-shirts and creaky bed frame? Townsend doesn't know what has happened in her life over the past two years, but something has changed her, turned her into someone nefarious. "What did Amanda tell you? Where is she?"

"Forget Amanda," says Meera. "I'm just taking back what is mine. You owe it to me."

Facing off from opposite ends of the couch, Townsend studies her, looking for the chink in her armor. There's no denying that she has more information than he would like—but would she ever actually do anything with it? He thinks of the complaints Talia has made in passing about her friend: lazy, flaky, apathetic. Not someone who would have the gumption to ruin his life, since she isn't even willing to fix her own. "Believe what you want," he says, "but the fact is that I don't owe you anything. Not as my girlfriend's friend, not as someone I used to hook up with, and not even as someone I simply pity."

Meera's face falls; clearly, this isn't the response she anticipated. "Talia deserves so much better than you."

"Right. Sure." Townsend is fired up now, spoiling for a fight. "Don't pretend you're such a great friend to Talia when you've been lying to her, keeping our past a secret all this time. Talia is a good person. She covered for your ass at work, and this is how you repay her? From now on, you fix your own problems. Don't expect me or Talia to bail you out."

With this, Meera stands, a bit wobbly on her feet, and suddenly it occurs to Townsend: the brick. Could Meera have tossed it through his car window? But she can barely get off the couch; it's hard to imagine her lobbing a brick with enough force to shatter a rear window. Once she's successfully gotten herself on steady ground, she turns to face him.

"You're an asshole," she says, "and you deserve all the shit that's coming your way."

"I welcome it," Townsend replies. He keeps his cool, but her words are ominous—is she talking about the collapse of his business? Amanda's continued harassment? Or something even worse?

They stare each other down for a moment, and Townsend knows the question on her mind, because he has the same question for her: *Are you going to tell Talia about this?*

But neither of them voices it, and eventually, Meera leaves.

Townsend tries him twice, but the private investigator that Carter hooked him up with doesn't answer his phone. It's a Friday night; the guy presumably has a life. Still, it's fucking annoying. This creep is getting a lot of money from Townsend to track Amanda down, and he needs to work faster. Clearly, Amanda is talking. Clearly, she needs Townsend to shut her up for good.

He's just poured himself a drink (yes, he's trying to cut back, but tonight, he needs one) when Talia calls. All he wants is an hour to himself, so he doesn't answer; maybe she'll assume he's working. But after a minute, she calls again. *Well, fuck,* he thinks. Meera probably went and told her everything. Time to face the music.

"Hey, babe," he answers. "Sorry I missed you the first time. What's up?"

Her tone sounds clipped, her words rushed—not because she's pissed, he quickly realizes, but because she's afraid. "Townsend? You there? Please, you need—"

Silence. "Tal? Need what?"

She doesn't respond. Instead, the phone beeps in his ear, signaling that the call has been dropped.

Within a few minutes, he's in his newly repaired BMW, speeding his way to Talia's place in SoCo.

During the fifteen-minute drive, a dozen different thoughts cross his mind: Amanda has broken in again and left another note. Or worse, Amanda has broken in to hold Talia hostage and currently has a gun trained on her face. He thinks he's exhausted every possible option—but nothing can prepare him for what he experiences when he turns down Talia's street: sirens. Flashing lights. Fire everywhere.

At first, he's too mesmerized by the flames—ten feet high, spitting and crackling like something alive—to think straight. Then he realizes those flames engulf Talia's home. A fire engine roars down the street behind him, and he pulls over to the side to jump out of his car, barely taking a few steps before collapsing to his knees.

Talia. Head spinning, he calls out her name, fumbles for his phone, tries to get to his feet—but before the panic can fully set in, she's running right into his arms. For a moment, they just sway in silence, shaking even as they attempt to hold each other steady.

Sobs rack her body. "Townsend," she cries. "My house. It's gone."

All he can do is repeat the same words of comfort, again and again: "You got out. You're okay. You're safe."

They both know the last part is a lie.

Chapter Thirty-One

Talia

Sitting in the police station, Talia feels numb.

Her home—the fruit of her labor—is gone, burned to a crisp before her eyes. All because some unstable bitch couldn't let Talia have something of her own.

Next to her, Townsend squeezes her hand, and she squeezes his back. He's already offered (multiple times, even) to let Talia live with him for as long as she needs, which she appreciates, but it isn't what she wants or needs to hear right now. Moving in together should be a momentous step, not a temporary fix. But at this point, she may not have a choice.

Talia closes her eyes and lets her head fall to her chest for a moment, but not a minute later, Townsend is shaking her shoulder. She sits up to find Detectives Harris and Burrows—the same detectives who visited Townsend's condo back in June to ask about Amanda—looking down at them.

"Ms. Danvers," says Harris, "I'm going to have you come with me. Mr. Fuller, you're going to go with Detective Burrows."

"Wait." Talia looks back and forth between the two of them. "Why can't you speak to us together?"

"We'd prefer to speak to you both separately."

"But . . ." For the second time that night, Talia feels like things are completely out of her control. "I'm not in a good place right now. I'd really like to stay with Townsend."

Harris gives a tight smile. "This won't take long."

Talia can tell from Harris's expression that she's not budging on this. Could they possibly still suspect Townsend of hurting Amanda? Doesn't her harassment campaign prove that she's alive and well? "Fine." She gives Townsend's hand another squeeze and then stands. "Where are we going?"

"Follow me."

Harris leads Talia down the hall to an interview room, complete with a bare table, two chairs, and what Talia imagines to be a one-way mirror, like they're on the set of a police procedural drama. The detective settles into one chair and gestures for Talia to take the other.

"Can I get you anything? Coffee? Tea? Water?"

"I'm fine. Thank you."

Harris shrugs in a way that seems to say *Suit yourself.* "Listen, Ms. Danvers. I know you've been through a traumatic experience tonight, and I don't want to take up too much of your time. For that reason, I'm going to get right to the point."

Her heart beats wildly. *Please, please don't say you suspect Townsend of doing anything wrong,* she thinks.

"How well do you know Meera Ratnam?"

This isn't at all what Talia expected to hear. "Meera? We've worked together for over three years."

"Would you consider her a friend?"

"I'd consider her my best friend."

"Okay." Harris takes a deep breath. "You're probably not going to want to hear this, but we think Meera might be responsible for what happened tonight."

If her home were not a pile of ash and charred wood right now, Talia might have laughed. "You think she set my house on fire?"

"We suspect that she's responsible for a lot more than that, actually. All those threatening text messages and emails? The slashed tires on your car? The note in your bathroom? The brick through Townsend's window? We believe Meera may be the architect behind all of that."

"The dead bat in my office desk drawer?"

"I'm sorry?"

"Never mind." In her distress, Talia may have forgotten to report that one. She shakes her head, then leans forward, cradling her skull in her hands. "This doesn't make any sense," she murmurs to the floor. Then, looking up at Harris, she says, "Amanda Reade. *She* was the one who—"

"We're not convinced that Amanda Reade is still alive."

"What?" Talia's heart climbs into her throat.

"We think Meera may be responsible for killing her."

Talia opens her mouth, but no words come out. She tries again, and a single word escapes: "Why?"

Feeling more numb than ever, Talia listens as Detective Harris walks her through the chain of events that led them to this conclusion. It isn't a surprise when she's told that Meera crossed paths with Townsend years before Talia met him herself—she knew this much, at least—but when Harris mentions a summer romance, her jaw drops open in shock.

"There's no way Meera and Townsend ever hooked up. She would have told me. *He* would have told me. Plus, she hates him."

"Well, it sounds like things didn't end well between them," Harris says, "which is probably the reason *why* she hates him. And why she's been obsessed with him all this time."

Talia's temples throb. "I think I will take that water, actually."

After Harris sticks her head into the hallway to request a bottle of water, she joins Talia back at the table, where she continues to outline her evidence. The IP address from some of the threatening emails matches Meera's work laptop, she explains. And during their search of Meera's house, they found a black-and-white modeling shot of a topless Amanda—the eyes gouged out with a knife—hidden under Meera's bed. Their theory: Meera killed Amanda in a crime of passion and used her as a scapegoat during her campaign of harassment, all in the hopes of getting Talia to break up with Townsend.

"This is ridiculous." Talia squeezes the plastic bottle in her hand so hard that it folds in half with a loud crunch. "Meera isn't capable of any of this. She's my best friend. She can't be a killer."

"Obsession can drive a person to do things they'd never imagined themselves capable of," says Harris. "Especially if they believe they've been wronged."

"But . . . how could she have been posing as a stalker all this time? And why would she pretend that Amanda was still alive?"

"To cover her tracks." Harris gives a wry half smile. "You can't be accused of murder if no one knows the victim is dead."

A tingle races down Talia's spine. Looking back, it's shocking how her best friend so perfectly fits the role of suspect. "The texts, the emails, the tires, the sticky note, the dead bat—almost every time I found some new threat, Meera was right there next to me," she says. Thinking out loud helps; Talia can see the puzzle pieces sliding into place, creating an image she doesn't like but that at least makes sense. "And those photos Meera received of Gracie playing in the park? Those could have easily been faked." She pauses, almost afraid to ask her next question: "What's going to happen to her?"

"Well." Harris interlaces her fingers. "Until we can find a body, we don't have enough evidence to make an arrest."

"So Meera is just running free right now?"

"We sent officers by her house an hour ago. She isn't there, and her ex-husband and daughter haven't seen her either. We think she may be hiding."

"Oh, my God." Talia buries her face in her hands again.

"We just need you to lay low. We'll continue our search, and we'll be checking in on you along the way. You and Townsend both."

Talia perks up a bit at the sound of his name. "Can I see him now? Townsend?"

"I can check to see if Detective Burrows is finished speaking with him." Harris stands. "You stay safe, okay?"

As unsettled as she feels, Talia knows this: She'll always feel so safe, so long as Townsend is by her side.

Later that night, they sit on Townsend's living room couch, both still shaken from their visit to the police station. But while Talia is eager to talk, to act—it's been Meera all along! They need to get away from her!—her fiancé seems reluctant to even meet her eye.

"Are we really just going to stay here?" Talia finally asks. "Like sitting ducks?"

"We haven't slept," he says. "Before we do anything, I think we need to get some sleep."

Talia stares at him, incredulous. "How are we supposed to sleep right now?"

"Because we're safe here."

"But Meera knows where you live."

"Yes, but we spoke to security, and they're not letting her past that front desk. We've locked the door. We've set the alarm. We're safe here."

Her eyes well up. Before she can stop them, the tears begin to spill. "I thought I was safe in my house too," she says. "But now it's gone. Now I don't feel safe anywhere."

Townsend takes her hand. "We're safe here," he repeats. "You're safe here. I wouldn't lie to you."

"You wouldn't lie to me?"

"Not on purpose."

She doesn't want to pick a fight, not now. But she needs to ask: "Then why did you never tell me that you and Meera dated?"

"Because we didn't. We hooked up a few times more than two years ago. I didn't think it was worth mentioning, because it literally meant nothing."

"It meant enough for Meera to burn my house down over it."

Townsend sighs, almost sounding annoyed. "She didn't send those messages and make those threats and do all that shit she did because we dated. She did it because she's a fucking insane person, okay? Had I known that, I never would have hooked up with her, just as you wouldn't have spent the last three years being friends with her."

He's tired, she tells herself. *It's been a long day. He's not angry with you. He loves you.* "You're right," she says after a moment. "I know you're right. I just feel so . . . betrayed."

"I know you do. I do too. Now please"—Townsend slips off the couch, tightening his grip on her hand—"can we get some sleep?"

She doesn't budge. "What if we just leave? We could throw some stuff in a bag, take my car, and just drive. Townsend, please." She can feel herself getting worked up, basically asking him to run away together like two reckless teenagers.

"Shhh." Townsend rubs her arm with his other hand, but the gesture feels forced to Talia. "The police are working on locating a body. Once they find Amanda, they'll be able to get Meera, and then we'll be free of this nightmare. Until then, we should do as we're told and stay here."

"Fine." Giving in, Talia follows him to the bedroom. She needs him to believe that she trusts him—and she *does* trust him. She just wishes he'd agree to pack a bag and run away with her, to some place where they could get a fresh start. A place where the ghosts won't be able to follow them.

Chapter Thirty-Two

Townsend

Next to Townsend in bed, Talia snores softly. *Lucky her,* he thinks. He's so tired he can feel the blood pumping behind his eyeballs, but sleep just won't come. Instead, he lies awake, watching out the window as the sun starts to rise over Downtown Austin. It's Saturday, Townsend realizes numbly. It's a new day. His company's fraudulent data is possibly moments away from being exposed, his ex is likely dead, and the police haven't caught the psycho who's threatening both him and his fiancée—but it's a new day, and Talia looks so beautiful, her sleeping form illuminated by the glow of the rising sun.

A few hours have passed since he and Talia left the police station, and Townsend still can't wrap his head around everything he's learned. Amanda, possibly dead this whole time, while someone else has been posing as her just to harass him—it's insane.

After Talia went off with Harris at the station, Townsend followed Burrows to a separate room, where the detective didn't waste any time dropping his bombshell. Apparently, Amanda wasn't Townsend's stalker after all . . . and she may not even be alive. Regret washed over him when he heard this—not for having broken up with Amanda but for having vilified her for so long. It was certainly tragic to see a beautiful young woman gone too soon (as damaged and self-destructive as she may have been). However, he wasn't in the right headspace to mourn—not yet. He was too distracted by his pent-up resentment, which now needed a new target.

"If Amanda wasn't behind all those messages and threats," he asked Burrows, "then who was?"

"Well." Burrows cleared his throat. "We have reason to believe it could be Talia's coworker, Meera Ratnam."

Once again, Townsend felt his stomach drop. "Meera? Are you sure?" Meera, his fiancée's best friend, who just that night was in his home, alone with him. She could have done anything she wanted to him, and yet, all she did was leave him with a threat: *You deserve all the shit that's coming your way.* Was it possible she then tried to burn Talia's house to the ground while she was inside it? She had proved herself savvier than Townsend had realized, sure . . . but could she really be that unhinged?

Burrows gave him a curious look. "You don't seem convinced."

"It's just . . ." Townsend thought back to Meera's unexpected visit to his condo, to those grunts of pain she'd made as she got on and off his sofa. "She has Hashimoto's disease, right? From what I understand, it makes her pretty weak. Talia told me she always struggles in their Pilates classes. I just have a hard time picturing her breaking into a house, or throwing a brick through a window, or committing arson and fleeing the scene before she's caught."

"Valid point." Burrows didn't seem particularly surprised by this argument. Really, he didn't have much of a reaction at all.

"Plus, she has a kid." The more Townsend thought about it, the more doubt crept in. "She has this seven-year-old daughter who is her whole world."

"Mothers can't be criminals?"

"I just don't see her doing anything that would endanger her kid, you know?"

"Right. Well, we are exploring other theories," said Burrows.

"What other theories?" Townsend asked warily.

Burrows ignored Townsend's question and asked one of his own. "Has Talia ever mentioned feeling threatened by anyone? Possibly someone from her past?"

Townsend hesitated; it didn't feel wise to mention this, but if it meant tracking down the possible killer after him and Talia, then it was worth it. "This is going to sound a little crazy."

"Try me."

"You have to understand that my mom is . . . kind of nuts. She thinks she's being protective but"—Townsend shook his head—"I don't know anyone else whose parent would hire a private investigator to spy on their girlfriend."

Burrows raised his brows. "Your mother had Talia followed?"

"Like I said, she's nuts, and I told her to fire the guy. Luckily, Talia has no idea that my mom was having her tailed, though she *did* know a PI was following her. And she told me . . ." Again, Townsend paused.

"What did she tell you?"

Whatever. He was just going to say it. Maybe it could help. "She thought the PI was hired by her ex-boyfriend's parents."

"Why would she think that?"

"I don't know. I guess things didn't end well between them." Townsend hadn't really asked questions; he was just relieved Talia didn't suspect his mother.

But now, lying restless beside his snoring fiancée, Townsend wonders why he hadn't asked for the full story about Talia's ex. Maybe it's because he doesn't really care what happened in Talia's life before him, instead choosing to focus on the new life that they're building together.

Or maybe he's afraid of what he'll find out.

He's about to close his eyes, to make one last attempt at sleep before getting up for the day, when he hears it: a muffled thumping that he can't place.

No, wait, he knows what that sound is—it's a fist bashing against his door.

"Oh, my God." Talia shoots up next to him, her hand clutching her chest. "Is that her?"

"She can't get in." Townsend tries to sound calm, even as his palms go slick with sweat. "I'll call the front desk. They'll take care of her."

"She already got past them. What are they going to do?"

The banging subsides, and Townsend allows himself to exhale. However, just as quickly, the rhythmic pounding of Meera's fist is replaced with a series of high-pitched beeps.

Talia gasps. "Does she know the key code?"

If Meera *did* know his key code, she certainly hadn't learned it from him. "She didn't use it when she came over earlier."

"She was here earlier?"

Townsend ignores this question. "Call 911," he tells her. "And stay here." Throwing the blankets off himself, he hurtles to the front door.

He arrives just in time to see Meera burst in. And she looks angry enough to kill.

Chapter Thirty-Three

Meera

It's four in the morning. Best case scenario, Townsend is fast asleep—and, ideally, alone.

Meera sneaks past the front desk and knocks loudly enough on his door to wake him. No answer. With a hesitant finger, she touches the keypad on his door, and it lights up like magic, illuminating the dark hallway. Then she remembers something Talia told her nearly a year ago, when she and Townsend were first starting to get serious: *He changed the key code on his door to my birthday. Isn't that sweet?*

She holds her breath as she enters the code—1-1-0-5—and lo and behold, the keypad chirps and blinks green. It worked. Now she can get inside, wake Townsend, and finally—

"Meera, please." Already standing just a few feet behind the front door is Townsend, hands held up in surrender. "Don't do anything stupid. Let's just talk, okay?"

He seems apprehensive. Afraid—of *her*, she realizes. As though Meera is some wild animal escaped from her cage.

"Is Talia here?"

"No. She's at home."

Meera almost laughs as she watches Townsend shift from foot to foot. He's always been a shitty liar. "I would believe you," she says, "but I just drove by her house. It was burned to the ground."

Townsend's brow furrows. "I don't know what the fuck kind of game you're playing," he says, "but Talia isn't here, and you need to leave."

"I'm not here to play games." Why is he looking at her like that, like she's a criminal? She's only doing what she needs to do. "I'm here to warn you. I . . ." There's no easy way to tell him this, to make him understand what she finally realized herself. "You're sure Talia isn't here?"

"For the last time, yes."

"Okay." Meera steels herself with a deep breath. "Then you should know that your girlfriend isn't who she seems."

"Fiancée," Townsend corrects. "And what the fuck is that supposed to mean?"

"All that awful stuff about her past? She made it up, Townsend."

Meera's suspicions first began the other day, reading that stupid romance book of Talia's. Her eyes nearly glazed over until they snagged on a familiar name: Neveah's Oasis. The home for unwed mothers where the protagonist's sister went to give birth. The same place where Talia claimed her own sister had been sent. Maybe it was a coincidence? Meera googled it. Outside the world of *Meat Cute* by Kennedy J. Abbott, it seemed Neveah's Oasis did not exist.

Bewildered, she leafed back through the opening chapters, reminding herself of the plot details she'd failed to absorb the first time through. It was all there. The pious butcher father, the hard-drinking mother, the wayward sister sent away after getting knocked up . . .

At the time, Meera had just felt vaguely uneasy. Why would Talia invent a personal history, stolen from the pages of a fiction book? Perhaps her childhood had been so uneventful, so conventional, that she'd felt the need to borrow tragedy. To give herself a sense of intrigue. That Meera couldn't condone, but she could at least understand.

But then she returned from Townsend's last night to find a box of her personal effects from the Cuff office outside her door. In it, a note from Aarav: *Don't trust your friend.*

"Neveah's Oasis, where Talia's sister was supposedly sent? It's a made-up place," Meera explains desperately. "For all I know, Talia doesn't even have a sister."

"Who would ever lie about that?"

It isn't Townsend who asks this, but Talia, and at the sound of her voice, Meera jumps. She whirls around to find Talia standing in the bedroom doorframe, wearing a Penn crewneck and what looks like a pair of Townsend's boxers.

Townsend lets out a low snarl. "Tal, I told you to stay in my room. And why do you have my paintball gun?"

That's when Meera sees it: the metallic object clutched in Talia's right hand. But that isn't a paintball gun. That's a real fucking gun.

Chapter Thirty-Four

Townsend

"Fuck, Tal. Where did you get that?"

Talia ignores Townsend's question, still keeping her gun trained on Meera. "The police are on their way," she warns. "You're not going to get away with this."

Slowly, Meera raises her hands. "I'm not here to hurt you—either of you." Despite the fact that she literally just broke into his home (and despite what the police laid out for him just hours before), Townsend has to admit that she seems like she's telling the truth. Her fear is palpable, real.

Meera looks away from the gun just long enough to glance at Townsend with pleading eyes. "This is what I was trying to tell you. Talia wants—"

Before she can finish, Talia cuts her off. "I want you to finally tell the truth. I want you to admit that you're in love with Townsend."

Meera's mouth opens and then closes again. For a moment, it looks like she might even laugh. "You can't be serious."

"That's the reason you've been torturing me. Because you love him, right? The police told us everything. We know you killed Amanda."

A look of genuine shock from Meera. She can't be this good an actor. "She's dead?"

But apparently, her reaction isn't convincing enough for Talia. "Just stop it with the act," she says. "Stop lying."

"You're the one lying. How do you explain your sob story coming straight from a book?"

This conversation is happening too fast for Townsend to keep up. He's still trying to process what Meera has told him about Talia's past, about her sister. Now that he thinks of it, he *does* remember Mother trying to tell him something about Talia's sister, which she learned through the PI . . .

As though reading his mind, Talia says, "I did lie about my sister. I'm sorry, Townsend." Tears start to fall. "But I only did it because the truth is so terrible."

"What do you mean?" He really wishes Talia would put down that gun. It's still by her side, held like an afterthought in her hand, but he'd feel much better if it weren't there at all.

"I liked the idea that I had a sister out there—and maybe even a niece—who I could find one day. It's a story I've told myself and others for so long that it has started to feel true."

"But you don't have a sister," Meera says. "Right?"

More tears. "I used to. She died when we were still kids. A drowning accident."

Is that what Mother was trying to tell him? Townsend wishes he'd listened. He wishes he'd known. Slowly, he approaches Talia and wraps his arms around her. "You could have told me the truth."

"I know. And I'm sorry. I'm so sorry."

"I am too," he says. Then, as soon as he feels Talia's body relax into his, he wrestles the gun out of her hand and into his own.

She yelps in surprise. "Townsend, what the fuck? What are you doing?"

"You were going to hurt yourself, Tal. I got us into this mess. I should be the one to handle this."

Feeling like an action hero, Townsend moves to stand in front of Talia, keeping the gun trained on Meera. *This is how it should be,* he thinks. *A man in charge.* He puffs out his chest as Meera presses herself back into a wall.

"You. Talk. Why are you here?"

"I—" Just as when Talia first stepped into the room with the gun, Meera's face is twisted with fear. "I didn't do anything wrong." She inclines her head toward Talia. "She's trying to frame me."

Behind him, Talia growls. Townsend's head is spinning. The gun begins to feel heavy in his hand. "Frame you for what?"

"All of it." Meera starts to reach for something in her pocket, and reflexively, Townsend jerks the gun back up.

In an instant, Meera's hands are back in front of her, held up in surrender.

"Please, I just—in my pocket. It's my termination paperwork from Cuff. Read it, and you'll see." Slowly, she reaches into her pocket and pulls out folded pieces of paper. She stretches out an arm to hand the documents to Townsend while keeping as much distance as she can between them.

Townsend's eyes skate over the page, his adrenaline too high for the words to make any sense.

"I thought I'd just been fired for accessing your messages with Amanda," Meera explains. "But they claimed I'd been *sending* messages from a user's account. They traced the impostor messages back to an IP address linked to my devices. But I *swear* I didn't send them—"

"Who was the user?" Townsend asks. Even though the thump in his gut tells him that he already knows the answer.

"Townsend—" Talia, still behind him, says his name like a warning.

Meera's voice comes out in a whisper: "Amanda Reade."

For just a moment, Townsend's hands loosen their grip—but it's all the time Talia needs.

Chapter Thirty-Five

TALIA

She's never held a gun before.

This one is small, built for a woman's grip. Talia can't stop running her hands over the cool, shiny surface. It makes her feel powerful, in control. Two things she rarely feels in life. And she needs the protection now more than ever.

Talia takes a breath, attempting to steady herself. *Inhale for a count of four, hold for a count of seven, exhale for a count of eight.* It's no use. The betrayal she's felt since yesterday in the police station—reignited now that Meera stands before her—threatens to tear her in two.

"It's been her this whole time," her friend is saying. "She's been pretending to be her own stalker."

"No," Townsend says. "That's impossible." Even in her anger, Talia feels a twinge of pride at his loyalty. He knows her too well to believe Meera's lies. He loves her too much to let Meera stand in the way of their future.

Below, sirens wail. It's time to do what she needs to do.

Talia takes another deep breath—*inhale for four, hold for seven, exhale for eight*—and pulls the trigger.

The blood comes first. Blackish-red liquid pools and soaks into Townsend's eggshell-colored rug like a scene from a slasher flick. Except that the growing puddle isn't made from corn syrup and red food coloring—it's blood, gushing from her leg.

Finally, the pain hits. Talia drops to the floor.

"Jesus Christ," she hears Meera say.

"Talia." Townsend's footsteps approach. "Talia, what did you just do?"

"Stay where you are," she tells him. Darkness starts to cloud her vision. "Stay right there. I need to do this. For us."

With her last bit of strength, she aims and pulls the trigger again. She hears a scream. A thud. A parade of heavy boots stampeding into Townsend's condo.

Then voices. "Police. Police. Put your hands where we can see them."

The last thing Talia sees is Townsend's face, blurred and swimming in the distance.

Just before he slips out of sight, she tells him again: "I did this for us."

Chapter Thirty-Six

Kaitlyn

First thing Saturday morning, Kaitlyn drives straight to Amanda's apartment building. There she finds Roger the landlord in the lobby, staring dead-eyed at his phone screen. When he looks up at her, his brows raise, and she wonders if that's because she looks as crazy as she feels.

Because right now, she feels mad enough to snap.

She barely slept the night before, if she even slept at all; she was too occupied with thoughts of her almost-certainly-dead sister, and her sister's potential murderer, and her pistol, suddenly and inexplicably missing from the trunk of her car. If Kaitlyn ever wants to sleep again, she's going to need some answers. Figuring out who's been paying Amanda's rent feels like a good place to start.

"I need to see the security tape," she says without preamble, and then just as quickly adds, "please."

"Right." Roger pockets his phone and waves her back into his office. She doesn't need to tell him there's urgency to this situation; he obviously feels it.

It takes the landlord an agonizingly long time to find the right moment, but eventually, he does. In silence, they watch the grainy footage of a dark-haired woman entering the lobby, exchanging a few words with Roger, and handing him an envelope.

"I can't see her face," Kaitlyn says, her heart sinking. Maybe she's not going to get the answers she's looking for after all.

Roger shushes her, even though the video has no sound. "Wait for it."

Finally, the woman turns. Roger pauses the video, catching her face in profile.

"Know her?"

Kaitlyn squints at the screen, expecting to see the Indian woman with the nose ring she was shown yesterday at the police station. Instead, she sees another familiar face: that of the sharp, accomplished woman she's been watching for months. "I do know her," she admits, because on that screen—handing over money to her sister's landlord—is Townsend's girlfriend, Talia Danvers. "Well, I don't, but I do."

Like a pile of bricks, the realization lands on her with a shattering blow. For so long, Kaitlyn assumed Talia was a victim, someone who'd attached herself to a rancorous (and possibly murderous) asshole without knowing any better. But it's clear now Kaitlyn was wrong. So wrong. Because Talia can only have one reason for paying Amanda's rent: She's the one who killed her.

"Okay," Roger says, as though her response makes any sense. He gestures to the screen. "So what do you want me to do with this?"

"Let me think for a minute." Kaitlyn stands and then—the office suddenly feeling too hot, too crowded with their two bodies—steps outside.

Surely Robert Frost didn't have anything like this in mind when he talked about those two roads diverging in a yellow wood, but still, this is how Kaitlyn feels: like she's looking down two different paths, wondering which one will lead to any semblance of peace. Pointing her gun at that amorphous human silhouette at the shooting range is nothing like pointing a gun at a living, breathing person; she knows that.

And she knows that, even if she were to find herself poised and ready (and even if her gun were not currently missing), she would never be able to pull the trigger. She is angry in a way that feels unshakable, a permanent part of her personality from here on out, but she isn't a murderer.

Perhaps ShrinkGPT can help. After pulling out her phone and opening the app, Kaitlyn asks, "How do you know if you're capable of killing?"

The app plays "Opus No. 1" as the chatbot generates its response. But when the answer is finally provided—something about patterns of deception and an escalation of violence—Kaitlyn notices right away that something is off. This isn't the AI voice she is used to, the soothing baritone reminiscent of Morgan Freeman. This is another voice entirely.

The app confirms it: Though a half dozen new voice options have been added following the latest software update, the voice she's become so accustomed to hearing—Male Dulcet Tone—is gone.

Great. Even her fucking AI-therapy chatbot has left her. She has no choice but to figure this out on her own.

For what feels like the hundredth time in the past few months, Kaitlyn wonders, *What would Amanda do?* If she closes her eyes, she can almost hear her sister's voice, can almost feel her standing beside her.

Talia needs to get fucked, Amanda would say. *Talia needs to pay.*

Before she can change her mind again, Kaitlyn calls the police. "This is Kaitlyn Reade," she says, her voice shaking, "and I have evidence that Talia Danvers killed my sister."

Someone asks her to hold, and a moment later, a voice she recognizes as belonging to Detective Harris answers the phone. "Ms. Reade?"

"I have evidence," she repeats. "I know Talia did it."

Harris pauses. "Would you come back to the station?" she says at last. "Talia Danvers was just shot."

Chapter Thirty-Seven

Talia

It takes a few minutes, but eventually, the hospital room comes into focus around her, and Talia realizes why she cannot move her arms: She is handcuffed to the bed.

Carefully, she tests the limits of her cuffs, tugging her left arm, and then her right. Pain radiates from her wrists, rubbed raw from friction, but it doesn't eclipse the throbbing of her left shin. *You need something to drink,* her brain informs her. *You need something to drink, and you need to stay calm.*

"Water," she cries out for a second time. "I need water."

The uniformed officer standing outside her door doesn't turn to look at her—and in fact, he starts to walk away.

"Come back." Talia's throat throbs with the effort of yelling, her command coming out as little more than a squeak.

Her heart sinks when the officer rounds the corner, leaving her sight, but just as quickly, he returns with a nurse in tow. Wordlessly, the two enter the room.

"Could I get some water, please?" she tries again.

The nurse doesn't respond, avoiding Talia's eyes as she switches out her IV bag.

"Are you able to take off these cuffs? They're really uncomfortable."

Still no response. Talia turns to the officer—a lanky, curly-haired guy who looks no older than twenty—standing solemnly in the corner of the room.

"There's no reason for me to be restrained. I didn't do anything."

The officer's eyes meet hers for just a moment before he snaps his focus out the window again.

The nurse peels back the dressing wrapped around her shin, and for the first time, Talia sees the bullet hole, gaping and oozing like something from a horror movie. Without warning, two gloved thumbs press into the wound, and Talia rears back, nearly blacking out from the pain.

"Ow!"

"Sorry," the nurse says, not sounding sorry at all.

She doesn't understand why she's being treated like this. She was just shot. She is a *victim*. Again, Talia tries appealing to the officer. "I need to know: Is Meera dead? And where is my fiancé?"

"Detectives Burrows and Harris will be here soon," he says, addressing the wall behind her. "They will speak to you."

Fuming, Talia lies in silence and allows the nurse to take her vitals until, at last, Burrows and Harris enter the room. Harris nods to the younger officer, and he and the nurse shuffle out of the room, leaving the two officers at the foot of the bed and Talia chained and vulnerable before them.

She asks again. "Please, can you tell me if Meera Ratnam is dead? You know what she's capable of, and you know I'm not safe if she's still alive. I mean, look at what she did. She shot me." Talia attempts to gesture to her leg before remembering she can't move her arms.

Harris pulls two chairs up to the side of the bed, and she and Burrows sit. "We'll get to that," she says. "First, I'd like to ask you about Malcolm Gray."

Talia feels lightheaded. She wonders what that nurse put in her IV bag. "What about him?"

"You went to high school with him, yes?"

"And college. He was my boyfriend. But what does—?"

"Did you know his wife, Clara Belle Linhart? She met Malcolm at Auburn University, yes?"

Annoyance creeps in. Do these detectives not understand what she's just been through? Can they not see that she needs to rest? "You're asking questions," Talia says, "but it feels like you already know the answers. What is the point of all this?"

"Three years ago, Malcolm and Clara Belle's home in Opelika was burglarized. Clara Belle was bludgeoned to death, and Malcolm was left with a traumatic brain injury. He still hasn't regained speech."

"I remember hearing about that. It was very upsetting."

Harris continues as though Talia hasn't spoken. "Police never found their suspect, and the attack was ruled random. However, Malcolm's parents have their theories, mostly having to do with a woman named Natalia Danvers who had a crush on him in high school and followed him to college." She nods at Talia. "That's you, correct?"

"I didn't follow him to college. He was my boyfriend. We were in love, and we agreed to go to college together."

"That's not how Mr. and Mrs. Gray seem to remember it."

"They're lying. They never liked me." Talia tries to sit up, and her chafed wrists scream in protest. "Could I please get these cuffs removed?"

"In the five years that passed between Malcolm's graduation at Auburn—when he first started dating Clara Belle to the night of the home invasion—Malcolm's parents say he received hundreds of emails and messages and texts from you. They say he only neglected to get a restraining order because he felt bad for you."

"Well, we dated for years. It would be weird if we simply stopped talking."

"Okay," Harris says, "but is it true that you moved to Austin right after Malcolm's accident three years ago? That you legally changed your name to Talia, cut off ties with your family, and started a new life?"

"I wanted a fresh start. Is that a crime?"

"No." Burrows's mouth twitches, as though he's tempted to smirk. "But it was a crime to kill Clara Belle Linhart and to nearly kill Malcolm Gray. And it was a crime to murder Amanda Reade three years later."

No. No, no, no. This can't be happening. The words spill out of Talia's mouth faster than she can even form them. "Clara Belle was killed in a random burglary gone wrong," she insists. "And Amanda disappeared. No one knows what happened to her. She was unwell. She stole my boyfriend. She harassed me for months."

"I think you've been telling yourself these stories for so long that you actually think they're the truth."

"I'm telling the truth. I didn't do anything wrong."

Burrows gives Harris a subtle nod, and the two stand. "We'll continue this later," he tells Talia. "Why don't you get some rest?"

"How am I supposed to rest while I'm chained up like this?" Talia asks, but she doesn't get a reply. The door swings shut behind the detectives, and once again, she is alone.

Her head spins. Her wrists throb. The silence is oppressive. All Talia wants is for Townsend to come into her room and wake her from her nightmare. Willing herself elsewhere, she closes her eyes, and she must nod off, because the next thing she knows, someone is pulling back the curtain around her bed.

Townsend, she thinks. *He came for me.*

But when she opens her eyes, it's not Townsend who stands at the foot of her bed but Meera, looking positively murderous.

A scream erupts from deep in Talia's belly, so raw and feral it threatens to split her throat in two. "Guards! Help!"

Meera rears back, horrified. "Talia, please—"

"Someone help me! This woman tried to kill me!"

"Please, Talia." Meera takes a tentative seat next to her bed, letting out a small groan as she does so. "I'm not going to hurt you."

Talia takes a deep breath, tempted to release a fresh round of screams, but what is the point? No one is coming to help her. No one here believes her. "What do you want, then?"

"I just want to talk to you. I just want to know why you did this to me."

Here Talia is chained to a hospital bed with a hole in her leg, and Meera still wants to throw a pity party. "What do you think I've done to you, Meera?"

"Well, for starters"—Meera pulls aside her own hospital gown, showing a bloodied bandage on her hip—"you fucking shot me."

"In self-protection."

Meera stares at her for a beat too long. "Do you really believe that?"

"You broke into Townsend's condo to hurt me. Maybe even to kill me. So yes, I do believe I was protecting myself."

Still Meera continues to stare. "Oh, my God. You've convinced yourself that it was all real, haven't you? In your twisted mind, you actually believe I posed as Amanda and sent all those messages and threats just to screw with your relationship."

None of Meera's words are making sense. "Amanda *did* send those messages."

"Amanda is dead," Meera snaps, "and you know that. What I want to know is when you decided to frame me for her supposed crimes."

"I don't. I didn't." There must be drugs in this IV bag. Something malicious is running through her veins, muddling her thoughts. They want to confuse her.

Meera continues, undeterred. "I trusted you more than anyone, and you betrayed me in the worst kind of way. You cost me my livelihood and my daughter. What did I do to deserve that?"

Is Amanda the real stalker, or is it Meera? Talia can't keep track anymore. Either way, Meera is frightening her. If only Townsend would appear and make her go away.

As though reading her mind, Meera says, "I just don't understand why you would do all of this for Townsend. You caused so many people so much grief, and for what? For a guy who cheated on you?"

Pain shoots through her limbs, stinging worse than when the nurse pressed down on her wound. "He's changed. He loves me. Amanda meant nothing to him, and he regrets what he did to me every day."

"Then why did you feel the need to kill her?"

Blood pumps so loudly in Talia's ears that she can barely hear her own response: "Because she almost ruined everything."

That's when everything goes black. Did she have a stroke? Did Meera kill her? Shivering, Talia clenches her hands into fists and squeezes her eyes shut, praying for that glorious moment when she'll wake up in Townsend's bed, having realized this was all a bad dream.

But then: the squeak of shoes on linoleum. Someone new has entered the room. No, two somebodies. "You have the right to remain silent," a voice says. "Anything you say can and will be used against you in a court of law. You have the right to talk to a lawyer for advice . . ."

Still Talia doesn't open her eyes. To open them would be to acknowledge what's happening, and she's not ready to do that. Instead, she mutters to herself the few things she knows to be true, as though the words will absolve her and make this all go away:

I had to do it. I had to do it for Townsend. It would be like she never existed. We could be happy. I deserved to be happy.

I had to do it.

Chapter Thirty-Eight

Meera

The police found a body in Town Lake.

According to the news, they actually found it three months earlier in May, but they weren't able to identify it at the time. Without knowing where Talia disposed of the body (she maintains that she has no memory of what happened), compounded by advanced decomposition and a failure to locate the necessary dental records, the Jane Doe was presumed to be Amanda.

Meera doesn't like to think about this—about Amanda's bloated, mutilated corpse sitting on the bottom of the lake, unrecognizable from the vibrant woman she'd been in life. She doesn't like to think about all the half-naked young people who floated above her body while drinking beers in boats, unaware of what lay beneath the water's surface.

All she wants to think about is the fact that Talia has been caught. She's been put away, and Meera is finally safe. Even if Amanda wasn't so lucky.

She felt a little funny about it, but still, Meera went to Amanda's funeral. It took place at a church in Georgetown, not far from where she and her sister were raised. In her eulogy, Kaitlyn talked about her sister hiding peanut butter sandwiches beneath her bed as a kid, a story that was somehow disgusting and touching at once. "I may not have loved being her roommate," she said in conclusion, "but I'm honored to be the keeper of her memory. And I will make sure that her memory lives on through me."

Later, Meera approached Kaitlyn as she stood by the symbolic casket, a receiving line of one. After introducing herself, Meera said, "I'm sure your sister would have loved the ceremony," because what else was there to say?

At this, Kaitlyn smirked. "No, she wouldn't have. She would have hated it. But at least she wouldn't have been able to give me shit about wearing all black for once." Then she looked around the crowded room, seemingly lost in another memory. "So many people loved her," she said, more to herself than to Meera. "I knew she had all those followers online, but I didn't realize she had so many people who loved her in real life too."

Neither of them mentioned Townsend, who was conspicuously absent. Who Meera half expected and never expected to show.

Townsend crosses her mind now as she sits at her desk in the empty Cuff office, putting together a presentation for her latest project. Capture the Red Flag, she's decided to call it. The feature will give Cuff users access to a suite of safe-dating tools—including background checks, reverse image searches, reverse phone number lookups, and criminal record searches—they can use before ever arranging a date with someone. Her hope: to help users (and women, in particular) avoid cheaters, and catfish, and creeps. And potentially much worse.

If Amanda had known Townsend was a cheater, maybe she would have never agreed to go out with him. Maybe she would have never made an enemy of Talia, and maybe she would still be alive. It's unlikely, but it's a nice thought. It gives Meera comfort to know that—in designing this new feature—she could potentially save someone else's life, even if it's too late for Amanda.

Cuff's COO, Betty Jeong, was surprised when Meera accepted her job back. "Frankly, I didn't think you'd want anything to do with this company after the grief we put you through," she told Meera. "And I imagine it will be difficult to come back, considering . . ."

Betty didn't have to finish her sentence; Meera knew what she was thinking. How could she continue to work at the place where she'd met Talia, the woman who nearly ruined her life? But that's precisely why Meera decided to return. She doesn't want to use other people as an excuse for giving up anymore. She's been dealt a bad hand, but she isn't ready to lay down and die because of it. No, she's ready to fight.

Aarav the custodian steps into the ML mod pod then, still empty save for Meera. "How is my Gracie girl doing?" he asks in Tamil.

"She's great," she says. "And as of last week, she's eight."

He smiles. He knows about everything that happened with Talia and Townsend and Amanda and Kaitlyn; Meera filled him in when he came to remove the contents of Talia's desk. She also asked him about the note he left her, warning her not to trust Talia. How did he know that Talia wasn't to be trusted? What did he notice that Meera herself had missed?

"I could see what she was doing, even if she never saw me," he told her. "People don't look over their shoulder if they don't feel guilty."

To Meera now, Aarav says, "I'm glad Gracie's doing well. And I'm glad you're doing well."

"I am doing well," she replies, and she means it. Her new doctor is helping her better manage her Hashimoto's symptoms. Gracie is back home. And for the first time in a while, Meera is excited by her work.

Best of all, Talia is locked away in a place where she'll never be able to hurt Meera again.

It's almost eight thirty; the rest of the ML team will be here any minute. Meera tosses out the empty Diet Dr Pepper can she stole from her coworker Otto, because he's an asshole and she likes to mess with him. Soon it will be time to present her new project, to prove to herself and her team what she's capable of doing when she's passionate about something.

But first: It's time to get closure.

A letter sits on Meera's desk, sealed and addressed to Talia Danvers, and she hands it to Aarav. "Would you mind dropping this in the mail for me?" she asks.

He nods without asking for an explanation. "Sure thing." He seems to understand that Meera needs to do this, to say her final piece, even if she never gets the answers she wants from Talia in return.

She doesn't expect a reply, nor does she want one. She doesn't want to hear any more of Talia's lies for as long as she lives.

Chapter Thirty-Nine

Kaitlyn

Kaitlyn used to think that moving on would be impossible without knowing the truth. Now she's not sure that one version of the truth even exists.

She tells her new therapist this during their first session together, to which Dr. Chavez says, "I'm not sure what you mean."

Admittedly, Kaitlyn isn't quite sure herself. She just knows that Talia—who, from the sound of it, oscillates between lucidity and delusion, depending on the day—claims to be as in the dark about what happened to Amanda as everyone else.

"Talia broke into Amanda's apartment while she was out," Kaitlyn explains to the therapist. "She's owned up to that. But from there, her story always changes. Sometimes she confesses to attacking Amanda first. Sometimes she says Amanda attacked her and she acted in self-defense. But the weirdest thing . . ."

Hearing her trail off, Dr. Chavez gives a nod of encouragement. "What is the weirdest thing?"

"Talia refuses to admit she killed her. She keeps insisting that Amanda was still breathing when she left. That when she returned to the apartment later, my sister was just gone. It's like she thinks that will absolve her, pretending she had no idea that Amanda was actually dead."

"What if it's like you said? What if this is Talia's version of the truth?"

"Then she's even more insane than I thought."

Dr. Chavez cringes; Kaitlyn suspects the therapist is about to chastise her for using this word, *insane*. Instead, she says, "Talia can't give you the answers you're seeking. Or, at least, that's the impression I'm getting. Should that keep you from moving on?"

As much as Kaitlyn would like to exact her own revenge—to make Talia pay for all the anguish she's caused Kaitlyn and Meera and for whatever the fuck she did to Amanda—she can't let that be the last thing she does. Already she's squandered months of her life searching for a woman who no longer exists; why spend the rest of her days rotting away in a prison cell? No, it's time for Kaitlyn to conclude this chapter. She will not allow Talia to steal another minute.

For the first time in a long time, Kaitlyn is ready to face forward rather than look back. Maybe she'll apply to law school. Adopt a dog. Get back on the dating apps. Do all the things she's been meaning to do but put on the back burner until her sister was found. Kaitlyn no longer has an excuse for pressing pause on her life, and that scares the shit out of her. But it also means she's free.

"No," she tells Dr. Chavez. "I won't give her that power."

What she doesn't tell her new therapist: That last night, after posting an old photo of herself and Amanda to Instagram, she'd received a "like" from a user named @geminibaby530.

Clicking on the handle revealed nothing—no posts, no profile picture, only a few bots for followers—but still, it was enough for Kaitlyn to entertain a fantasy.

To imagine a world where her sister was still out there, lying in wait. Plotting a way back to her.

Chapter Forty

Townsend

When it arrives, the subpoena feels less like a surprise and more like an inevitability. Of course the Securities and Exchange Commission is investigating Townsend's company. Of course this would happen on top of everything else.

The email is brief and unambiguous. . . . attached subpoena is being issued to you as part of an ongoing investigation . . . can report to the Fort Worth Regional Office on October 1 to provide testimony and requested documentation . . . failure to comply may force the SEC to bring an action in Federal Court, resulting in a fine or even imprisonment.

He'll forward the message to Carter Bonier, just to confirm, but Townsend doesn't need a law degree to know that his business—not to mention his life—is utterly, irrevocably fucked.

He wonders who ratted him out. Did Sage Clinic blow the whistle after looking at his books? Or was it that piece of shit Orson Livingston? It's also possible that freaky data science professor decided to screw him over. It doesn't matter, really—but still, Townsend would like to know who he needs to make pay after he gets things sorted out.

For thirty-four years, Townsend has led a charmed life, his small missteps and failings expunged from his record before they could fester into anything resembling consequences. The looks, the money, the girl—he had it all, and while he felt he deserved those things, even he could admit that there was something preternatural about the way his luck ran.

Now it seems as though his luck has run out. Starting with the girl.

From his living room couch, he can see it: the rust-colored stain that's now a permanent part of his rug. It's the only remnant of that woman—that *psycho*—remaining in his condo, and once his new rug arrives next week, the mark she left will be gone too. Then he just needs to contact the post office and refuse any letters from her. He may have to endure Mother saying *I told you so* indefinitely, but he's done being tormented by a crazy ex.

His phone rings, and Townsend answers without looking at his screen, expecting Carter. Instead, he hears the scratchy voice of the private investigator Mother used to follow Talia.

"I have an update for you on that woman you asked about, Amanda Reade."

"I watch the news," Townsend tells him, restraining himself from adding *you stupid fuck*. "I know she's dead."

"That's the thing, though." The guy chuckles. "They never actually identified that body as hers."

"Okay." Where is he going with this?

"And my sources say they saw a chick at a rest stop in Houston matching the description. Blond hair? Five foot four? About one hundred and thirty pounds?"

"You just described half the female population of Austin."

"Gemini symbol tattooed on her right hip?"

This gives Townsend pause. "I think you've got bad intel," he finally says, "because Amanda is dead." Still, even hours after hanging up the phone, Townsend can't help but wonder.

He knows Amanda isn't alive, because Talia killed her . . . but what if she didn't?

No, she can't be. It isn't possible.

But is it?

Chapter Forty-One

Amanda

The worst part of that stupid book Amanda had to read for her community college Arthurian literature class, *Le Morte d'Arthur*? The ending.

After being saved from execution, Queen Guinevere decides to shut herself away in a convent, an act of penance for the sin of fucking whoever she wanted. It was bullshit, Amanda thought. Queen Guinevere shouldn't be sorry. She should be pissed at everyone who spoiled her fun. She should be *livid*.

She should want revenge.

Amanda thinks about this now as Paul (or is it Peter?) drives west along State Highway 71. His hands—manicured, soft, free of knuckle hair, and bearing a gold band on a particular finger—tell a story: meticulous. White collar. Married. Of course, this man wouldn't have agreed to drive Amanda the two and a half hours from Houston if his marriage mattered to him. But neither his motivations nor his expectations are Amanda's concern.

Maybe she'll screw him as thanks. Or maybe she'll run off before he can ask for gas money. Her only concern right now is getting where she needs to go.

As though reading her mind, he suddenly asks, "So what's at Austin State Hospital? Visiting a friend?"

"Something like that." Anyone else would probably tell this guy to fuck off and mind his own business, but Amanda doesn't mind a little conversation. She's been too quiet for too long.

"You know," Paul-or-maybe-Peter continues, "this isn't a regular hospital. It's a"—he lowers his voice dramatically—"*psychiatric facility.*"

"I know."

His eyes flick to the scar above her left eyebrow—months old now, but still fresh enough to look tender—before returning to the road. "You must be a good friend. I hear that place is haunted."

"I don't think it's all that bad," Amanda says. "In fact, my friend who's there? I think she deserves to be somewhere much worse."

Epilogue

I have a confession to make: I knew you were going to be there.

You thought it was fate, that day we reconnected on Town Lake and saw the bats fly out from under the bridge. But Brett Livingston posted an Instagram Story from the lake earlier that day with you in it, so I knew you would be there. And I knew it was my chance to get you back.

May 18th—I'll never forget it. That would make a great wedding date, now that I think about it. I would love a spring wedding. I can already picture myself carrying a bouquet of oversized calla lilies, like Kennedy J. Abbott did at hers.

I'm sure you're worried about how I'm doing, but I'm fine. I promise. It's nice here (even though it used to be called the Texas State Lunatic Asylum—did you know that?), and I don't mind it, especially since I know it's only temporary. I'll be back home with you soon enough. There's a gym so I can exercise, and the food is decent, and I get the newspaper every day so I can read about what's happening out in the world.

It's strange to read about myself in the paper. I don't like seeing my face in print. I don't like hearing their version of events, which—as I'm sure you know—is all wrong. Just like with Clara Belle, what happened with Amanda was a mistake. But you already know that. I know you believe me.

I read a story the other day that made me think of you. You know the I-35 expansion project? Apparently, it's displacing thousands of bats that live under the highway's bridges. The colony at the Congress Ave Bridge is going to be fine, thank God. But thinking of all those other bats losing their homes made me sad. I used to be afraid of bats, you know. You changed my mind. You showed me that they were harmless and misunderstood—beautiful, even. That's one of the many things I love about you. You see me—all of me, the good and the bad—and love me anyway.

I should have listened to you when you warned me about Meera. I should have known you could see things that I was too blind to see for myself.

She wrote me a letter. She told me your company is being investigated by the SEC. She seemed almost glad about it, and she said you were finally going to get what was coming to you. Completely delusional, as usual. I wish you would have told me yourself, but I understand why you didn't. Just remember, you can always tell me the truth. You know that I would never hold anything against you.

I would have just told you what you already know: You're going to get through this, like you always do. The investigation will end, the hospital will let me go, and you and I will finally begin our lives together, like we were always meant to do.

By the way, do you have an update on Grandma Birdy's ring? Is it still getting resized? I would love for it to be ready by the time I come home. It would be so romantic for you to slip it on my finger when you pick me up. And maybe, once I become Mrs. Talia Fuller, people will finally stop asking me about Amanda Reade. She's all anyone wants to talk about here. She's all I see when I close my eyes. Even when I try to dream of you, she invades my thoughts and turns my dreams into nightmares.

She won't stop haunting me.

I don't want you to worry about me though. I'm going to be okay. I just wish I could hear from you. I keep asking for your letters, but the hospital claims you've never written. I don't know why they're lying to me, so just keep writing, like I know you are. I'll wear them down someday. No one can keep me from you.

I have to go now. They've just told me I have a visitor. I hope that it's you.

I love you, Townsend. I'll write to you again tomorrow.

Yours always, Talia

Acknowledgments

The road here wasn't easy, but I'm eternally grateful for the people who helped me make it to this place.

To Stephen Barbara and Maria Whelan: I'm so lucky to have you in my corner. Thank you for reading every messy draft, answering every neurotic email, and convincing me that the rejection would all be worth it when I finally got a win.

To Lauren Oliver: Thank you for choosing me and for introducing me to that dark, wonderful mind of yours. You are a one-of-a-kind talent.

To Jenna Brickley: I've never had more fun writing than I have while working with you. I'm a better storyteller because of you, and I'm so thankful for your guidance.

To Liz Pearsons and the Thomas & Mercer team: You shared my vision, and you said yes. That means more to me than I can say.

To Angela James: Your incredible eye has made this into a sharper, tighter, and creepier novel than I could have dreamed.

To Jennifer Close, Swan Huntley, Georgia Clark, Rufi Thorpe, Lauren Fox, and Elisa Albert: I'm forever in your debt for blurbing my first novel and for giving me the confidence to call myself an author.

To my coworkers at *Cosmopolitan*: You inspire me. You cheer me on. Most importantly, you keep me young. Thank you for that.

To Mom, Dad, Kat, and Devin: I wouldn't be living my dream if it weren't for your endless support. You make anything feel possible.

To Mickey: Had we not matched on Tinder back in 2014, I don't know who or where I would be. You're more than just my perfect partner—you're the best friend I've ever had.

To Natalie and Skylar: You've made this novel quite challenging to write (particularly you, Skye, who arrived before I could finish the first draft). You've also helped me become the best version of myself. You're the last people I see when I close my eyes and the first people I think about when I wake up.

About the Author

Photo © 2025 Rona Liana Ahdout and Sabrina Toto

Corinne Sullivan is the senior news editor at *Cosmopolitan*, where she covers celebrity and entertainment news. She graduated from Boston College in 2014 with a degree in English and creative writing. She went on to receive her MFA in fiction from Sarah Lawrence College. Her stories have appeared in literary magazines such as *Night Train*, *Knee-Jerk*, and *Pithead Chapel*, among other publications, and her 2018 debut novel, *Indecent*, was included on several "best of" lists.

Corinne lives with her family in Jersey City. Stay up-to-date with her latest work by following her on Instagram (@corinnzo).